Night Whispers

by

Matthew J. Pallamary

Mystic Ink Publishing

MATTHEW J. PALLAMARY

Mystic Ink Publishing
San Diego, CA
www.mysticinkpublishing.com

ISBN 10: 0692518177 (sc)
ISBN 13: 978-0692518175 (sc)
Printed in the United States of America
San Bernardino, California

This book is printed on acid-free papermade from 30% post-consumer waste recycled material.

Library of Congress Control Number: 2015914091

Book Jacket and Page Design: Matthew J. Pallamary/ San DiegoCA
Author's Photograph: Matthew J. Pallamary -- Gibbs Photo/Malibu CA

DEDICATION

This book is dedicated to Colleen Kennedy.

CHAPTER ONE

The sound of a key sliding into the front door lock jolted him out of semi-consciousness. The musty smell of old perfume whispered in his mind, reminding him that he'd been waiting for hours. His feet ached. He strained to see more, but the closet remained shrouded in darkness. Razor thin silver light shone through the door leaving a slice of moonlight across the clothes hanging in front of him.

Disoriented at first, he gradually remembered what he had to do. Part of him didn't want to go through with it, but the voice wouldn't allow him to think of anything else.

As if in answer to his thoughts, it whispered in his mind. *Remain silent*, it hissed. *Do not move. You mustn't be found. Breathe slow. Deep. In measured breaths. You are the divine instrument of God's will. His hand will guide yours.* Sweaty fingers slid over the handle of the sickle at his side.

His back felt stiff. His legs shook. He longed to move, but the sounds from the hall outside the bedroom told him that to do so would mean discovery.

The bedroom light clicked on and a slash of gold stabbed through the crack in the door, stopping inches from his face. He cringed, catching his breath. She came straight toward him. He held his breath, tightening his grip on the sickle. The pretty blonde stopped with her hand on the door as if lost in thought, then turned away and began undressing.

He exhaled slow, studying her through the opening. Cascading blonde hair and smooth curves. When she pulled an angora sweater over her head he saw firm breasts and smooth, delicate shoulders. He nearly gasped when she unzipped her jeans and wiggled out of them. Her panties followed. Seeing her in this intimate way sparked long atrophied desires.

That's not why you're here, the voice admonished. *Put those filthy thoughts out of your mind.* The harsh words made him feel hot and prickly; the way he felt when his mother used to scold him.

She turned toward him again and stared. He tensed, then remembered the mirror on the closet door. She cupped her breasts and turned from side to side, examining herself. His gaze darted between her breasts and the honeyed patch of pubic hair that graced her smooth, toned thighs. If not for the voice, he might have gone for her then, but fear kept him in check.

When he reached the limits of control, she turned and disappeared from view. The sound of running water came from the bathroom, then the toilet flushed. When she passed the closet again he saw that she put on a nightgown, then the light went out.

The dull glimmer of moonlight filled his consciousness once more, followed by the creak of bedsprings and the beeping sound of her cell phone.

"Ken?" She said softly. "Yes, babe, I'm home, tucked in and thinking about you." A pause. "I know. I miss you too. We'll spend tomorrow night together. All night." Another pause. "I'm sorry too. I love you." Pause. "Goodnight, babe."

More creaking came from the bedsprings, then the sound of her breathing, strong and regular at first, then slowing.

Soon, the voice said. *When the silence nears perfection. God will guide your hand.*

He drifted with the voice, trusting it as it strengthened him; an old, reliable friend. He couldn't remember when he first heard it, only that it gave meaning to his life and promised him happiness and fulfillment. Tonight he would give in to its insistence and it would reward him.

He remained still until no other sound came except her breathing. Slow and even.

Moving with the patience of a snake stalking prey, his hand glided forward, fingers touching the smooth door, stopping when his hand made full contact. He applied pressure until the closet door swung open noiselessly. The voice had seen to it that he oiled the hinges before settling in to wait.

He inched forward, slipping between her clothes, once again catching the lingering scent of her perfume, extricating himself from the confines of the closet, emerging into the full glory of the moonlight.

Fear, love, frustration, and unbearable longing held him immobile when he beheld the graceful curves of the girl beneath the sheets. If only...

She stirred.

He froze while she rolled onto her back and licked her lips, mumbling something before slipping back into peaceful slumber. He moved closer, pausing again to admire the childlike innocence of her face, stifling the urge to stroke her hair.

Do it! the voice commanded.

He flinched, then raised the sickle, momentarily fascinated at the silver glinting off its blade.

Her eyes snapped open. Wide. A sharp intake of breath. Her mouth opened forming an "O" before the tip of the sickle plunged down, turning what might have been a scream into a raspy gurgle. The stark fear in her eyes dulled as he pulled the sickle out, dimming further with each successive strike.

CHAPTER TWO

Nick Powers felt the ground tremble and the wall shaking at his back. The rumble gained momentum as it rushed toward him, reaching a peak before subsiding into a cacophony of shrieking steel that announced the subway's arrival. A rush of dank air, heavy with the smell of stale urine blew the doors of Dorchester's Shawmut Station open, sending the loose pages of a newspaper fluttering by.

The word "Decapitation" in the headline of the *Boston Globe* caught his attention. He stomped down, catching the paper under his foot and picked it up. The picture of a beautiful blonde girl below the headline caught his eye. "Goddamn waste," he muttered. "Why does it always have to be the pretty ones?"

Oblivious to the people exiting the station, Nick admired the girl's picture a moment longer before reading the story below.

POLICE INVESTIGATE CAMBRIDGE DECAPITATION

The headless body of Lynn Ford, a twenty-three year old Boston College student was found in her Cambridge apartment late yesterday afternoon.

The victim's head is still missing.

A source close to the investigation is quoted as saying, "There are no suspects and no apparent motive, but forensic specialists speculate that the ritual nature of the murder indicate a pattern that may be repeated."

The discovery of Ford's body was made by her boyfriend Ken Reeth who was held for questioning, then released by police. Reeth is not a suspect in the slaying. An official spokesman for the Boston Police refused to comment on the murder pending further investigation.

SEE MURDER PG. A7.

Weird shit, Nick thought, flipping through the paper finding that page A7 wasn't among those he'd snared. Oh well. He stuffed the paper into an overflowing waste basket that said "Keep Boston Clean". An unusual amount of cans and bottles filled the trash.

What was this world coming to? Gorgeous babes getting their heads chopped off by lunatics and homeless trash pickers going on strike. It wasn't like Obie to let such a treasure go ignored for so long. Rounding the corner of Shawmut Station, Nick saw an abandoned shopping cart, recognizing it as Obie's. Speak of the devil. Only Obie had bright orange Hefty bags and an army blanket.

What was wrong with this picture? He'd never seen Obie without his cart. Nick leaned against the railing bordering the subway and stared at the cart, puzzled. Come to think of it, Obie hadn't been around for a couple of days. Where would he go? Maybe he found some new dumpsters to scavenge. Now that he thought about it, it dawned on Nick that in the past few weeks he had seen more street people in the neighborhood than usual. It had to be that new rescue mission across from Town Field. Maybe Obie was hanging out there getting free grub, but he would never leave his trusty shopping cart. He usually made enough selling cans and bottles to feed himself. Chow had be pretty good if Obie did go there. Nick shrugged, stuck his hands in his pockets and started up the street.

Close to six feet, with jet black hair and probing blue eyes, Nick seemed older than his eighteen years and he liked to dress the way his old man had. Leather jacket, jeans and engineer boots. People who didn't know them mistook them as brothers. Like his father, Nick combed his hair straight back. The neighborhood girls said he was a cross between Robert Downey Jr. and Tom Cruise.

Because of his father's connections, Nick knew everyone on the streets, who had what drugs, what they charged and who specialized in what kind of stolen goods. He knew all the bookies, hookers, and pimps on a first name basis. People knew he was a stand-up guy who could get in on the action any time, but he did his best to steer clear. His father had been into too much of it and got busted for selling cocaine to an undercover dick. They sent him away to Walpole where he died three weeks after Nick's fifteenth birthday; the victim of some asshole from Southie's shiv.

His father's absence had made Nick independent and if he learned anything from his father, he learned not to follow his example. None of that jive talking, street hustle shit. Best to keep away from Johnny Law and keep The Man off his ass.

He dreaded the thought of being another unhappy drunk spending the rest of his life trapped working for the fucking post office or some other mindless civil service job. He dreamed of going to college and becoming an airline pilot so he could get out of Dorchester, but he couldn't afford the schooling. His mother could barely feed him as it was and he hated living at home. It made him feel like he wasn't pulling his weight, especially with the not so subtle reminders from his mother's asshole boyfriend Mike, but he had no money to go anywhere else and he wasn't going to give in to the easy money that those loser crack heads with their fancy pimpmobiles in Codman Square bragged about. Fuck that.

After graduating high school, he worked as a construction laborer, but they laid him off back in September and he hadn't been able to find work since. At least he had a place to stay. Guys like Obie didn't. They slept in dumpsters, subways, or back alleys. If they were lucky, they found a place like the rescue mission across from Town Field.

"What the hell are you talking about?" a voice said from behind him. "You crazy son-of-a-bitch!"

Nick wheeled around to see a lanky old man wearing a grimy Red Sox ball cap, soiled trench coat, and a battered pair of Converse All Stars. The bill of his cap shadowed hollow eyes sunk in a gaunt, sunburned face that looked straight at Nick, but nothing registered in the man's glassy stare.

No one else was in sight.

"Fuck religion," the man said. "I don't believe in that bullshit." He frowned and clenched his fists. "What? You go right on thinking that if you think it's gonna do any good, but..." Anger clouded his face. "Listen, fool, you can't tell me nothing!"

Who the hell's he talking to? Nick thought as the man shuffled by, oblivious to him. Must be a hell of an argument. Never saw him before. Definitely not a regular.

"Goddamn religious fanatics are all the same," the man said, arms flailing. "Talking all that shit about God's will."

Nick shook his head and watched the man continue down the street caught up in his heated debate, then he turned and leaned on the railing, directing his attention back to Obie's shopping cart. Maybe he's going to hang out with Obie?

His thoughts were interrupted by a squeal of rubber, followed by the sound of a racing engine. A gold "73" Camaro with a brown vinyl top turned the corner of Dayton Street. Nick recognized the tall, curly haired driver when the car pulled up alongside him.

"Joey," he said when the driver rolled down the passenger window. "Long time no see. Thought you were still doing time for stealing cars."

"Got out this morning."

Nick stepped back, admiring the Camaro, then let out a low whistle before sticking his head in the window. "Nice looking sled. Another hot box?"

Joey wiggled the keys. "It's my uncle's. Get in. Let's take a cruise."

Nick hesitated. It didn't feel right. "I don't know, Joey..."

Joey wiggled the keys again. "It ain't no hot box, Nicky. What are you waiting for? I ain't seen you in months. Get the fuck in and fill me in on what's been going down."

Nick felt uneasy, but got in anyway. As soon as he closed the door, he smelled liquor and knew he made a mistake, but before he could say another word, Joey jerked the gearshift down into first, popped the clutch and laid down a short strip of rubber.

He smiled at Nick. "Thing's got some balls, huh?"

"Hey, Joey, if this thing's your uncle's, how come..."

The screech of another car's tires cut off his sentence. A Boston Police cruiser fishtailed around the corner behind them, blue lights flashing. Joey stomped on the gas and the car jumped forward. Nick cursed himself for being so stupid.

"I thought you said this wasn't a hot box," Nick said, grabbing the dashboard.

"I lied." Joey yanked the wheel to the left. Nick hung onto his door, looked back and saw the cops whipping around the corner in pursuit. Joey flew past Saint Mark's School hitting sixty, barreled into Dorchester Ave., known to the locals as Dot Ave. He turned a hard right, skidding over into oncoming traffic. A car swerved out of the way. Nick closed his eyes when he saw them heading for a bus. Joey swerved to the right, missing it by inches. The sirens seemed to fade. Nick opened his eyes and looked back to see that the distance between them and the cruiser had grown.

He punched the dash. "You son-of-a-bitch, Joey. What the hell's wrong with you?"

Joey let out a crazy laugh, pulled a pint of Jack Daniels out of his jacket and tossed it in Nick's lap.

"Shit!" Nick picked up the bottle as if it came straight from an oven and tossed it out the window.

"What'd you throw it out for, Nicky?"

Nick checked the rearview mirror, afraid that if he turned around, the cops would recognize him. The distance between them and the cruiser hadn't changed. Joey ran the stop light at the intersection of Dorchester and Talbot Ave.

A car hit their left rear fender, sending them sliding into a row of parked cars. Joey stomped on the gas and sideswiped three of them. Nick threw his arms up to shield his face from a shower of glass and mirrors. The cops didn't come through the intersection.

Joey cut hard to the right, taking a corner on two wheels and skidding into another parked car before shooting down a side street. They both looked back, half expecting to see blue lights. When they looked ahead again, a ball bounced out from between two parked cars, followed by a small boy.

"Fuck!" Joey swerved. The Camaro careened off of a pickup truck and bounced up over the curb, sending trash cans flying everywhere.

Nick looked out the side window, catching the shocked look of the kid, then looked ahead in time to see a chain link fence ripping up over the hood.

"We're screwed." were the last words out of Nick's mouth before they plowed into the front porch of a three-decker apartment, slamming him into the dashboard.

CHAPTER THREE

Tattered clouds drifted in front of a crescent moon making the murky shadows of the graveyard shift and slither. Creeping lines and angles from bare tree branches mingled with a spray painted pentagram and other graffiti desecrating the side of a white marble tomb.

OZZIE RULES

SYMPATHY FOR THE DEVIL

SATAN LIVES

Max Broderick leaned against a weathered gravestone, clutching a half-empty bottle of Thunderbird. The smell of the cheap wine on his clothes overpowered the lingering scents of damp earth and burning leaves. Max studied the graffiti. Kids, he thought. Stupid doped-out little punks and gang-bangers. He hated these stakeouts. Aside from their monotony they gave him the fucking willies, but bizarre assignments came with the territory and no one could do them better -- at least that's what they told him.

Graduating at the top of his class at the F.B.I.'s National Academy, Max had been asked to join the Investigative Support Unit at Quantico as the youngest criminal-personality profiler in the history of the unit. After five years in the field, his undercover skills had become as legendary as the weird circumstances of his stakeouts. Now Special Agent Broderick had the distinction of being the sole member of the U.S. Justice Department's Occult Crime Unit.

At thirty-six, the one man O.C.U. still looked boyish. His tousled, dirty-blond hair, the dimple on his cheek, and his mischievous blue eyes made women wonder what went on behind them. Cops teased him, saying that he looked more in his element at the country club carrying a tennis racket instead of on the streets packing a thirty-eight. He looked perfect, except for a small pink sickle-shaped scar over his right eye, compliments of an amped-out tweaker wielding a ritual dagger.

Two months ago the Boston Police had asked for his help. Over a three month period, fifteen bodies had been dug up from the Cedar Grove Cemetery in Dorchester. Three had been recovered -- minus their heads.

In contrast to everyone else's horror, Max expected some heads to be missing. He'd run across it before, but never on this large a scale. High whacko concentration on this one. Crazy fucks were probably having a convention. How to get a head in life - - or death. He smiled at his own black humor. No, these boys were serious. Human skulls went for five hundred dollars or more on the black market.

At most of the exhumation sites, the Boston P.D. found bones from animal sacrifices and other signs of ritual worship which wasn't unusual in body snatching cases, but the alarming frequency of disinterments and evidence of the same M.O. here pointed to a large, well organized cult. Their unchanging routine piqued Max's interest, especially when the Boston P.D. sent him copies of the crime reports. In every grave robbing, detectives found sprigs of mistletoe beside the open graves and among the residue of whatever ritual had been performed.

Calling cards.

A chilled New England November wind soughed through the trees. The sound of dried leaves skittering across the grass of the graveyard sounded like a small army of rats. It was going to be a long night. Max shivered and pulled the collar of his ragged field jacket closer to his neck, thinking of all the places he'd rather be, like in front of a warm fireplace with...

The sound of a car engine followed by tires on gravel made his heartbeat quicken. He slid his hand inside his jacket, resting it on the butt of his thirty-eight. The feel of it gave him comfort, but not enough. In a place like this, a crucifix would probably do a better job.

Looking in the direction of the noise, he saw an eerie blue light filling the graveyard. A moment later a police cruiser topped a rise and rocketed toward him, skidding to a stop a few feet away. A uniformed cop jumped out, the beam of his flashlight sweeping the headstones until it came to rest on Max.

So much for the stakeout.

"Broderick?"

Max stood and stretched to his full six feet, working the kinks out of his back. Getting too old for this shit. "Yeah. What's up?"

"Lieutenant O'Grady sent me. She wants you over at a crime scene in Cambridge."

"Cambridge? Shit. I don't work for O'Grady. She's supposed to be working for me."

The cop shrugged. "I'm just following orders. I come to get you, you yell at me. I can deal with that. I go back to her without you, I got to listen to her shit. Have a heart, will ya?"

"I see your point. Aw, what the hell, the stakeout's blown anyway."

The cop opened the door of the cruiser and gestured for Max to get in. "We've got a stiff over there with no head and some pretty spooky shit."

"No head?"

"That's right."

Max thought about a connection between the headless bodies recovered from the grave robbings and this new murder. He shook his head. Too much of a coincidence.

"Whew." The cop held his nose. "That's a hell of an aftershave you got on there. Fit's right in with this shithole neighborhood."

Max climbed into the cruiser and they headed for Cambridge, half-listening to the cop tell him what he knew about the murder. They took the Southeast Expressway toward downtown, then followed Mass. Ave. while the uniform rambled on. Max grunted and nodded at the right places, but his thoughts dwelled on his liaison with the Boston P.D.'s Lieutenant Colleen O'Grady, a thirty-three year old striking, red-haired beauty from South Boston.

She was a stubborn go-getter with a legendary Irish temper who was getting to be a royal pain in the ass, but he would cut her a lot of slack. O'Grady was a good cop.

Recently divorced from a homicide dick with a drinking problem, she took great pains to come across cold and indifferent, but Max saw fire smoldering behind those incredible green eyes, and on the other side of all that heat, tenderness. She had high cheek-bones with a hint of faded freckles that appealed to Max. Her looks combined with the way she carried herself made her a natural for a career in acting or modeling, but she wanted to be a cop.

What a waste.

They turned off of Mass. Ave. and took side streets until they stopped in front of an old Brownstone with newer glass doors and modern fixtures lighting the building. Two cruisers and an unmarked parked out front. Another uniformed cop stood sentry. Max hopped out of the cruiser, thanked his driver and went up the steps, nodding to the cop by the door.

"Second floor," the blue said, pointing. "209".

"Thanks."

Ducking under the police ribbon on the second floor, Max went down the hall. Another uniform stood outside the apartment. Max flashed his shield. The cop knocked once, then pushed open the door, letting him in.

The apartment smelled of Patchouli. Overstuffed pillows and braided rugs covered newly varnished floors. Woven baskets and oriental fans hung on pastel walls. A mauve colored vase sat in one corner with large peacock feathers sticking out of its top. Max heard voices from a back bedroom.

Rounding the corner, he collided with O'Grady. His hands flew up, instinctively grabbing her by the waist. His surprise passed quickly, replaced by the pleasant feel of the curve of her hip beneath her blazer. The sweet fragrance of Dare cut through his own soured odor of stale Thunderbird.

She stiffened at his touch, her eyes flared, and she jerked her head back.

Max let go. "Sorry, didn't hear you."

A puzzled expression flitted across her face, then her features softened and her eyes met his. "Thanks for coming." She looked away, then pointed over her shoulder. "In there."

Max walked past her into the bedroom, stopping when he saw leaves on the floor which struck him as out of place in an otherwise neat apartment. Maybe they blew in a window left open by the killer? He turned his attention to the aftermath of the carnage in front of him.

Spotlights lit the area where a surgical-gloved forensics technician with frizzy brown hair and thick eyeglasses took samples from reddish-black pools of congealed blood saturating the bed where the body had been. Two homicide dicks in dark jackets stood in a corner, heads together in close discussion. Max nodded to them.

The headboard and window behind it were splattered crimson. The words:

Cromm Cruaich

were scrawled on the wall in blood. Max studied the words. Celtic?

"She was probably sleeping when he found her," O'Grady said from behind him, her voice composed.

Pretty cool customer, Max thought watching her in the mirror. Bet she's seen a few stiffs in her day, but I doubt they were as pretty as this one.

"He got into the apartment some time during the early evening and waited for her in the closet," O'Grady said. "This one's definitely strange."

Max turned back to her. "That's an understatement."

"What I mean is, he was very careful. Thought things out beforehand. Went through a lot of trouble to conceal himself. Even oiled the hinges on the closet door so she wouldn't hear him coming out." She nodded toward the two homicide detectives who still hadn't spoken to him. "We know from the arterial spray on the wall and window, and the neck wounds, that this guy used a sharp instrument with a long, curved tip."

Max thought of Richard Ramirez, Southern California's Night Stalker climbing into people's bedrooms and murdering them in their sleep. Ramirez wasn't part of a cult, he was a self-proclaimed Satanist, but that had been bullshit too.

O'Grady nodded toward the bed. "This is where it gets really weird."

Max looked from the bed to the forensics tech. "We've got some good hair and tissue samples," the man said pointing to his lab case.

Max turned his attention back to O'Grady who shook her head.

"He left his prints everywhere. We found them on the window outside, the closet door, the walls. He went to such great pains to sneak in without getting caught, then got sloppy."

Max nodded. "What makes you think it's connected to my body snatchers?"

"I wouldn't have thought anything about it if I hadn't read about it in the paper. I figured I'd better come over and take a look."

"I have to admit, I was pissed about you pulling me off my stakeout, but figured you wouldn't yank me here because of what you read in the paper. What else you got?"

A hint of a smile flickered at the corner of her lips. She caught herself and motioned for him to follow her into the living room. "I've gathered from the crime reports of the bodies that have been recovered, that none of the heads have been found, right?"

"That's right."

"And mistletoe was found at all the exhumation sites alongside evidence of animal sacrifices, right?"

"Sacrifices are common in cases like this, but mistletoe is unusual, especially at *all* the sites."

"That's what I thought. We've done a cross-check on the blood samples. Not all of it is human." With trembling hands, she pulled out a folder and spread a handful of photos out on a coffee table.

Close-ups of a headless female body.

Her midsection had been eviscerated, the entrails piled neatly on her breasts as if placed with great care. Mistletoe poked up from the stump of her neck and arranged alongside the gutted organs.

"We still haven't found the head," O'Grady said.

CHAPTER FOUR

Somewhere in the darkness Nick heard the wail of a siren as if it came from the end of a long fuzzy tunnel. He struggled to figure out where he was and what had happened.

The siren grew louder.

Panic surged through him, urging him back to consciousness and a flurry of whispering voices passed through his mind like trash scattering before the wind, then the blare of the siren drowned them out. His head hurt.

He opened his eyes and saw the idiot lights of the Camaro glaring back at him from the dashboard. Engine stalled. Windshield spider webbed. Joey gone. Shit!

He heard the roar of an engine racing toward him from the end of the street. Pushing himself up, he looked in the rearview mirror and saw the flashing blue lights of a cruiser bearing down on him.

"Son-of-a-bitch!" He slid across the seat and stumbled out of the open door on the driver's side, standing on wobbly legs. Over the roof of the car he saw a little kid holding a ball, staring first at him, then at something above him. Looking up, he saw a woman in an old pink bathrobe and curlers glaring down at him from the porch of the house they'd hit.

The sound of the cop car's tires screeching to a stop hit him like a shock. Doors opened.

"Freeze!"

Nick bolted down an alley beside the house. The cop's footsteps echoed on the sidewalk behind him.

"I said freeze, punk!"

Nick thought he recognized the voice, but didn't look back fearing that the cop might see his face. Two gunshots hammered his eardrums. Warning shots. He turned the corner, rounding the back of the house. Another shot. The bullet zinged by the corner of the house. No more warnings.

He ran through the yard, passed another alley and spotted a second cop running toward him. Leaping onto a rickety wooden fence between the yards, he flipped himself over, landing on his tailbone. A knife point of pain shot up his spine.

"Put in a call for assistance," he heard the first cop say. "Then get over to the next street and cut him off." He heard a grunt and the fence shook, looked up and saw two arms coming over the top. Nick sprinted for the back fence, hoisted himself over and came down on his feet. He heard the cop landing in the yard on the other side, then a vicious growl followed by the rattling of a chain. A snarling Doberman sprang toward him.

He scrambled away from the dog, tripped and fell. The Dobie lunged, jerking short at the end of the chain, its teeth inches from his face. Nick's breath stuck in his throat. His head pounded, pain slamming his temples like twin mallets.

The back door of the house opened. Nick rolled away from the dog, jumped up and ran through the half-opened gate. Glancing back over his shoulder, he saw the top of the cop's head over the fence. The Dobie turned its attention toward the cop.

Yeah, go ahead. Jump *that* fence.

He ran down another alley and sprinted across the street, ducking into a clump of high bushes as a cruiser skidded to a stop across the street.

The first cop ran out of the alley, pointing toward him. "Over there, in the bushes." Both cops trotted across the street, guns drawn. Nick recognized one of the cops. Sullivan. He had more than one run-in with Sully in the past.

Running between the houses, Nick ducked behind one as the two cops burst through the bushes. Out of the corner of his eye, he spotted a storm cellar, its doors laying open at ground level. He hopped down onto the stairs and found the cellar door closed. Footsteps closed in. He wouldn't make it out of the yard. Crouching against the concrete steps, he lowered his head.

His breathing came hard, the slamming in his head keeping time with his ragged breath. He wiped sweat from his face, took his trembling hand away and saw blood. Jesus, how the hell did I get myself into this?

Sully and the other cop ran into the yard, stopping less than two feet away. Putting his hand over his face, Nick struggled to breathe through his nose.

"Maggot must have hopped the fence," Sully said, gulping for air. "Go call for someone to cover the next few streets. We know which direction he's heading."

The cop looked straight at Nick, not seeing him, then trotted back the way he came. Sully climbed up on the fence and scanned the surrounding yards. Nick saw him clearly. Short, wiry hair. Dark, hollow eyes. Long nose jutting from his gaunt, pockmarked face. He looked like a pissed-off terrier.

Nick scrunched up his forehead trying to quell the agonizing pain throbbing behind his eyes. He put his head against the cold concrete. Dirt and grit stuck to the film of blood and sweat of his face.

He flinched when he heard someone whispering behind him. Lowering his head, he turned and saw the padlocked cellar door. No one. When he faced the yard again, Sully turned toward him, spotted the open storm doors and started toward the house. The other cop came running into the yard. "Two streets over," he said breathlessly. "They've got a suspect."

Sully stared at the cellar a moment longer, then followed his partner out of the yard.

Nick listened as the doors of the cruiser slammed, then waited. When his breathing came easier, he wiped blood off himself and went out to the street, working his way down, staying close to the side in case he had to run.

Keeping to back streets, he made his way to Ashmont Station and caught the subway to Shawmut. As the train rattled through the tunnel, he kept looking behind him, his head jerking each time he heard a flurry of whispers that sounded like butterflies with sandpaper wings.

CHAPTER FIVE

"The results are back from the lab."

Max looked up from the file he'd been studying, pleased to see O'Grady at the door to the office the Boston P.D. had set up for him deep within the rat maze of offices that made up the District Eleven station. She wore a conservative police-blue skirt, matching blazer and a white blouse with ruffles down the front. Feminine, but all business. Max looked past her and saw plainclothes detectives and uniforms drifting in and out of offices, shuffling paper, carrying files, coffee, evidence bags, bagels and doughnuts.

"Come in, Lieutenant." He stood and motioned to a chair beside his desk. "If you don't mind my saying so, you look very nice today."

Mild surprise flashed in her green eyes, then her face flushed, adding to her appeal.

"Please, have a seat," he said, anxious to put her at ease.

She sat across from him, crossing her legs. Max had all he could do to keep from staring. "So what have we got?" he said, nodding toward the file.

"The girl's name was Lynn Ford," O'Grady said in a monotone. "Only child. Daughter of Joan and Eric Ford. Twenty-three year old senior at Boston College, majoring in journalism." She flipped through the file. "Far as we can tell, good kid. No priors. No known criminal connections. Her blood test showed slight traces of marijuana and alcohol. "We got a good DNA sample from the hair and tissue we found and fingerprints. The M.E. said she had intercourse recently, but there's no sign of rape or struggle. Her boyfriend confirmed that they had sex earlier that night. Serology tests show that the semen found in her vagina matches his."

Max listened, studying the intent expression on her pretty face, admiring her thoroughness. He wished she was an old battle ax. It would make things easier.

She looked up as if reading his thoughts. Max smiled and her expression softened. He thought she might return his smile, but the old poker face swept back like a drawn curtain.

Max pushed his feelings aside, concentrating on the task at hand. "You guys had any murders in the past couple of years that might follow a pattern like this?"

"We haven't had anything close to this since DeSalvo back in the sixties. We've contacted Walpole, Bridgewater, and all the other mental health professionals in Massachusetts and New England to see if any violent sex offenders have escaped or been released recently, and we've run the fingerprints through our database." She shrugged. "So far we've come up with nothing. The blood samples are due in this morning, but I called ahead to a friend of mine in Forensics. She gave me the preliminaries over the phone. Most of the blood belonged to the girl. The animal blood came from a chicken."

"Let me see."

She handed him the file.

Max studied it. "I think I'm going have a couple of my boys run these DNA and finger prints through the VICAP computer. What about the writing on the wall? What was it? Cromm Cruaich? Anybody come up with anything?"

"We're still working on it."

"I think it's Celtic. I have some books and files being shipped here by Fedex to your attention. Figured they'd get to me quicker. Nobody up here knows me."

She grabbed a piece of paper from his desk and jotted a note. "I'll get them to you as soon as they reach me."

"Thanks. I have a hunch about the mistletoe. When I get my books I'll be able to follow it through." He leaned back in his chair and stretched his legs. "What do you think of all this?"

She pursed her lips and her eyes took on a faraway look. "With the mistletoe, chicken blood, and the unusual murder instrument it makes me think it has to be some kind of weird Satanic thing. I thought for sure there'd be more than one perp, but the test results indicate only one, so it makes me think of a loner."

Max nodded. "I was thinking along the same lines, but I don't think it's Satanic."

"No?"

"The mistletoe and the writing on the wall point to something pagan."

"Like witches and warlocks?"

"They have the same roots and many of the same practices, but I don't think we're dealing with witches. I'm talking about pre-Christian religious practices. Nature worship, fertility rituals..." He stopped. "Listen," he said lowering his voice. "Keep this under your hat. I don't want a bunch of rumors getting out, but my gut tells me our subject's going to keep going until we nail him -- and my gut's never wrong." He tapped the file. "A lot of things don't fit. The oil on the hinges, the method of entry, the way he hid in the closet. Our subject is very intelligent and knew exactly what he was doing. This was a mixed organized - disorganized presentation. Sociopathic and organized until he was done with the girl, then sloppy. That's what puzzles me. Left his fingerprints all over the walls as if he didn't care anymore."

"That's been bothering me, too."

O'Grady's cell phone rang. She reached inside her purse, pulled it out and looked at the display, then tapped it and listened. "Your Fedex is here. I'll go pick it up and get the forensics report while I'm out." She grabbed her purse, stuffed her cell phone back into it and started out the door.

"Hey, O'Grady."

She stopped and turned back to him.

"You were right about the connection between my body snatchers and this murder. Good work."

She graced him with the first full smile he had ever seen from her. "Let's nail this son-of-a-bitch," she said.

CHAPTER SIX

A rush of people came in on a train from downtown when Nick reached Shawmut station. Expressionless faces, oblivious to the stench of stale wino piss swarmed by him, all drained from a day's work in downtown Boston. He hoped his mother wasn't among them. Those who acknowledged him stared as he made his way up the stairs. Each step made his head pound and his stomach felt queasy. He stopped on a landing and grabbed the hand rail to let the throbbing subside.

No one stopped to ask if he was all right. He saw no concern in their eyes; only fear in that brief moment before they turned away. The people behind him made a wide berth, obviously uncomfortable by his disheveled appearance.

Thank God for daylight savings, Nick thought when he walked out of the subway. Streetlights flickered on as he hurried home keeping in the shadows, ducking into alleys and side streets whenever he saw headlights. A chill November breeze rustled what leaves remained in the trees, giving Nick the eerie feeling that the whispers he heard earlier followed him.

He wanted to rest and give the sledgehammer in his head a chance to back off, but he didn't dare stop. He had to get home before his mother. He couldn't explain his present state and he certainly didn't want to have a run-in with her boyfriend Mike.

He saw no lights in the apartment from the street so he went down the alley and hustled up the back steps to the third floor of the wooden three decker apartment house that defined Dorchester. He hurried to the bathroom, locked the door and sat on the edge of the tub until the pounding in his head subsided, then he stood and saw himself in the mirror.

"Holy shit," he muttered. "No wonder those people acted weird in the subway." Blood and dirt smeared his forehead and the side of his face. A crusty scab had formed over his eyebrow. He touched his head gingerly and felt a lump beneath his blood-stiffened hair.

He filled the sink with water and washed the blood and dirt from his face, carefully cleaning the area around his eyebrow. Once clean it didn't look so bad, but the lump beneath it remained tender. He put a bandage on the cut and changed his shirt. He felt better, but a muted pain still stabbed through his head like a dull knife. After swallowing two Excedrin, he stretched out on his bed with a cold towel on his head.

Somewhere between wakefulness and dozing he heard a chorus of whispers, as if they'd been waiting for a quiet moment to insinuate themselves into his brain. He tried to block them, but they continued in hushed urgency.

He couldn't make out words, only that the whisperers wanted something. He struggled to hear more clearly, and for a moment thought he would, when the sound of the front door unlocking startled him awake.

Cold sweat. He heard his mother and Mike coming through the front door, going down the hall to the kitchen. When he heard his mother starting dinner, he realized his stomach still churned. Better get up and tell her he wasn't hungry. No sense in her cooking for nothing. Easing himself out of bed, he made his way to the kitchen.

His mother had her back to him, washing dishes. Mike sat at the kitchen table, his hairy potbelly hanging out from beneath his too small tee-shirt, the ever-present can of Bud resting on his gut. Nick smelled his shoeless feet. A blue Bay State Trucking shirt hung off the back of his chair. His curly hair was uncombed and he needed a shave. Mike looked up from staring at Nick's mom's backside and fixed Nick with that slightly bug-eyed look of his.

"What the hell happened to you?"

Nick's mom turned. She looked small and frail, as if Big Mike had sucked the life out of her. Wispy strands of dark hair dangled from the bun on top of her head. She wore a pink blouse and a beige suit. Her worry lines cut deeper into her forehead.

"I tripped on the subway stairs."

Mike took a swig of beer and belched. "Right. You were probably loaded and fell over your own feet."

The slur in Mike's words told Nick that he had already had a few. Fat, stupid, and smelly has spoken, he thought. You ain't got no room to talk, you pot-bellied lush, he almost said, but he caught himself. Keep the peace. For ma's sake.

"Nicky, are you all right?" He saw the concern in her blue eyes as she dried her hands. She tucked the dish towel into the refrigerator handle and put a hand on his forehead, eyeing his bandage.

"I'm okay, ma. It's just a scrape."

"Nicky, are you all right?" Mike said, imitating Nick's mom in a mincing voice. "Jeezuz Christ Louise, don't baby him. You want to turn him into a little pussy?"

Nick's insides tightened. No, she wants me to be fat and stupid, like you. A real man, he thought.

Louise turned to Mike, putting her hands on her hips. "I won't have you talking like that in my house."

"Don't start mouthing off to me, Louise, otherwise I'll…"

Mike's threatening tone made Nick's adrenaline surge like steam through a blown valve. He backed away from his mother. "Otherwise you'll what?"

Louise froze and Mike's eyes bugged out even more.

Nick felt himself shaking. "Listen, Buddha, you think you're so tough, let's step outside. You're gonna look awful funny when the neighbors see you get your ass kicked by a little pussy!"

"Nicky!"

The mallet in his head slammed harder. His face felt hot. "Sorry, mom…"

Mike pushed himself away from the table, made a dismissive gesture and retreated to the living room. "He wouldn't be getting' loaded and fallin' down the subway stairs if he got off his ass and got a job."

When his mother turned to look back at Mike, Nick gave him the finger. You fat fuck.

His mother faced him again.

"Sorry, mom, I didn't mean to mouth off like that."

She put her face in her hands. "I don't know why you two can't get along." She looked up and her eyes started to fill. "He's not a bad man. He means well. Works hard. It's just that when he gets a few beers in him…" She glanced over her shoulder.

"Which is every night."

"He's had a few hard knocks, that's all."

"Sure, ma." Nick hugged her. "Don't worry about me, I'm okay."

"You sure?"

"Yeah."

She kissed him on the cheek and went into the living room. Nick shook his head in disgust. A few hard knocks. Shit. He clenched his fist. Buddha keeps it up, he's gonna get a few more. He went back to his room, closed the door and shut off the light. His exchange with Mike had intensified the pounding in his head.

Climbing into bed, he lay on his stomach with his face on the pillow, pressing his palms into his forehead. As he relaxed the pain lessened. Shadowy dreams and half-formed images lapped at the edge of his mind. Each wave carried a whisper that seemed to caress, then wash over him. He knew pain waited for him if he rose to full awareness, so he let himself drift down, hoping to escape into sleep.

Deeper away from the pounding the whispers grew stronger, following him down into the depths like bats attacking a moth. *Andrasta.*

The chorus came to him on a chill wind, as if a combination of the many voices had strengthened. Why were they calling him? Looking up through the gnarled branches of barren oak trees he saw a gibbous moon bathing him in silvery light. The wind gusted, bringing with it a damp loamy smell and the scents of burning wood and cooking meat. Ahead, he saw an orange glow flickering on the other side of a hill.

Andrasta.

Torn between the compulsion to explore and the urge to flee his feet moved forward as if driven by another will that overshadowed his. The rising intonations came from the direction of the glow where bare twisted oaks dotted the hillside in a landscape that appeared ghostlike and lifeless. Nick crested the hill, stopping to gaze at the hollow before him. Nothing grew within it but the stubble of a few stunted oaks. A circle of rough-hewn stone pillars surrounded a place where firelight flickered and danced sending fingers of light darting into the surrounding blackness.

Nick breathed deep. Earthy smells filled him. Ancient smells. He held his breath and listened, hearing the fevered chorus. *Andrasta,* followed by unintelligible words and haunting cries. The name seemed to pull him toward those who uttered it as if it had a power and intelligence of its own. He worked his way down the hill, moving furtively from oak to oak, staying in the skewed shadows until he came to the perimeter of the circle.

Crouching, he crept into the shadow of a stone pillar and straightened, his face pressing against cold stone. The chants rose in volume and power, then diminished, only to rise again. He didn't understand the language, but its hypnotic cadence lulled him. He closed his eyes, letting the strange words flow over him.

An anguished scream cut through the droning chorus, startling him out of his stupor.

He inched his head around the pillar and peered into the circle. Dark figures in hooded robes held hands and chanted as they revolved around a massive bonfire. Some wore garlands of mistletoe around their necks. Nick struggled to see where the scream came from while the group chanted on.

Nick looked up and saw a flat rock spanning two shorter columns above him. Finding a handhold, he hoisted himself to the top for a better look. Halfway up, he heard another scream.

As he scrambled over the top, the crowd parted. A bloody stone altar draped with mistletoe and oak leaves sat in front of a backdrop of roaring orange. A line of skulls lay side by side along the front of it. Four wooden posts stood at each corner. A human skull hung from each of them. A nude, heavy-set girl with sagging breasts, flabby thighs and long dark hair lay sprawled on the altar, her hands and feet tied to the four posts by leather straps. Her wrists and ankles bled where the leather cut into them.

A single hooded figure stood over her chanting "Andrasta" in a distinctive, cultured sounding voice that rose above the rest. It felt both familiar and repulsive.

The assembly grew quiet.

The girl squealed and thrashed from side to side, wide eyes glinting in the firelight like a trapped animal. Nick could almost make out the man's features when he surveyed the crowd, then the leader raised a golden sickle high above his head with two hands.

Nick tried to cry out but couldn't find his voice.

The girl's features distorted. She opened her mouth, but no cry came forth. Only a flash of gold.

Blackness rushed in. Nick's stomach knotted. He tried to scream.

Vomited. Turned to jump. Fell. Struggled to his feet on legs that felt useless. Willed his body forward. It moved awkwardly, as if tangled in rope. Something rustled behind him.

When it descended, he forced himself to look, not believing his eyes. A figure with a fluttering black cape reached toward him.

He went rigid when a hand grabbed his shoulder, then he did scream...

...and awoke to find his mother standing next to his bed, hand on his shoulder, a shocked look on her face. "Nicky, wake up. You're having a nightmare," she whispered.

He looked over and saw his curtains flapping in the breeze from the open window.

CHAPTER SEVEN

This corner of the Cedar Grove Cemetery didn't look as sinister in the light of day; in fact the cover of darkness had done it justice. Its broken down, dank mausoleums smelled of urine and moldering shit. Many of the headstones had been toppled. Among a scattering of beer and liquor bottles, Max found a bra, torn panties, and two spent condoms. He hoped the girl had been willing.

"No respect," he muttered pulling his trench coat closer. He wrinkled his nose when he caught a whiff of the Thunderbird he doused himself with. After the first flurry of investigation following the Ford murder, no further leads had surfaced. All he had to go on was O'Grady's hunch about the murder and his body snatchers. He hoped by coming to the cemetery in day light dressed like a bum, he could get a better look at possible clues or suspicious activity while blending in with the other denizens of the approaching night.

At a shaded corner of the graveyard he saw a stooped figure in front of a newly filled grave. He doesn't look like a grieving family member, Max thought, stepping up his pace.

"Yo, Greg. Check out the honky wino."

The man bent in front of the grave straightened. Max saw something small by his feet, then he glanced back in the direction of the voice. Three black teenagers sat with their backs against a tomb, sipping wine and passing a joint. The man by the grave couldn't see them. The tallest kid wore a baseball cap with the bill toward the back of his head, sweat pants, a windbreaker, and bright red Converse All Stars. The heavier one beside him had on blue nylon gym shorts over sweat pants, a Boston Celtics jacket, and battered Reeboks. His baseball hat had the bill turned to the side. The third wore jeans, a hooded sweatshirt and a nylon stocking over his hair. A toothpick danced between his lips.

The one with the toothpick regarded Max with slit eyes. "Mother fucker looks like he shit his pants," the heavy one said.

Max ignored them, hoping they would lose interest in him. He turned his attention back to the man by the grave, aware of the reassuring weight of his thirty-eight in his shoulder holster. He wasn't going to let these punks rattle his cool.

The man stood motionless, staring in his direction. Max noted ragged clothes. Another honky wino. Small world, isn't it? Maybe my cheering section will back off. He kept shuffling toward the man.

"I don't know if he shit his pants or not," the first voice said from behind him, "but I'll bet I can make him."

Shit. Back off junior. I don't need any of your shit right now.

A chuckle. "Git down with your bad self, home boy," one said. "You gonna make the whitey drop a load in his drawers?" All three laughed. "I gotta see this."

The hairs bristled on the nape of Max's neck. Having his back to them made him feel vulnerable, but he didn't want to blow his cover. He had to find out what the homeless man was doing by the grave.

He kept a steady pace, putting more distance between himself and his antagonists. The man by the grave hadn't moved. For a moment Max didn't hear anything, then footsteps closed in behind him. Son-of-a-bitch! Sliding his hand inside his coat, he rested it on the butt of his gun and leaned forward as if in pain. A hand grabbed him by the shoulder and spun him around. Two smiles greeted him.

Toothpick didn't smile.

His eyes narrowed into slits. He held up a switchblade and flicked it open, jabbing it toward Max. "Hey, motherfucker. What you think you're doing walkin' 'round here stinkin' up my neighborhood?"

"Hey, brother," Max said lowering his voice. "I'm just minding my own business. I don't want any trouble."

"Brother? Shit!" Toothpick drew a gurgly inhale through his nose. Max knew what was coming. "I ain't your brother." Toothpick spat a wad of phlegm on his chest. "Do I look like your brother?"

Max stifled his kindling rage. You're pushing the wrong buttons, homeboy. You already stepped someplace you don't want to go. "Aw, c'mon, give a guy a break," he pleaded. "I'm having hard times. I don't want trouble."

"Ain't we all." Toothpick leaned closer, the blade of the knife dancing inches from Max's chin. "What the fuck you talkin' 'bout trash. Hard times is my middle name."

These assholes weren't going to back down. More than anything, Max wanted to look behind him to see if the homeless man still stood by the grave, but he didn't dare. If he made a scene, the guy at the grave would see -- if he was still there. If he backed down...

Toothpick poked him in the chest with the tip of the knife. "Hey, fool, don't be talkin' that shit to *me* 'bout hard times."

Fuck it. "No Mr. Hard Times, *you* don't understand."

"Whoo-oo. Whitey's jumpin' bad. What the fuck you gonna do, shitbum?" The knife danced closer. "You think you bad enough to show me hard times?"

"You're a funny guy, ain't you? Real bad when you got your home boys with you."

Toothpick blinked in surprise, then his eyes flashed hard. "Shit, motherfucker. I'll show you funny..."

Max stepped back, drawing his gun. "No you won't, punk. *I'll* show you funny." He pulled back the hammer and pointed it at Toothpick. "Drop the blade, bitch."

Toothpick stared open-mouthed at the gun, then the knife slid from his hand. Max picked it up, then grabbed Toothpick by the ear and pressed the barrel of the gun to his temple and wiped the spit off himself with his antagonist's face.

"I think this is funny, don't you?"

He glared at the other two wide-eyed kids, then turned Toothpick toward them, stuck his gun in his belt and poked Toothpick in the ass with his own switchblade, making him dance. "Know what else is funny?" He growled into Toothpick's ear. Funny is how you're going to look with this knife shoved up your ass."

The other kids bolted.

"Guess you ain't so bad now, are you?" Max said, feeling the kid trembling in his grasp. He pocketed the switchblade and pulled the thirty-eight from his belt. "How 'bout I pop a cap in that thick head of yours, homeboy, then stick you in the ground with the rest of these stiffs?"

"Say, brother, I was only having some fun." Toothpick's tough voice came as a whine. "I didn't mean nothin' by it."

Max pulled his ear harder. "I ain't your fucking brother. Do I look like your brother?"

"N-n-no, sir."

"Let me tell you something about fun, homeboy. You got it all wrong. Fun is sneaking around at night, finding punks like you, capping them and burying them where no one can find them."

"No, man," Toothpick started crying. He wiped his running nose with a shaking hand. "Don't kill me. Please."

"You see this cemetery?" Max said, letting his anger carry to his rising voice. "This is where I like to hunt. I see you around here again and you're fair game. Got it?" Max twisted his ear harder, bringing the kid to his knees. Toothpick fell forward on all fours. Max planted a foot on his backside and pushed. "Take a hike, bitch!"

Toothpick scrambled to his feet and disappeared in a flurry of arms and legs. Max shook his head and turned to see that the homeless man had gone.

Dammit! Something small sat at the foot of the grave. He trotted over and found a sparrow. Its wings were spread and pinned to the fresh dirt of the grave with two small wooden stakes like a butterfly displayed in some otherworldly collection. The bird's stomach was slit lengthwise, its entrails arranged beside it. Blood blackened the dirt beneath it.

That old bum must've seen it and bent down to check it out. My little dance with the soul patrol must have scared him off.

He hustled to the gate of the cemetery, slowing his pace when he caught sight of the homeless man hobbling along the sidewalk. Max heard him talking to himself, but he couldn't make out the words.

Keeping a half a block behind, Max followed him down Adams Street, through Lower Mills to Dorchester Ave. where the man crossed the street and headed north. They stayed on Dorchester Ave. a long time until the man turned into a storefront at Field's Corner across from Town Field. Max crossed the street and checked out the building from the other side.

A long sign painted in green letters ran the length of the building.

ST. AUGUSTINE CENTER FOR THE HOMELESS

Max waited around for a few minutes before giving up. *Just another poor slob down on his luck. Looks like I'll have to keep staking out the boneyard.*

He walked the few blocks to District Eleven, pleasantly surprised to find O'Grady waiting for him in his office. Today she wore a police-blue pantsuit, white blouse and a red silk scarf. *For cop fashions, this lady had it all. Her ponytail made her look like a little girl.* A huge Fedex box sat in the middle of his desk.

"I thought you might be here, so I dressed for the occasion." Max smiled and pulled open the front of his trench coat like a flasher. "Even put on your favorite aftershave."

O'Grady shook her head and let a tiny smile escape, but it quickly disappeared, replaced by her usual businesslike demeanor. Max threw his coat over the back of a chair and sat on the edge of his desk. "It's okay to lighten up," he said. "When it comes to this sickness, I'm as serious as a heart attack, but if I didn't clown around, I'd go nuts."

She opened her mouth, but Max held up a hand. "I know you've seen a few bad things in your day, but this twisted little world we're dealing with is lower than whale shit. If you want out, I'll understand and I won't think any less of you."

"You're right," she said, nodding. "I don't know what I can or cannot take. I've seen more than my share of stiffs, some of them decomposed, some bloody, but the wounds for the most part have been clean. Knives, bullets, you know. But that poor girl -- mutilated like that."

"It's all right." Max lowered his voice. "I'm sure it's going to get worse before it gets better. You need a sense of humor, dealing with this shit. Sometimes it gets so bad, all you can do is laugh or cry. I choose to laugh. I don't like seeing this shit any more than you."

"I promise to work on loosening up." She extended her hand. "I want to stop this insanity as much as you do, if not more. The only way I'm leaving is if you throw me off the case."

Max took her hand and saw a resolve in her eyes that both scared and attracted him.

She reached into her bag and pulled out a file. "Here's a copy of the completed forensics report on the Ford girl. They confirmed that the murder weapon has a long, curved blade. Longer than a dagger. They're intrigued by the wounds. Apparently the blade has quite a curve."

God, I love this girl. All business. A trooper. Tougher than a lot of men I've known. "Let me see."

She handed him the file. "No match-up on the prints yet. It's as if the guy doesn't exist. We're still working on it."

Max studied the file. "I've got some friends working on the prints. They're coming up empty too. Doesn't look like we're getting very far with the physical evidence."

He dropped the file on his desk and opened the Fedex box. "The murder weapon and the writing on the wall. Cromm Cruaich. Those are the leads I want to investigate. I think we're going to find more answers in this box than we will in the lab." He looked up. "This may take awhile. You eat yet?"

"No."

"Tell you what." He reached in his pocket. "You fly, I buy. How about it?"

O'Grady smiled. "As long as you don't make me look at crime scene photos while we're eating. I do have limits."

Max handed her a fifty dollar bill. "I won't put you through that for at least another couple of weeks."

"You're all heart." O'Grady left and Max went to the locker room to shower and change.

Back at his office he opened the Fedex box and reached in. The moment his hand touched the first book, O'Grady burst into his office, breathless.

"They just found another one. Same M.O.."

CHAPTER EIGHT

Andrasta.

The word popped into Nick's head the moment before he realized he was awake, followed by a flurry of images. He opened his eyes, blinking at the sunlight filling his room. The pounding in his head had gone, replaced by a dull pain. He gingerly fingered the bump on his head. Tender. His tailbone ached where he'd fallen on it. Better take it easy today. Lay low. Cops might be looking for me. At least they don't know who I am, otherwise they'd have been here by now. If Joey got busted he won't snitch. Nick shook his head. That's the last time I get in any car with him, no matter what he says. How could I have been so stupid? He sat up, rubbing his eyes when he saw the clock on his nightstand. Twelve-thirty. Damn! Slept fourteen hours.

After the voices and the nightmare he laid awake half the night staring at the ceiling, finally sinking into a deep dreamless slumber. This morning, in spite of his hung-over feeling, his head felt quiet, as if the voices themselves had been a nightmare. He thought of the word again. Andrasta. It wasn't even a word.

Easing himself out of bed, he took more Excedrin and a hot bath, then made himself a sandwich and a cup of coffee before settling down on the living room couch. After channel surfing he shut the T.V. off in disgust. Idiot box.

Even though he slept a long time, he still felt tired. Lying back on the couch, he closed his eyes. His nightmare of the preceding night replayed itself through his mind. When it came to the part where the robed man swooped down on him his eyes snapped open. A tingle skittered across his shoulder where the man had touched him.

Why am I having such weird dreams? And what's this Andrasta shit? And that guy in the robe. Was he some kind of magician? Was he the guy with the sickle? Andrasta?

He caught himself. What the hell am I thinking about? This is nuts. Had a bad dream, that's all. Got a good crack on the noggin. Rattled my brains a little.

Not wanting to dwell on his nightmare, Nick switched on the T.V. again and flipped through the channels, stopping at channel four, his attention drawn by the news commentator's words.

"...the second murder of its kind. Sources close to the investigation suspect cult activity or the work of a lone killer."
Nick went cold. Images from his nightmare flickered in his mind. Goosebumps danced over his body. A picture of the pretty girl he saw in yesterday's paper flashed on the screen.

"The head of Lynn Ford, a twenty-three year old Boston College student murdered in her Cambridge apartment, has still not been found."

The commentator, an attractive brunette, came back. "The second victim, identified only as a Charlestown resident, has been withheld pending notification of family members."

Nick hit the power button on the remote and took a deep breath. No way, Jose. Now I know I'm losing it. First I hear voices. Then I'm having sick dreams and tripping out over the five o'clock news. What the hell's going on? Why am I even thinking these things?

Keys rattling in the front door made him jump. Jesus Christ, Powers. Get a grip, will ya?

He heard his mother and Mike coming down the hall. A moment later she stuck her head into the living room. "Hi, honey, how's your head?"

Spinning off into the Twilight Zone. How's yours? "It's all right, ma. Just a little sore."

"You startled me with that nightmare."

"Yeah. I scared myself."

"You looked it. You going to have dinner with us?"

"Sure. I can eat."

Dinner passed uneventfully. For the most part his mom talked about work while he listened. Mike's nose stayed buried in the sports page which suited Nick. Talking to Mike about anything other than the Bruins, Celtics, Red Sox or Patriots was like discussing quantum physics with a chimp.

While Mike read the paper and belched, Nick helped his mother with the dishes, then retreated to his room and went to bed early. As soon as his head hit the pillow he thought about the newscast, sparking another ripple of goose bumps.

Don't know why that newscast made me feel so weird, he thought. It doesn't mean anything. I need a good night's sleep that's all. At least I'm not hearing any more voices. I was starting to wonder if I was going to end up in the Bozo barn. Shit, enough is enough. Tomorrow, I'll get up early, get my ass out the door and start pounding the pavement to see if I can find a job.

Closing his eyes, he drifted down into a restless sleep followed by a chorus of hushed whispers.

CHAPTER NINE

Barbara Brice's severed head sat beside her body.

Like Lynn Ford's, it had been cleaved off with a sharp curved instrument. Max studied the remains of the heavy-set girl sprawled on her poster bed. Her hands and feet were tied to the bed posts by leather straps. Blood crusted on her wrists and ankles where the leather had cut into them.

Her breasts had been cut off and placed over her mouth and a stake driven through her. Like the Ford girl she had been eviscerated, her entrails arranged on her stomach. Mistletoe stuck out of the stump of her neck and alongside her gutted organs.

Max spotted leaves on the floor of an otherwise neat apartment. Oak leaves. Same as the last murder. The same frizzy-haired forensics technician took samples from blackened splotches of congealed blood that saturated the bed. The walls of the room were splattered crimson. The word Andrasta had been scrawled on one wall in blood.

On the window sill lay a sparrow, its wings spread and pinned with two small wooden stakes like the one he saw at the foot of the grave. The bird's stomach had been slit lengthwise, its entrails arranged beside it, a miniature of the debacle on the bed.

"He must've waited 'til she was sleeping," O'Grady said beside him, in a shaky voice.

Max walked over to the closet. "Got into the apartment sometime during the day and waited for her. Same as Ford." He sniffed the hinges on the closet door, then turned to the forensics tech. "Did you get a sample of the oil on these hinges?"

The man pointed to his lab case. "Got that and more hair and tissue samples." He shook his head. "I don't get this guy. Left his prints everywhere. The closet door. The walls. He went to such great pains to sneak in without getting caught, then got sloppy."

"Definitely the same guy," Colleen, said. "Same M.O., right down to the oil."

"Hey, O'Grady," a gruff voice said. "What's a skirt like you doing here?"

Max and Colleen turned to face a sharp-featured, heavy-set man with a crew cut. Steel gray eyes probed Max. Whatever line might have divided the man's thick neck from his broad shoulders disappeared beneath the collar of a herringbone jacket. Max caught a whiff of gin when he came close.

"Working, what does it look like I'm doing, Flynn?" Colleen's voice sounded colder than Max had ever heard it.

"Aren't you a little out of your league here? This is my beat." Max flashed his shield. "Special Agent Broderick. U.S. Justice Department. She's working with me."

Flynn studied Max's badge and snorted. "I didn't hear nothing about the feds."

"We're to give him complete co-operation," Colleen said.

"That's fine as long as he knows who's in charge." Flynn pushed his way past. "Looks like they had a little picnic here."

This asshole likes to throw his weight around a little too much, Max thought, but I'll give him some slack. Who knows, maybe's he's good?

Flynn rubbed his chin and rocked back and forth on his heels as he studied the girl's remains. "Fucking Satanists."

Max crossed his arms. "What makes you say that?"

"It's obvious." He pointed to the writing on the wall. "Look at all this devil shit."

"I wouldn't be so sure."

Flynn glared at him. "I'm sure all right."

"Well I'm not."

"Hey, don't tell me my fucking job," Flynn snapped. "I've seen shit like this before. It's those fucking tweakers. Devil worshipping little pieces of shit."

Max shook his head. "That's your opinion, but you know what they say about opinions?"

"What?"

"They're like assholes."

A frown.

"Everybody's got one."

A blank expression, then something registered behind hard eyes. Flynn glared at Max. "Fucking smartass, huh?"

Max returned his stare. Guess he figured that one out. "Better than being a dumbass."

Flynn blinked. His hand clenched into a fist. He started toward Max. Colleen stepped in, blocking him. Flynn backed away, mumbling.

"Look, Flynn," Max said, putting his hands in his pockets. "I'm not here to argue about who's in charge. I'm here to stop the killing. I'll do whatever it takes."

"Long as you got my say-so."

Max held up his hand. "Fine. I have to phone in a report to Washington." Max winked at Colleen, then nodded toward Flynn. "You got a handle on things?"

"Sure."

Max went into the kitchen, closed the door and tapped the numbers on his cell phone. After two rings an operator picked up.

"U.S. Justice Department."

"Hi, can you put me through to extension three-ninety-seven, code twenty four."

"Right away, sir."

Two more rings, then a gruff voice. "Gibbs."

"Tony. Max here."

"Max. What have you dug up?"

"Funny."

"Sorry, can't help it."

"S'all right. You get my report on the Ford girl?"

"Yeah, you said you think it's linked to your body snatchers. You're authorized to upgrade your investigation to code blue. You need anything we're ready."

"Good, 'cuz we got another one. Same signature."

"Your boy's been busy, huh?"

"Fraid so. I'll send the latest as soon as I get it. Do me a favor and run it by Hart in Behavioral Science. See what kind of a profile he comes up with."

"No prob. You need some bodies up there to do legwork, say the word. We'll have some people on the next plane."

"I'll be all right for now. I have some good help."

"Getting along with the locals okay?"

"That's one of the reasons I called. Can you do me one more favor?"

"Name it."

"I had a little run in with some prick named Flynn. Charlestown homicide. I'm afraid he might fuck things up. He needs to be humbled. Can you call the governor's office and get him yanked off the case?"

"Done."

"Thanks, Tony. I'll check in with you in a couple of days. If you get something hot, you know where to find me."

"Okay, Max. Watch your ass."

"You bet." He hung up and scrutinized the rest of the apartment before going back to the bedroom. He heard Flynn's raspy voice on the other side of the door. "He's a fucking smart-assed, flaky fed."
Max put his hand on the knob.

"He's a damn good cop," O'Grady shot back. "And a gentleman. He's got more class in his pinkie finger than you've got in your whole drunken body."

Max smiled. Well, Miz O'Grady, I had no idea. He pushed the door open. "I'm not interrupting anything, am I?"

O'Grady spun toward him, green eyes flashing. "No. Flynn was just leaving."

Flynn glowered. "Listen hotshot, maybe you didn't get me before. I'm in charge of this case..."

"Past tense. Were in charge."

"What the fuck you talking about?"

"You're off the case."

Flynn laughed. "Still a fucking comedian. I had about enough of your shit. I'm going to get on the horn and get your ass bounced out of here..."

"Sounds to me like you've been blowing your horn enough, Flynn," O'Grady said.

Before he could answer, a uniform poked his head in the door. "Hey, Flynn, you got a call."
Flynn waved him away.

"From the commissioner," the cop said. "He's pissed. Royally. Wants to talk to you. Now."

Flynn looked at him and squinted, then glared at Max before stalking away, shaking his head.

Max caught O'Grady's smile out of the corner of his eye.

"How soon can you have a report for me?" Max asked the forensics tech.

"First thing in the morning, sir."

"That'll be great. One more thing."

"Yes, sir."

"Don't call me sir. You seen enough here, O'Grady?"

"Yes, sir."

"Funny." He turned and walked out of the room.

"You need a sense of humor, dealing with this shit," she said from behind him.

He didn't let her see him smile. "Flynn's kind of anal, isn't he?"

"He's a mean, loud-mouthed drunken slob who likes to hold a grudge -- and he's a sneaky son-of-a-bitch. He's not going to let this go by. Be careful, he'll be looking to get even." They reached the street and walked side by side to their unmarked.

"Sounds like you know him quite well," Max said.

"I used to be married to him."

Max took a moment to let that one sink in. "Hey, O'Grady," he said lowering his voice in a passable imitation of Flynn.

"What do you want, Broderick?"

"Lunch. I'm still buying."

CHAPTER TEN

Nick awoke feeling used and dirty. His dreams had been disjointed and bizarre; as if he experienced someone else's thoughts. The sights and sounds of sacrifices and people in dark robes flitted through the shadowy recesses of his mind. Ancient temples reminding him of Stonehenge. Chanting. The magician.

It felt like something dropped him into the rushing waters of a madman's thoughts. It took all of his willpower to cling to the slippery rock of his own rationality to keep from being swept away in the alien flood.

Now that he was awake the images lost their vividness, but the voices still passed through his mind like phantom stations on a radio receiver drifting in and out of tune. If he concentrated he could block them out, but if he relaxed they came floating back.

In spite of the specter of the voices, Nick felt better. The bump on his head still ached, but his headache had passed. Today he planned to go through the want-ads of the *Globe* to look for a job -- any job at this point, then he'd start pounding the pavement.

After climbing out of bed and throwing water on his face, he went to the kitchen for coffee. Mike grunted and lowered the newspaper, regarding him with a blurry-eyed stare. "Look what the cat dragged in," he mumbled.

"Morning, Nicky" his mother said from the stove. "You want some eggs?"

"Just coffee. Hey, Mike, can I see the paper when you're done?"

"What you gonna do, look at the pictures?"

"Funny."

His mom set a cup in front of him. "Don't you two get started this morning."

Nick took a sip and looked up. The headline caught his eye.

SECOND DECAPITATION IN CHARLESTOWN
HEADS STILL MISSING

His throat went dry. "Mike." His voice felt husky. "Can I see the front page?"

The paper lowered and Mike glared. Nick expected trouble, but to his surprise, Mike handed him the front section without argument. Taking it with trembling hands, Nick scanned the headline, following it down the page, stopping at the picture. The skin on the top of his head felt like it tightened and crawled backward across his scalp. Time seemed to freeze, suspending Nick inside a thick bubble-like cocoon, then the dream returned in a lightning flashback.

The girl in the picture.

The same one he saw sacrificed in his dream.

The words My God! went through his head. He wanted to voice them, but his mouth wouldn't work.

A subtle whisper caressed his thoughts.

Andrasta.

"Nicky, what's wrong?" This voice sounded stronger than the first. Somewhere outside him. "Nicky, what's the matter?" More urgent. A hand shaking him. "Nicky!"

He blinked and the kitchen swam back into focus. His hand rose as if under its own power, then his voice returned. "I'm okay," he said breathlessly. "I'm okay, mom." He put his hand on his chest and took a long, trembling breath.

"What's wrong with you?" she said.

"Mom. I know you're not going to believe me -- but the girl..." He pointed to the paper. "I saw her killed."

"What?"

"In my dream." He had trouble catching his breath. "I banged my head. Started hearing voices. Then I dreamed the murder. I saw the girl in the picture. Saw them kill her. The magician tried to get me. That's when I woke up."

"Nicky, what on earth are you talking about?"

He heard the edge in her voice. Way to go, stupid, he thought. Now you've got her upset.

"That's it. I'm taking the day off. You're going to the hospital..."

"Forget it, Louise." Mike set down the sports page. "The kid's on drugs. Can't you see that? That's why he fell down the stairs. If you take him to the hospital, take him to rehab. Turn him in for treatment. He's probably having one of those flashbacks from smokin' that crack shit."

Nick forced himself to breathe slower. "I'm all right. I don't do drugs." He stared at Mike. "I bumped my head. Had a nightmare, that's all."

His mother gently stroked his hair. "Maybe you should stay in bed today."

He looked up and saw the alarm in her eyes. "I'm all right." He picked up the paper and turned to the want-ads. "I want to hit the streets today. See if I can find a job."

"You sure?"

"Jeezuz, Louise, quit babying the kid, he's wimpy enough as it is. He can take care of himself."

Wimpy enough to whoop your ass, slim. "Hey, ma, for once I agree with Einstein. I don't need to be babied. Go ahead and get ready for work. I'll be okay, really."

She gave him a lingering look, then went back to the stove.

He took the subway downtown and went from business to business filling out applications, then spent the afternoon in South Boston applying for work at the fish packing houses on the waterfront. As long as he kept his mind occupied, the voices remained at bay, but as soon as he settled into a quiet moment, they drifted back.

He didn't look forward to going to bed that night.

Though dusk approached when he reached Shawmut station, Nick didn't want to linger there. The cops might still be looking for him, but he wasn't ready to go home yet either. He didn't want to think about what would happen when things got quiet. He decided to take a walk.

Starting off along the transit, he spotted Obie's shopping cart, still unclaimed. Someone had made off with his blankets and possessions, leaving his orange Hefty bags. It wasn't like Obie to leave his cart. Not for this long. Maybe he was at that new rescue mission. Could soup kitchen food be that good? He started walking again. If something's happened to Obie nobody would know. Nobody would care.

He saw a cop car parked half a block up the street. Nick didn't think they'd hassle him, but decided to play it safe, slipping into a side yard and hopping a back fence. The next street over looked deserted as streetlights winked on. Good. He stepped up his pace, anxious to put distance between himself and the cops, ending up at Wainright Park.

With the exception of a lone shopping cart tipped over in a corner and scattered bits of broken glass, the basketball courts looked dark and deserted. For some reason, Nick felt drawn to the upended cart. A trash bag full of smashed soda cans spilled onto the blacktop, along with a bundle of ratty looking blankets and a paper bag stuffed with clothes. He smelled old piss and flashed on Obie's cart abandoned by Shawmut Station. Like Obie's, this one seemed out of place without an owner. He picked up the bag of clothes between his thumb and forefinger, wondering if the cart's owner was hanging out with Obie. Maybe it was time to check out that rescue mission near Town Field?

A beam of light blinded him.

"Don't move!"

Shit! Nick dropped the bag. His breath stuck in his throat. Jesus, scared the shit out of me!

"Keep your hands where I can see them."

He saw his hands shaking in the glare of a flashlight beam. Get a grip. He forced himself to breathe. The light bounced toward him.

"Well, well, look what we've got here."

Nick recognized Sully's voice before he saw his short, wiry hair and pockmarked face.

"Fucking Powers." Sully directed the beam of the flashlight into Nick's eyes. Nick put his hand up to block the light.

"Been taking any joyrides lately?"

"What're you talking about?"

The light lingered a moment longer, then switched off. "You and Arbing. The other day. Gold Camaro."

Nick shook his head. "Don't know nothing about it."

"You don't, huh? Well we popped your buddy, Joey."

"So?"

"So, he told us everything. We know you stole the car." He lowered his voice. "Why don't you tell us your side?"

Now that the light was out, Nick's eyes began to adjust. He studied Sully's gaunt features and dark hollow eyes. He's full of shit, Nick thought. Trying to weasel it out of me. Joey wouldn't snitch. "If you already know, why you asking me?"

Sully pulled out his gun, grabbed Nick by the arm and pushed him up against the fence. "Okay, smartass. Put your hands on your head, turn around and spread 'em."

Sully kicked his feet further apart and patted him down. His hands seemed to linger a little too long below Nick's waist. "I don't know what you think you're gonna find. I ain't got nothing."

"Listen, maggot." Sully turned Nick back toward him and put his face in Nick's.

Bad breath.

"I know you stole the car and I know you're the one I chased."

"I don't know what you're talking about."

Sully flipped on the flashlight and pointed it at Nick's head. "Then where'd you get that bump?"

"I fell."

He nodded. "You're the one I chased."

Enough of this shit. "Look, I have someplace to go. Either bust me or back off."

Sully gave Nick a hard-ass stare. Nick returned it.

"Yo, Sully," a voice said from out of the darkness. "There's an O.T. over on Adams, let's go."

Sully looked toward the voice, then turned his attention back to Nick. "You think you're getting away with something," he growled. "But let me tell you something, punk. You ain't."

His partner yelled again, louder now. "Come on. Let's go!"

"I'm going to nail you for that hot box." Sully started to leave, then stopped. "If I don't, I'll find something else to nail you for."

Nick stuck up his middle finger as Sully disappeared into a flurry of blue lights.

CHAPTER ELEVEN

The wind gusted sending a swarm of dry leaves skittering around Max's feet as he stared down into the empty grave. Either this guy works fast or there's more than one, he thought. It'll be interesting to see the profile Hart comes up with.

One of the uniforms sifting through the pile of dirt beside the grave tapped him on the shoulder.

Max turned to a beefy cop smoking a cigar. He pointed toward the pile with the stub of his cigar. "We found the sparrow under the dirt, right where you said it would be. How'd you know?"

"I think I saw someone put it there the other day."

The cop frowned. "Why didn't you question them?"

"Some asshole blew my cover." He waved his hand. "Don't ask. It's a long story."

Max started toward the dirt pile. "What've we got so far?"

"Same M.O. as the others, only this time we found two sacrificed animals. You were right about one to mark the grave and the second after the digging. We've had teams examining the other exhumation sites. We're finding the same thing. Don't know how we missed it before."

"Don't feel bad. I'm supposed to be the expert and I missed it. It doesn't follow a normal pattern."

"A *normal* pattern?" The cop made a sweeping gesture with his cigar. "What the fuck is a normal pattern when it comes to this shit?"

He had a point. The concept of normal became increasingly alien with each passing day. Max smiled. "You don't want to know."

The cop stuck the cigar in the corner of his mouth and nodded. "You're right," he said between clenched teeth. "You sure you don't want us to put a detail out here? If our guys come through every night and check ahead of time, we might be able to nail this prick when he comes back to do the digging."

"Not unless they're good undercover men. This animal sees any shit going on, he'll get spooked and bail on us."

The cigar came out again and danced through the air as the cop punctuated his statements. "Somehow I don't think anything can spook this guy. If you ask me, *he's* the spook. Tell you what. I'll put in a req. for the manpower, see what the cap'n says."

"Fair enough. Do me a favor and let me know before anybody goes out. I want to brief them."

"You got it. I'm going to call in a report, then head back to the station. You seen enough?"

"Yeah." The wind kicked up. A piece of paper fluttered toward Max, lodging against his jacket. He picked it off and started to toss it back into the wind when a flash of red caught his eye. A cross. The writing on it said "ST. AUGUSTINE'S RESCUE MISSION MEAL TICK..." A tear cut across the rest of the printing. Sticking the paper in his pocket, he followed the cop back to the car.

Max saw transients milling around outside St. Augustine's when they passed it on the way to District Eleven. He fished the scrap of paper out of his pocket. Maybe it's a coincidence, or maybe it's a drifter, he thought. The guy I saw talking to himself the other day didn't come across as capable of planning things like oil on the closet door hinges. He stuffed the paper back in his pocket.

Back at the station he unpacked his Fedex box and began going through his texts, passing on *The Diagnostic And Statistical Manual Of Mental Disorder* and *The Crime Classification Manual*, finally settling on a book specializing in religions of ancient England. In the index he found a listing for sacrifices and a subheading titled Druidic.

He scanned the text, stopping on a quote attributed to a Roman named Diodorus Siculus.

> Their victims were stabbed and the convulsions of the dying were studied for the purpose of divination. The entrails were also examined.

Max set the book down and let that sink in. Their entrails were examined. Maybe he had something. He picked up the book again.

> In his Natural History (A.D. 77) the elder Pliny says that the Druids 'held nothing more sacred than the mistletoe and the oak, and they never perform any of their rites except in the presence of a branch of it'.

There's my mistletoe and the leaves on the floor, he thought. I'll bet the stakes are oak too. Heartbeat quickening, he kept reading.

> 'They choose groves formed of oaks for the sake of the tree alone. They specially venerated the mistletoe that grew on an oak, regarding it as a particular sign of the divine favour. When one was found, on the sixth day of the moon preparations were made for the sacrifice of two white bulls which were for the first time tethered by the horns, and for a banquet under the trees; a priest clad in white then cut down the mistletoe with a golden sickle.

The last two words sent a chill slithering down Max's spine. Either my man thinks he's a druid or he's taken up their habits. Wait'll O'Grady gets a load of this. Druid sacrifices. What were those names? He rifled through his notes. Cromm Cruaich and Andrasta. He looked up the names in the index, finding Andrasta first.

> Among the British Celts, human sacrifice continued in 77 A.D. Dio Cassius tells of the atrocities practiced on female victims in honor of the goddess Andrasta. Their breasts were cut off and placed over their mouths, and a stake driven through their bodies.

Christ almighty -- the Brice murder. His mouth went dry. His hands shook as he looked up Cromm Cruaich.

> From the Dindsenchas we learn that "the firstlings of every issue and the chief scions of every clan" were

offered to Cromm Cruaich -- a sacrifice of the first born. At one festival the prostrations of the worshipers were so violent that three-fourths of them perished. Though the mythic tales of the Dindsenchas are considered incredible, they were doubtless quite credible to the pagan Irish, and the ritual notices were certainly founded on fact.

Jesus, he's making sacrifices to Druid Gods. None of the locals are going to believe me, but I have good documentation and you can't ignore the parallels.

Anxious to get it all down, he spent the rest of the morning poring over his books and typing up his findings. Four hours and a stiff neck later, he rolled his head and rubbed his eyes, then decided to take a walk to clear his head.

When he came back he smelled O'Grady's perfume outside his office. Inside he found her hard at work at his desk. She wore her traditional police blue blazer with an aquamarine blouse, green scarf and a matching ribbon in her hair. The effect of the scarf and ribbon against her red hair made her eyes look even more startling.

She held up a sheet of paper. "This just came in for you." She nodded toward the file spread out in front of her. "After you read it, I've got the preliminary workup on the Brice killing."

He took off his jacket. "Good."

O'Grady started to rise from her chair.

He held up his hand. "No, no, it's okay, stay there." Sitting across from her, he handed her his notes and turned his attention to the Brice report.

Barbara Brice had been sacrificed to the Druid goddess Andrasta. He set the report down and rubbed his chin. Cromm Cruaich and Andrasta. Which sacrifice was next? He had to sort this out. He looked up and his eyes locked with O'Grady's. "Ford was an only child, wasn't she?"

O'Grady flipped through some papers and did a quick scan, then nodded. "How'd you know?"

He picked up the paper she had given him, noting that it came from Hart in Behavioral Science.

PSYCHOLOGICAL PROFILE

The placement of the ritual objects – the severed breasts, the stake through the body, the Mistletoe, and the positioning of the body all indicate compulsiveness amidst a frenzy of disorganized mayhem. I expect him to be on, or at least have been on some kind of prescription medication. His placing the victim in the degrading ritualistic posture tells me he had no remorse about the crime.

As you know, in most cases, the victims of bizarre murders are women or children. The killers are invariably men and the killings are usually intraracial. This seems to be the pattern here. Statistically, since these women have been white, most likely the killer is white. He's probably in his mid-thirties to late fifties. In spite of his mixed organized-disorganized presentation, the crime scene demonstrates methodical organization.

His painstaking attention to detail, particularly in the arrangement of the organs and his pattern of dismemberment combined with the lack of neatness in the surrounding crime scene lead me to believe that our unknown subject is in a highly disorganized mental state. The oil on the hinges indicates that when he is lucid, he is highly intelligent and calculating, but he has a hard time distinguishing between fantasy and reality. He's probably on the fringes of society, unable to function within the normal social constructs. Most likely a transient.

Max stopped reading and thought about the talker he followed. Maybe talking to himself was an act? Maybe he's smarter than I think? He leaned forward again and read the rest of the report.

His twisted visions of religious ecstasy indicate that earlier sexual traumas induced in his childhood were most likely forced on him under the guise of God and religion. He's probably heavily involved in a church and religious activities.

Max fingered the scrap of paper in his pocket.
Like Saint Augustine's Rescue Mission.

CHAPTER TWELVE

Nick stepped into a subway car on a Tuesday morning, heading downtown. As the doors hissed shut behind him the train lurched into motion. He grabbed a handhold as the train picked up speed shrieking along the tracks and remembered the whispers. He hadn't heard them for a couple of weeks.

The shrieks reminded him of the girl in his nightmare. Its horror lurked at the edges of his mind like a spider stalking its prey. Except for a few whispers passing through his mind the night he had the run-in with Sully at Wainright, Nick's sleep had been deep and dreamless.

With the passing weeks, the murder he dreamed and the shock of seeing the picture in the paper seemed more and more unreal, like one long non-stop nightmare.

Each day he walked by Shawmut, Nick looked for Obie. The shopping cart had remained in the same spot until this morning. Nick had a strong feeling that it wasn't Obie who claimed it. The thought bothered him. Sure, Obie was just another bum, but he was a neighborhood fixture as far back as Nick could remember.

Obie used to buy beer for Nick and his buddies when Nick was in junior high, back when his dad was still alive. He bought for the older kids too and their older brothers before them. Good Old Obie. He always came through, happy to get the change Nick and the gang could scrape together. Obie could be dead and no one would know.

The subway car shot out of the tunnel's blackness into bright sunshine and sped toward Field's Corner station. As it slowed, Nick felt an urge to get off and see if he could find Obie at the new rescue mission.

He walked down the ramp to Geneva Ave and headed toward Town Field where he saw some of the homeless hanging out by the bleachers.

Obie wasn't among them.

Nick walked up the street to where street people hung around a storefront with the ST. AUGUSTINE'S RESCUE MISSION sign running the length of the building in freshly painted red letters, a cross at each end.

Nick studied the faces in search of Obie's, but saw only soiled, toothless, haggard men and women in ill-fitting, mismatched clothes worn to a shine. Unsavory smells of body odor and boozy bad breath long past any attempt at hygiene made him think of Mike in the mornings. The lingering stink of urine, vomit, and unwashed hair threatened to overwhelm him.

Most of them grasped tickets. The writing on them was too small to read, but Nick recognized the red crosses. Getting close to chow time. He went inside. Fresh paint covered scarred, barren walls. A small platform and a pulpit sat at one end of the large room, tables at the far side. More tables took up the space in the middle of the floor. The heat felt oppressive, the air thick with the dregs of humanity. Nick stood well inside the doorway, scanning the expectant faces of those lining the walls and sitting at the tables.

No Obie.

Someone tapped him on the shoulder. Shit, someone's going to hit me up for spare change, he thought as he turned, ready to voice the word "No", stopping when his gaze met the darkest blue eyes he'd ever seen.

The depth in the older man's eyes emanated a calmness that Nick thought he could get lost in; as if they had the power to swallow him.

"Can I help you, son?" The man's voice sounded soft and reassuring, with an Irish accent. His broad open face inspired trust. Thick eyebrows, salt and pepper hair and an aquiline nose made him look distinctive. He wore a black suit, matching jacket and a clerical collar. "I'm Father Derlen."

This man had *it*, Nick thought. What was that word? Charisma. Aside from the free chow, Nick could see why the homeless flocked to him.

"Yeah, I umm, I was looking for a friend."

A slight frown. "In here?"

"He's a homeless guy. I've known him all my life. He's disappeared. I thought he might've come here. Maybe you've seen him. His name's Obie."

Derlen rubbed his chin thoughtfully. "Can't say that I have. We get a lot of people in here." Derlen held out his hands. "I try to help them all, but there's so many."

The more the priest talked, the more Nick thought he recognized his voice, but he had grown up with Irish-Catholics. Lots of people had accents like Father Derlen's. The older man studied him, as if waiting for him to say more. Suddenly Nick felt stupid and wanted to get out of there. "Well, umm, thank you, Father. Sorry to bother you. I'm sure you're busy and I can see that Obie isn't here. Thanks for your time."

The priest smiled and patted him on the back. "Take care of yourself, son."

Nick walked out feeling perplexed. Sure is a nice guy, he thought. Not like that asshole Sully, or a selfish slob like Mike. This one's really helping people.

He walked home, puzzling over the mystery of Obie's disappearance. Without understanding why, he felt certain he would never see Obie again.

After making lunch, he spent the rest of the day cleaning house. It bothered him to see his mother work all day, then come home and have to clean. He helped whenever he could, especially since Mike moved in. The messes were bigger now and other than going to the liquor store, Mike never lifted a finger.

No sooner had Nick finished when his mom came home. A broad smile filled her face when she saw the clean house. Nick's heart swelled when she gave him a hug and made dinner for the three of them. After eating, Nick helped her with the dishes while Mike watched the boob tube.

When they finished, Nick went to lie on his bed. His certainty that Obie had disappeared coupled with the fact that no one noticed or even cared, troubled him. If Obie were dead, the cops would never know and if they did, they wouldn't do anything. Who'd make a missing persons report about a street person? He pictured himself walking into the District Eleven station and running into Sully.

He put his hands behind his head, closed his eyes and thought about it. No way Obie would leave his shopping cart like that. No way. Eventually he drifted into a restless sleep where disjointed images flitted through his mind, finally coalescing into a strange setting.

He smelled dirt. Loamy. Felt it against him. With the exception of dim moonlight, the sky looked dark. He looked up from the bottom of a freshly dug hole and thought he heard voices. A cloud passed in front of the moon and countless arms reached over the edge of the hole, slithering toward him. Impossibly long arms. Touching him. Lifting him.

He rose out of the dirt and the hands silently grappled him, covering every part of his body. Squinting, he peered into the darkness, trying to see the owners of the hands. He saw bodies, but couldn't make out heads -- they didn't have any! Adrenaline raced through him. His heart slammed in his chest. He tried to scream, but couldn't. He fought, unable to free himself. Arching his body backward, he saw a headstone. Though he looked at it upside down, he saw the name clearly.

NICK POWERS

He gasped and threw his head forward. His eyes met those of a hooded man with a gaunt, sunken stare.

The wind gusted and blew the hood off Sully's head. He laughed. "You're mine, Powers," he said between clenched teeth.

Hands closed around his throat, cutting short his breath. Nick opened his mouth, felt his eyeballs bulging...

...and woke up trembling, his body drenched in sweat.

CHAPTER THIRTEEN

"Tell me something," O'Grady said, nibbling on a French fry. They sat in Max's office, reports, books, and notes spread out on the desk between them. The continuous clicking of keyboards and ringing phones came from the surrounding offices. "You've been working on this occult mumbo-jumbo stuff for awhile now. Devil worshippers, cults, body snatchers, and now druid sacrifices -- and all the weird stakeouts you've been on and the warped people you've had to deal with…"

Max swallowed the last bite of his hamburger, and wiped his mouth. "Definitely on the fringes of religious freedom, wouldn't you say?"

"But is there anything to it?"

"What do you mean?"

"The occult and the supernatural. Ever had any weird experiences?"

Max chuckled. "As far as I'm concerned they're all weird."

"That's not what I'm talking about." She sipped her iced tea. "Have you ever run across any genuine supernatural phenomena? Do you believe in ESP?"

"Well…" He hesitated, enjoying the way her eyes widened. He could almost see the gears in her brain meshing. He shook his head. "I don't believe any of that off-the-wall cult stuff," he said, his tone somber. "But the people I've had to deal with do. That's what makes them dangerous. In every devil-worshipping case I've worked to date, there's been a link to narcotics. Meth to be exact. And let me tell you something." He pointed at her. "There are junkies who'd sell their mother for a fix and crackheads who survive by knocking over Seven-Eleven's, but there's nothing more sick or dangerous than an amped-out meth head who thinks the devil's on his ass." He leaned back in his chair. "And what goes on in their heads is scarier than anything I've ever seen in a movie theater. As far as I'm concerned, they are possessed by demons, only their devils are man made and chemically induced."

Colleen frowned and nodded slowly. "I see what you mean. It's spooky no matter which way you cut it." She picked up the trash from their lunch and tossed it in the wastebasket, while Max leafed through a file.

"Can you do a little digging for me?" he said, looking up from the file.

"Name it."

"Find out what you can about St. Augustine's Rescue Mission."

"On Dot Ave.?"

"Yeah. Be discreet, but I want to find out who's running it, where the money comes from, stuff like that."

"I'll get right on it. You think our man might be at the mission?"

"I followed a homeless guy there from one of my stakeouts. I didn't think anything of it at first." He reached in his pocket and pulled out the meal ticket stub. "Then when I went back to the cemetery to investigate the latest body snatching, I found this." He handed it to her.

O'Grady turned the stub over in her fingers then handed it back.

"Might be a coincidence," Max said returning the ticket to his pocket, "but it's a lead we can't afford to pass up. Besides we don't have anything more to go on at this point. I've found more clues from my books than I've gotten from the evidence."

"I'll get to work on it right away. What are you going to do?"

"More undercover work."

"At the mission?"

"Yeah..."

A gaunt patrolman with short, wiry hair and a pockmarked face popped his head into the office. "Excuse me," he said. "Didn't mean to eavesdrop, but I was walking by and I couldn't help overhearing that you were going undercover at St. Augustine's."

Frowning, Max looked at the cop. He must've been walking awful slow to hear all that. Their eyes met and the uniform averted his gaze. Max didn't like the way the guy popped in or the expression in his eyes. "Who are you?"

"I'm sorry." He held out his hand. "Officer Sullivan."

Max took his hand. The palm felt wet.

"My friends call me Sully." He looked at O'Grady, his gaze lingering a little too long. "I know Father Derlen." He turned back to Max. "A good man. I do volunteer work for him with the homeless. If there's anything you want to know, or you need any help, let me know." He looked back at O'Grady, his eyes doing another close inspection. She moved uncomfortably in her chair.

Just what I need, Max thought. A God-damned shifty uniform on my team, introducing me to my suspects.

"Thanks, Officer Sullivan," Max said. "I appreciate your offer. I'll contact you if we need your help."

Sully nodded. "No problem. Glad to be of service." He looked at O'Grady again. She turned her back and flipped through a file. Max started toward the door. When Sully didn't move, Max took his hand, shook it, patted Sully on the back and guided him out of the room. "Thanks for your offer, Officer Sullivan. I'll keep you in mind."

"Sully. My friends call me Sully."

"Okay, Sully."

Max shrugged at O'Grady and sat back at his desk without speaking, then rose again and poked his head out the office door. Sully knelt beside it tying his shoe. Max leaned against the door jamb and crossed his arms. Sully looked up with a sheepish smile. Max waited until he left and closed the door.

"Nice guy," O'Grady said sarcastically.

"A little too nice for my tastes."

"Well, now that we're being honest, he's a creep."

"Talk about it. I'm changing my undercover plans. That guy's bad news."

O'Grady put her pen to her lips and squinted. "Makes me wonder."

Max leveled his gaze at her. "Oh yeah?"

"Wouldn't surprise me if he's one of Flynn's boys."

"No shit?"

"I'm worried. It'd be just like Flynn to pull something like that."

"And interfere with an investigation?"

"When it comes to Flynn's ego, nothing is sacred. You handled him well, just be careful."

"You didn't do so bad yourself."
"Don't underestimate him. He won't forget."

CHAPTER FOURTEEN

Nick collapsed into the seat of the subway car after another grueling day at his new job; bus boy at Jimmy's Harborside on Commonwealth Pier. Shit work for shit money, but he couldn't afford to be picky. His finances had dwindled to nothing.

He closed his eyes when the train lurched ahead. Now that his nightmares had stopped, he looked forward to falling into bed each night, exhausted after long hours on the job. Since starting work, he woke up each morning with no memories of any dreams.

Because of his hours, he hadn't been on the streets much. His run-in with Sully seemed part of an unreal past. Things were finally looking up. He'd even managed to wrangle himself a date with one of the waitresses.

The train passed over Dorchester Ave. and braked for its stop at Field's Corner. Nick looked out the window and caught a glimpse of the homeless people outside St. Augustine's.

Never did find Obie, he thought. Wonder what happened to him? He remembered his meeting with Father Derlen and the way the man affected him. Too bad Obie didn't go to the rescue mission. Derlen would have taken care of him. The train stopped, disgorged its passengers and took on a few before leaving Field's Corner. Nick leaned back in his seat and shut his eyes again.

The train slowed when it approached Shawmut. Nick stood and stretched. When the door hissed open, he stepped out and hustled up the steps ahead of the crowd, slowing when he reached the turnstiles.

Apprehension gripped him the moment his hand touched the door to the street, as if an unseen truck hurtled toward him. He pulled his hand back. His legs started to shake. He looked around to see if anyone was near. Not a soul.

The train pulled out of the station, sending a blast of cold, dank, wino-piss air rushing past, and the first of the other passengers appeared above the top of the steps. The doors flew open in front of him as if beckoning.

He stepped out into the chilled night air. Disembodied words exploded into his mind with a force that made him stagger. *You have to do it!* He put his hands over his ears. His gut knotted. He bent over and grabbed his stomach. Images flooded his mind like a swarm of bats. The sacrifice. The girl's picture in the paper. Barbara Brice. His nightmares. The whispers.

They weren't whispers anymore.

You are the divine instrument of God's will. His hand will guide yours. The voice sounded normal now, as if its owner were beside him.

At least he stopped screaming, Nick thought, fighting to clear his head. Two or three people stopped to stare at him. Great. Sideshow time again. A neatly dressed man wearing a felt hat and glasses held a brief case in front of him like a shield. He shook his head at Nick and walked past. "Kids." He stopped and turned back to Nick. "Why don't you learn to say no? Keep away from that shit."

Nick wanted to flip him off, but stopped himself when a small, heavy-set woman clutching a shopping bag approached him. "Are you all right, son?"

You will never rest until my will is done. "I'm okay, ma'am. Must've been something I ate."

She put a hand on his shoulder. "Would you like me to call someone?"

He forced himself to stand up straight. "No, no thanks. I'll be all right." He looked around. The crowd had swelled. Better get the hell out of Dodge. He didn't need all this attention. If Mike or his mother ever heard about this... "I live just around the corner." He pointed. "I'm almost home. Thank you."

He pushed his way through the crowd and headed in the opposite direction. *The chosen few must be sacrificed for the greater good of all.*

The voice had calmed. Now it sounded like it was reasoning with a child. *You mustn't disappoint me. You know how much we've come to depend on you. Our future rests on what you do.*

Nick walked at a brisk pace, listening carefully. Where the hell have I heard it before? Why is it talking in my head?

Further down the street he spotted a dark figure huddled in a doorway. When he drew near he saw a bearded homeless man drawing his jacket closer. The light from the streetlight cast itself across the man's face, giving his weathered features a jaundiced pallor. His eyes glinted an unholy yellow.

Many are called, but few are chosen, the voice said as Nick passed.

"But I don't want to be called," the man in the doorway blurted. "I don't want to be chosen."

Nick's knees buckled. His head seemed to float above him as if filled with helium. Grabbing a car for support, he steadied himself. *You have no choice in this matter. The forces have chosen you. You cannot deny their authority.* Nick's heart fluttered and for one crazy moment, he thought it might explode. He forced himself to breathe deep.

"But I have a free will," the man cried from the doorway. "I can choose!"

You have given your will to me and you have given it to the powers that rule over us all. You are a divine instrument. Come to me and be blessed. Accept your fate.

"But I'm afraid."

Nick crouched low and ducked behind the car, watching the man carry on one side of a conversation while the voice in his head supplied the other.

"I don't want to do it. I can't do it. It's against -- it's against..."

There is still time. Come to me. Free yourself from your wretched existence. Be among the blessed. Embrace your destiny."

The man tottered onto the sidewalk. Nick let him get ahead before following him down Center Street. The voice in his head remained quiet. So did the man.

When they neared Saint Mark's school, Nick heard a car coming up the street and the sound of tires slowing. He wanted to look back, but decided to keep moving. The car stopped and he heard a door open and shut.

"Hold it right there, Powers," Sully said.

Shit! With a sinking heart, Nick watched the homeless man disappear into the darkness.

Just what I need. Sully must really have a hard-on for me. He's got a funny way of showing up at the weirdest times. Like he's got radar or something. He turned to face Sully, who came toward him slapping his nightstick into the palm of his hand. "What's up, Sully?"

Sully jabbed the nightstick toward him. "That you I got the complaint about, causing a disturbance down at Shawmut?"

"Do I look like I'd cause trouble?"

"Call said some dark-haired punk was going spastic in front of the station. Figured it had to be you."

Nick shrugged. "Sorry to disappoint you." He started walking. The nightstick shot out, stopping him.

"Where do you think you're going?"

I ain't got time for this macho shit, Nick thought. "Home. I ain't done nothing wrong."

"That's for me to say. Up against the wall and spread 'em."

"You serious?"

Sully smacked his palm. "Don't cross me unless you want your head decorated." He pushed Nick up against the wall and searched him, again spending a little too long below Nick's waist. When he finished he backed up. "Okay, Powers, turn around."

"What's your problem?" Nick said.

Sully acted as if Nick hadn't spoken. "Your pal Joey's looking at a stretch in Concord. He's taking the rap for you. How's that make you feel, tough guy?"

"You still hung up on that shit? I'm sorry to hear Joey's going away again, but it's not like it's the first time. He'll manage."

Sully leaned toward Nick, club raised. "Get in the cruiser."

"For what? You busting me?"

Sully pointed with the nightstick.

Nick hesitated. If he got in they'd take a ride, but it wouldn't be to the station. If he held his ground, Sully would have to prove himself here on the street. Either way, Nick figured he'd end up with a beating, then Sully would throw him in a cell and tell everyone how he'd been drunk and fell down the stairs.

"Hold on a minute." Nick held up his hands.

"Bullshit." Sully grabbed him by the collar. The club went up. Nick raised his arms to protect himself and an eighteen wheeler rumbled around the corner. Sully lowered the club.

Asshole didn't want any witnesses.

The truck rolled up the street, its air brakes hissing to a stop beside them. Nick's heart leaped when he saw the Bay State Trucking logo.

The door opened and for the first time in his life, Nick was glad to see Mike.

"What's the problem here?" Mike said, hopping out of the cab and rolling up his sleeves."

"Move along," Sully said. "This is none of your business."

Mike kept coming. "Whaddya mean, none of my business? Damn right it's my business." He stopped next to Sully and crossed his arms. Fear flickered in Sully's eyes. Mike stood a full head taller. "That's my son you've got there. You got a beef with him, you got a beef with me. What's the fucking problem?"

Nick felt Sully's hand go limp on his collar. "Just asking a few questions, that's all."

"Then you're done, right?"

Sully's voice lowered. "Yeah, I'm done."

"Good. Come on, Nick, supper's gettin' cold."

He followed Mike to the truck and climbed in the cab beside him. He smelled alcohol as soon as the doors closed. Mike had been hitting the hard stuff. He double clutched and shifted into first.

"Whew," Nick said as the truck started forward. "Saved my bacon there."

"What was that all about?"

"He thinks…"

Mike waved his hand. "Aw, forget about it. I don't want to know. Sully's a punk. Always was, always will be. A real dickless wonder. The only dick he's ever had was somebody else's. Fucking sausage smoking faggot."

"Thanks for showing up. How'd you know?"

"One of the neighbors called. Said you were having problems near Shawmut. Wouldn't say what it was, only that you looked sick."

"What about my mother?"

"She was at the store. She don't know nothin'. I ain't gonna say nothin' if you don't."

"Thanks. I don't want her upset."

"You and me both." He pointed at Nick. "You and me. We've had our differences, but when it comes to her, I think we see eye to eye. I been watching you the past few weeks. You been bustin' your ass at your new job. I respect that."

"Thanks."

"Besides, Sully's a fuckin' maggot. I'm sure you and me'll have some more run-ins in the future, but that's between us. Sully ain't got no business messin' with the family."

CHAPTER FIFTEEN

"When do you expect those forensics reports back from Washington?" O'Grady pulled the unmarked onto the Southeast Expressway and headed toward Dorchester. Leaden clouds hung low in a cold November sky. A gusting wind brought large raindrops splattering against the windshield. With no new leads and no new killings, she and Max had decided to re-examine the murder scenes in an effort to corroborate the details Max had gleaned from his books.

Max looked up from the file he was studying, his gaze passing quickly from O'Grady's legs to her face. Cop blue skirt today. "Funny you should ask. They're taking way too long. Should've been here a couple of days ago. I called to check up on them this morning. They asked me to bear with them a while longer." He shrugged. "Must have found something interesting. I expect the report this afternoon. Between you and me, since there haven't been any new murders and the publicity has died down, I think they're dragging their feet."

"Figures. Soon as we get another stiff, the media will be breathing down our necks, wondering why we haven't made any progress." She sighed. "Maybe we'll find something waiting for us back at the station."

"If we're lucky." Max went back to his files, studying the photos of the crime scenes again.

"You spend more time studying crime scenes than anyone I've ever met," O'Grady said, glancing over at him.

"If you want to understand the artist, you have to look at the painting," he said without looking up. "You have to put yourself in the position of the hunter like a lion who's trained himself to sense the weakest antelope in the herd. It's the same with people."

No new reports awaited them at District Eleven. "Shit." Max tossed the files he'd been studying on the desk. "We're stalling here. No new leads. A stakeout's chancy at best. We've got nothing hard."

O'Grady set her purse down and dropped into a chair, crossing her legs. "Maybe something will break when we get those reports."

"If we ever get them."

Max went around to the back of his desk, where he couldn't see her legs. Too distracting. "I'm going to make another call and put some heat on someone's ass. This is ridiculous." The moment his hand touched the phone, it rang. "Broderick."

"This the federal investigator?" a muffled male voice said.

"Who wants to know?"

"I have a tip."

"Who is this?" He looked at O'Grady and frowned. She leaned forward.

"A concerned citizen. I have information about the murders you've been investigating."

"How do I know you're legit?"

"You don't, but from what I hear, your investigation is going nowhere."

"Who told you that?"

"I have my sources. If you want information, meet me at ten tonight."

Max fumbled a pen from his pocket and grabbed a notepad. "Where?"

"Savin Hill Station. Come alone. Anyone else shows and I'm history. Got it?"

Max jotted it down, shielding it with his hand so O'Grady couldn't see. "Yeah, I got it. How will I know who you are?"

"I'll be at the end of the platform wearing a trench coat."

"I'll be there."

The caller hung up.

"Who was it?" O'Grady said when Max set the phone down.

"Don't know. Might have been that Sully creep, but I can't be sure. Says he has information about the homicides. He seems to know an awful lot about the investigation." He rubbed his chin. "Like he's a cop or knows one. I think it's a setup, but who'd set me up?" He looked at

O'Grady.

"Flynn," she said without hesitation. "That'd be just like him. Where does he want to meet? I'm going with you."

"He said I should be alone."

"That's too dangerous."

If he was going to be stupid enough to walk into this, Max didn't want to risk her getting hurt. He steepled his fingers and studied O'Grady, admiring the way her expressive features mirrored her thoughts. He felt like he could have a whole conversation without her saying a word. Her face did all the talking, especially those green eyes. "Yeah, I know," he said, watching her reaction, "but we don't have any solid leads. We can't afford to pass this one up. You can come, but I want you to stay in the car."

"Cut the shit, Broderick. Where's the meet?"

He held up his hand. "I'll tell you, but you have to promise you'll stay in the car.

She scowled.

"Don't worry. I need help, I'll scream."

"Where?"

O'Grady parked their unmarked half a block up the street from Savin Hill Station a little after nine-thirty that night.

"Okay." Max checked his thirty-eight and tucked it in his shoulder holster. "You keep watch from here. If you see anything funny going down, put in a call and come in with your shield out and your weapon drawn. Don't take any chances."

"I'm coming in with you."

"If you come in and this guy's connected to the department, they'll make you, then our lead's blown."

O'Grady pulled her thirty-eight out and laid it in her lap.

"Look, I'll tell you what." He patted her on the shoulder. "If it'll make you feel any better, give me ten minutes."

She gave him an uneasy smile. "Fair enough."

He glanced at his watch. Nine-forty-five. He glanced over at O'Grady and caught her studying him. He gave her his most reassuring smile. "Showtime." He stepped out onto the rain-soaked sidewalk and heard the sound of tires hissing on wet pavement. A light drizzle hung in the air. He put his collar up against the chill wind and walked up the street.

Three minutes later, he went through the turnstile at Savin Hill

Station. He checked his watch when he stepped off the bottom step onto the platform. Ten o'clock. The outdoor station looked deserted. Max glimpsed the outline of a man next to a storage room at the other end of the station. He wore a trenchcoat.

Familiar butterflies filled his gut, reminding him of his undercover days with the DEA. How many buys had he made? Fifty? Sixty? He pressed his arm close to his body, comforted by the feel of his thirty-eight, then slowly walked to the end of the platform. The man with the trenchcoat disappeared behind the storage room. Max slid his hand inside his jacket, resting it on the butt of his gun.

He flinched when someone coughed in the darkness. An old drunk slouched on a bench facing him. Taking a deep breath, he steadied himself and watched the drunk out of the corner of his eye, not liking the vibes.

When Max reached the end of the storage room the man with the trench coat stepped out. Startled, Max started to draw his gun, then stopped. The man had his hand extended in greeting. No weapon. About six-two and heavy-set, he wore a gray felt hat pulled low over his eyes and a matching scarf that covered the lower half of his face.

Max stepped closer. The man's eyes lit up in what Max interpreted as a warm greeting. Relaxing a little, Max tried to read what he could see of the man's face. The only distinguishable feature was a jagged scar across the bridge of his flattened nose. It had been broken more than once. Max pulled his hand out of his jacket to return the shake and the man's hand closed into a fist that pistoned into Max's stomach, knocking the wind out of him.

He doubled over and grabbed for his gun. A second fist caught him in the side of his head. Bright light exploded. He stumbled backward into someone's arms that tightened around his neck in a hammerlock. Shit!

"A present from Flynn," said the voice from behind.

The drunk. Should've known. A fist in the eye. A flash. His knees buckled. Hang on. He saw two feet. Blurry. Timing. One. Two. He launched his foot, catching his assailant in the groin.

"Uuuh."

Then he brought his heel down hard onto the instep of the man who held him.

"Aaarghh!"

The arms loosened and Max drove his elbow up and back, catching the man in his jaw. The man hit the platform. Max forced himself to breathe. His vision cleared. Out of the corner of his eye he saw a kick coming toward him. He turned and it glanced off him, but the force still knocked him down. Blackness threatened to swallow him. He reached inside his jacket, wrapped his hand around the grip of his thirty-eight and started to draw, but a kick from behind stopped him.

The first man kicked him in the gut. Max bent forward. Another kick from behind. On the second kick from the front, Max caught the foot and twisted it. The man's arms flew out and he went sprawling to the ground.

The platform started to rumble. A train. The man pulled his leg away and scrambled to his feet. Movement behind him, but no more kicks. The sound grew louder. Max fumbled for his gun as the two staggered away, but by the time he drew it, his assailants had disappeared.

A cold rush of wind hit him in the face as the train roared into the station. He holstered his gun and forced himself to sit up. Faces stared at him from the windows of the car as the train screeched to a stop. Two people disembarked from the other end. Max forced himself to breathe deep as the train pulled out of the station. Now that his adrenaline had slowed, he began to feel the pain of his injuries.

Reaching up, he felt wetness where his eye began to swell, then he looked at his hand. Blood. He went to stand and felt a sharp stab in his side. Better rest. He took out his gun, put his finger on the trigger and stuck it in his pocket, barrel forward, then pushed himself to his feet with a grunt and limped out of the station, stopping every few steps to rest. Climbing the stairs a few steps at a time, he made it to street level. He stopped outside the station and leaned against the wall to catch his breath.

Footsteps. Shit, here we go again. Then a whisper. "Check out that drunk. Bet his wallet's an easy snatch."
The footsteps came closer. Max waited until a hand touched his shoulder, then pulled out his gun and stuck it between the kid's eyes. "Fuck off, I'm having a bad day."

Dark eyes grew wide. "Y-y-yes-ss- s-sir." Two leather jacketed teenagers turned and bolted.

When O'Grady saw him, she came running, stopping a few feet from him. Her hand went to her mouth. "What happened?"

"I had a disagreement with a door. The door won."

"It was Flynn, wasn't it?" She reached toward him, tenderly touching his face, reminding him of his mother's reaction the time he'd come home from his first fight.

"You're a terrible liar, Broderick," she said, her voice husky. Then she seemed to catch herself. "Press charges. I want you to press charges."

"Look, even if something did happen, there's no way I could prove it was Flynn. Two guys jumped me. One of them said he had a present from Flynn." Max touched the cut over his eye. "Interesting delivery. Let's just forget it. There's no proof."

Her eyes narrowed. She fumbled a handkerchief from her purse and handed it to him. "You can't press charges, but that doesn't mean I can't do anything."

"Don't worry about it." Max put the handkerchief against his cut and smelled O'Grady's perfume. "I'll deal with it in my own way." She watched him in the mirror of her compact, but he knew she wasn't listening.

CHAPTER SIXTEEN

The whispers returned that night, drifting in and out of Nick's mind like ethereal dancers in a ballroom of gauzy light. He couldn't make out any words; only an underlying sense of urgency and unrelenting insistence. He fell asleep sometime after two, fully expecting nightmares, but none came.

In the first moments of silence following his awakening, the whispers came drifting back, then he heard Mike and his mother in the kitchen.

He thought about the previous night while washing his face and brushing his teeth. Spooky. Then Sully. A real horror show. If it hadn't been for Mike... Nick couldn't believe the way Mike had stood up for him. He found himself smiling through a mouthful of toothpaste. Put that weasel Sully in his place, that's for sure. Maybe Mike's not one-hundred percent purebred asshole after all. He might have some redeeming qualities underneath that Neanderthal exterior. He wiped his face, hung the towel on the rack and went out to the kitchen.

"Good morning," he said, taking a seat.

Mike lowered the paper and glared at him without answering. In that moment Nick understood that things hadn't changed. Whatever happened the night before meant nothing; as if there were two Mikes. Budweiser Mike, the belligerent, predictable, self-centered asshole, and Seagram's Mike, the cool, unpredictable bad ass who stood up for family because he cared for Nick's mother. Nick didn't know which Mike scared him more.

After half a cup of coffee, he left.

Outside in the brisk morning air, he felt refreshed, his perceptions tuned. A feeble November sun lit the street. He listened for the whispers, trying to get some sense of them. They grew louder as he neared Shawmut station, but the words sounded too soft to be distinguished. On impulse he called in sick at work and continued down Center Street; the same route the homeless guy had taken last night.

When he reached Dorchester Ave., Nick went left toward the rescue mission. To his surprise, the whispers grew fainter. He turned and started back toward Ashmont. When he passed St. Mark's church, he felt a jolt in his gut, then the voice grew stronger. He stepped up his pace, moving past Ashmont to Gallivan Boulevard. He could almost make out the words.

With the stronger voice, Nick gained a sense of its direction. He could "feel" the words in his head. If the sensation came from the side of his head and he turned away, he felt it at the back of his skull, as if someone had rested their hand there.

Through trial and error he ended up at the entrance of the Cedar Grove Cemetery on Adams Street where the voice stopped. Outside the gate he scanned the grounds, his gaze stopping on a blue Chevy Impala. An unmarked. He gave the rest of the graveyard a quick check. Two old women put fresh flowers on one grave. A young woman and a child stood holding hands next to another.

We must always escape detection, the voice said from his left. Nick turned toward the source. A lone figure, huddled in the shadow of a dark angel that towered over a black granite headstone. Nick felt a rush of adrenaline when he recognized the bearded man from last night. He also spotted two dicks from the unmarked. They too seemed interested in the homeless man. Nick shook his head. Boston's finest looked conspicuous by trying so hard not to look conspicuous.

The offering has been made. Tonight you will perform the final ritual. Consummate your loyalty.

Final ritual? The dream of Barbara Brice's murder flashed through his mind. Can't be.

He stifled the urge to run and tell the two dicks, but what would he say? "Hey, guys, arrest that bum. I've been hearing voices and they tell me he's a serial murderer." Right. They'd give him the royal treatment, complete with wardrobe and first class accommodations -- a strait jacket in a rubber room. No thanks. A chill tickled his spine. He shook it off and felt tightness in the pit of his stomach. Have to play this one solo.

Return to me, my faithful one, so I may bless you and send you on your quest.
The bearded man rose and started toward the cemetery gate. The two plainclothes cops turned away as if interested in something else. Nick backed out of sight, then crossed the street and waited. A few minutes later, the bearded man appeared, deep in conversation with himself. Nick waited to see if the cops would follow, but the unmarked didn't appear. He followed the man to Adams, then down Dot Ave. listening to the controlling side of the conversation in his head while the man muttered responses.

It didn't sound so strange now that he'd grown used to hearing it. Any resistance the bearded man put up had been subdued. He spoke to his mentor with the tone of an obedient child. Nick remembered the pain of the angry voice crashing through his mind and understood how someone would want to keep it pacified.

Now that it wasn't yelling, Nick thought he recognized the voice, but couldn't place it. The words carried a quiet authority that made it hard to tell. For the most part the statements were a repetitive hypnotic cadence that urged the bearded man on. Its rhythm lulled Nick and it actually felt comfortable and reassuring in his head.

Like an old friend.

The conversation lasted all the way to Field's Corner, then ended. Nick wasn't surprised to see the homeless man head for Saint Augustine's.

Across from the mission a small group had gathered. They weren't homeless people. It struck Nick as odd and out of place to see such a gathering in Town Field. He slowed and studied them as they burst into spontaneous shouts and clapping.

As if in answer to his question the crowd parted revealing a street magician, complete with top hat, cape, and tux. When Nick spotted the cape, his nightmare flooded his mind and for the second time in as many days he almost fainted. In a flash of insight he realized that the magician ended his act as soon as the bearded man appeared at the same time the voice stopped. Nick felt cold. He wanted to move, but his legs refused to obey.

The magician. The nightmare. The voice. The sacrifice.

Each image flashed through his mind. The magician turned his attention away from the bearded man and looked directly at him. Nick's heart jumped. The ensuing adrenaline brought his legs back to life. Stumbling backward, he fell over a bicycle, scrambled to his feet and ran, not daring to look back.

He kept running until he reached Shawmut station where he ducked into an alley. Pressing himself against the wall he fought to catch his breath. A flurry of disconnected images raced helter-skelter through his mind. With shaking hands he wiped the sweat from his face.

Damn it, settle down. Jesus. It's him. He's the one who's been talking in my head. In my dreams. Does he know I can hear?

He heard footsteps crunching on broken glass coming from the end of the alley. Shit, he's coming after me. He looked around, frantically searching for something to defend himself with. Seeing a long-necked beer bottle, he picked it up by the neck, smashed the end of it against the wall, and held the jagged end out. The footsteps receded. When his mind and the noise outside the alley grew quiet, Nick slipped out and walked for hours – away from the voice.

Darkness came and he headed for home, unable to stop thinking about the magician. He didn't want to go to sleep. Since his confrontation at Town Field, Nick hadn't heard any more voices, but when he finally dropped off to sleep, he thought he heard them stirring to life.

He tried to escape deeper in his mind, but they followed, sweeping him up in their frenzy, lifting him. He had the momentary sensation of floating above his bed before being whisked off into the darkness.

The voices grew quiet, then he experienced a confusing mix of perceptions. Part of him felt as if he floated, his awareness scattered about the ceiling of a tiny room, removed, yet part of the setting. Another part felt as if he stood in darkness. The air felt stuffy. Something hung in front of his face. The faint smell of old perfume filled him. His body felt alien. He wanted to move, but had no control.

He shifted his attention back to the ceiling and sensed that he could be both in the room and observe himself at the same time. He had a vague memory of experiencing this kind of dichotomy in his dreams.

Along with the sense of being the observer and the observed, he felt helpless. As far as he could tell, his awareness and the sensory impressions in the body were normal, but his will to act had vanished. A mixture of sour, acrid, and repulsive smells assaulted him. The same ones he encountered at the rescue mission.

His thoughts changed too. His mind felt poised and expectant, yet strangely blank. He remembered the term he learned in science class. Tabula Rasa -- blank slate. That's how he felt now.

He heard noises. A door opened. Someone coming.

Teutates. The voice boomed in his head, pulling his attention into the body. It jerked as if touched by a live wire and Nick became aware of its physical sensations. Feet ached as if he'd been standing for hours, then his awareness swelled, once more splitting into two vantage points; one oozing out into the tiny space surrounding the body, the other aware of what was happening inside it, as if watching.

"He must be appeased," he heard the body whisper.

As if in answer, the voice whispered softly in the part of him that floated inside the body like a bubble suspended in oil. *Remain silent,* it hissed. *Do not move, you mustn't be found. Breathe slow, deep, in measured breaths. You are the divine instrument of his will. His hand will guide yours.* Nick felt fingers moving, but not from any conscious effort on his part. Some other intelligence controlled the body. He felt something in its hand, dangling at its side.

A light clicked on. A slice of gold stabbed through the crack in front of him. He felt the body tense, hand tightening on whatever it held. The appearance of the light caused the "floating" half of him to disperse, as if rising higher above everything. The other half remained in the body as a passive observer.

Through the opening he saw a black girl with long, curly hair pull a blouse over her head and wiggle out of a skirt. Nick felt embarrassed when he saw her chocolate colored thighs and grapefruit breasts in stark contrast to white bra and panties. He wanted to cry out a warning, but couldn't.

What if she came over to hang up her clothes?

She tossed them onto a chair and turned away, then the light went out. He heard the rustling of sheets as she climbed into bed, then the sound of her breathing, strong and regular at first, gradually slowing.

Soon, the voice said. *When the silence nears perfection. Teutates will guide you.* The body remained still until he heard no other sound, but her breathing. Slow and even.

Rising panic shot through Nick. His thoughts raced as if someone had turned up the heat beneath the oil suspending them. He both watched and felt the hand glide forward, fingers touching the smooth door, stopping when it made full contact. The sensations felt eerie, as if he were sleepwalking with an invisible puppeteer controlling his movements. From his vantage point above, Nick thought of himself as the puppeteer, except that he had no control. The closet door swung open noiselessly. Another rush of panic.

The body lurched forward, slipping between the clothes, extricating itself from the confines of the closet. Both floating above and inside it. Nick saw the curves of the girl beneath the sheets in the semi-darkness. Big hips compared to her upper torso.

Do it! the voice commanded.

The body flinched, then stooped to put down the object. A sickle.

Nick's thoughts boiled. What's going on here? Why -- can't -- I -- stop -- it? He fought to assert control over the body.

A second pillow lay beside her. The body picked it up, then jammed it down over her mouth and nose. Her eyes snapped open, followed by a muffled scream. Her fists came up. Nick's consciousness jerked back and forth between the body and his ethereal self like a frenzied pinball machine. The body pressed harder with the pillow. The girl kicked, fear lighting her eyes. She scratched. Punched. The automaton climbed on top, putting his full weight on her. She wriggled beneath him, her struggle weakening.

Nick tried to rally his diminishing thoughts to push the mindless robot away, but the part of him trapped inside felt forced to watch as its inconsequential energy faded alongside the life of the girl. Her eyes glazed and she became still. The body kept the pressure on for another minute.

Both Nicks felt crushing guilt at the horror of the experience. He watched numbly as the body climbed off the girl, then fought once more to escape the walking prison. The robot picked up the sickle and held it above her neck.

His thoughts bubbled over.

He screamed when the blade plunged into the soft flesh of her throat, but no sound came from him; only blackness as he tumbled into the darkness...

...waking in the dim light of his bedroom, biting back his second scream.

CHAPTER SEVENTEEN

Max lay with his hands behind his head, staring at the ceiling thinking how all hotel rooms looked the same. One or two enamel framed prints on the walls, and above, four corners; white, empty, and impersonal. The ceilings more than anything drove him back to his work which became an obsession that pushed him toward his own high standards. Max lost himself in his work to escape the loneliness that swept over him if he gave it the chance.

He had spent his life living on the edge, two steps behind his drive to excel and two steps ahead of emptiness. Closing his eyes, he remembered the day Eric Hart, the Justice department's behavioral specialist had brought his compulsion to his attention.

"You're the best, Max," Hart said from behind his desk in a small windowless office somewhere deep in the depths of Quantico. "Makes me a little worried."

"Worried?"

He looked up. "I'm not a therapist, but I'm concerned about your -- how can I say this? -- your pursuit of excellence."
Hart's words puzzled him.

"It's admirable," he continued. "Everyone respects and envies you, but I don't see it the same way."

"You don't?"

"I see it as a symptom of something deeper."

"You can't be serious. I put everything into my work. It's my life. Without it I'd have..."

"Nothing."

Max opened his mouth, but couldn't think of a response. Never before had one word hit him with such impact. Not only the word, but the expression on Hart's face and the conviction with which he spoke.

"You like everything orderly," Hart said, stating it as fact. "You hold yourself up to your own ideal of perfection, which in itself is admirable, but you push too hard."

"What are you saying?"

"I'm saying take a good look at yourself. If you don't find some other channel for your energies, your drive is going to turn around and bite you in the ass. You have a lot going for you. Slow down. Find someone to share your life with. You might have fooled yourself and everyone else, but you haven't bullshitted me. Your drive is going to leave you burned out, spent, and bitter. Worst of all, alone."

Max opened his eyes and stared into the emptiness.

Alone.

It didn't matter where he was; New York, Chicago, Seattle, L.A., San Diego, Miami, Boston. The hotels all had the same effect. The decor didn't matter either; colonial in New England or the earth tones of a southwestern desert. They all had a sameness -- the lack of a personal touch that only a woman could provide. Frilly things. He smiled. Fru-frus. The touches that made a place home.

Max hadn't been any place he could call home since -- since he was nine. Prior to that his life and home had been warm and full of love. His mother had fussed over him.

All shattered one night by one asshole with a gun.

Max remembered playing with his Legos in the front room when the policeman came. His father opened the door and the cop smiled down at Max. He remembered the look before the cop asked his father to step outside, a fleeting uncomfortable glance that he pondered for years, finally recognizing it as guilt.

Little Max ran to the front door, pushed open the mail slot and put his ear to the opening, listening to the cop's hushed tones.

"Sorry to be the one to have to tell you this, Mr. Broderick..."

"What happened? It's Roseanne isn't it? What happened?"

The loss of control in his father's voice made Max's own throat tighten.

"There's been a robbery and a shoot out." A short hesitation, then the words gushed forth. "Your wife was caught in the crossfire."

"Is she? Is she?"

"I'm sorry Mr. Broderick."

His father let out a strangled cry. Max felt numbness wash over him. His thoughts felt suspended in Jello. His brain refused to process anything else.

"We need you to come down to the coroner's office and make an identification."

Max heard and understood the individual words, but strung together, they didn't have any meaning.

Then the expression on his father's face when he came back in -- not guilty like the cop's. More like the absence of a look. The absence of comprehension, yet it conveyed as much if not more than what the cop had.

Grief, denial, anger. Max passed through them all but the anger remained. The flush of emotions made him feel helpless, except for his anger. It made him strong. Gave his thoughts clarity. Focus. Max clung to it; a life preserver for his sanity.

Injustice, loss, helplessness, and anger. In Max's mind there were no other choices. He made a secret promise to his mother. He'd catch the bad guys. Stop them so they couldn't destroy other families.

Once a fun-loving, successful, corporate lawyer, the tragedy transformed Max's father into a cold, brooding, unhappy drunk. Gone were the smells of pipe tobacco and cologne. Now the stink of gin and cigarettes filled the house while Max's father drank himself into physical and financial ruin. He died two days after Max's fourteenth birthday.

The concept of a happy home was destroyed with the death of his mother. Any semblance of roots Max might have experienced vanished when his father died. Living on a small trust fund, Max's life became a blur of endless dormitories, foster homes, rented rooms and hotels.

In his own way, he was a homeless person. Ironic, wasn't it? Sure, he had food and warm places to sleep, but like the guys at the rescue mission, he had no one to go home to.

No place to call home.

How many nights had he lain awake in hotel beds, wide-eyed, staring at white, empty ceilings, longing for someone to talk to? Someone who would understand.

He thought of O'Grady, wondering what it would be like to spend time alone with her. Away from work. Away from the disinterred, dismembered, and eviscerated bodies that brought them together. Away from the stink of death that had become so familiar.

He reached over and picked up the handkerchief she'd given him and held it to his nose. The faint smell of her perfume brought a smile. What did she do when she was alone? What did her apartment look like?

Wherever it was, she made a home of it, he thought. Lots of frilly things. Pictures, knick-knacks. If it weren't for the job, she'd be someone to talk to, then again, if it weren't for the job he never would have met her. He shook his head. Ain't life a bitch?

His cell phone rang, startling him out of his reverie. He jumped and the aches from his beating came back. He looked at the clock on the nightstand. Four a.m.. Whoever it was, if they were calling at this hour, they weren't the bearer of good news.

His cell rang again.

He picked it up. "Broderick."

"It's Colleen. There's been another murder."

Two hours later, O'Grady stood transfixed in the doorway of an apartment before putting her hand to her mouth and backing out of the room. Max gagged at the stench, but held his ground. The same curly-haired forensics man who'd investigated the Brice and Ford murders looked up from his work. Max saw two glistening streaks beneath his nostrils. Vicks.

The forensics tech grinned. "Can't say that I blame her. Never do get used to it." He tossed Max the Vicks and a pair of latex gloves before bending back to his work. "We've got another bizarre one." He pulled out a tiny instrument and a bag, took the corpse's claw like hand and gently scraped the underside of a painted fingernail. "This one put up a fight. Good hair and tissue scrapings."

In spite of the open window, the pungent smell of death hung in the air of the Roxbury apartment like a malevolent fog. Max spotted the oak leaves while dabbing Vicks under his nose.

Thankful for the covering scent, he scrutinized the rest of the room before his gaze came to rest on the remains lying on the bed. Yvonne Perry's once tender, chocolate brown skin now looked sickly gray and wrinkled, like sun-beaten elephant hide. So much for the intraracial theory, Max thought.

Her hands, fingers and legs were bent and twisted as if she'd been trying to climb an invisible tree. Her body looked like a poorly posed, headless mannequin that had fallen over. Her withered entrails lay beside her on the bed, painstakingly arranged and garnished with sprigs of mistletoe. The word "Teutates" was scrawled with blackened blood on the sheets by her feet.

Yvonne Perry had died in a violent struggle. Like Lynn Ford and Barbara Brice, her head had been cut off with a sharp curved instrument. "He used a sickle," Max said.

"How do you know?" The forensics tech sealed a small bag and looked up, his eyes owl-like behind thick glasses.

"Trust me." Max crossed the room, studying the details of the crime scene. "I guarantee if you find one and compare it to the wounds, you'll get a match."

O'Grady reappeared, her face a stoic mask.

That's my girl. A real trooper. Max tossed her the Vicks and some gloves, then went to the head of the bed. Like the two before her, mistletoe had been stuck in the stump of Yvonne's neck.

"I already got oil samples from the hinges," the tech said.

"What did you say your name was?"

"Geist. Rick Geist, Boston P.D. M.E.'s office."

"You do good work, Geist. Listen, you've been on three of these now. Any more pop up, make sure it's you and no one else. I'll put in a formal request if you think we need it."

"You got it, G-man." Geist went back to work. "Not that it matters, but I put in the request after the second killing."

Max smiled and turned to O'Grady who looked pale. "What do you think, partner?"

She put the cover on the Vicks and handed it to Geist. "It has the same signature, doesn't it?"

Max nodded.

She looked around the room. "Blood smeared walls. Sloppiness after meticulous planning. Same guy." She moved around the room as if Max's question had set her in motion. "The bodies too. All arranged in the same way."

"Good call on the signature," Max said. "Our perp went through a lot of trouble to pose the bodies." He shook his head slowly. "We don't get many cases of posing."

"Posing?"

"Treating the victim like a prop to leave a specific message. They're crimes of anger. Crimes of power. It's the thrill of the hunt, the thrill of the kill, and the thrill afterwards of how the subject leaves the victim and how he's beaten the system. It's the opposite of staging where the offender tries to throw off the investigation by making cops believe that something happened other than what did, like a rapist who tries to make his intrusion look like a burglary. Posing is signature."

"He's telling us something," O'Grady said, stepping back and folding her arms. "This makes three. It's now officially a serial." She stepped to the foot of the bed, studying the sheets. "Teutates. Another druid god?"

"Bet on it." Max turned back to Geist. "Any way you can put a hurry-up on the preliminaries?"

"They're expecting heat from the press. I'll do all the work myself -- walk it through, then I'll get the results to you."

"Thanks, I appreciate that." This is the kind of guy I want, Max thought. "Great. When I see you this afternoon, I have some things to share. Might give you some ideas about what to look for when you put together your evidence."

"I look forward to it. I want to nail this sick fuck as bad as you."

A uniform stuck his head into the room. "Who's Lieutenant O'Grady?"

"I am," Colleen said.

"Call for you. They want you to get in touch with Charlestown homicide."

"Thanks." She fished her cell phone out of her bag. "Back in a minute, Broderick."

"What do you make of this?" Max said to Geist.

"Not sure." Geist pulled out a camera and snapped pictures as he spoke. "Some of the things this guy does are consistent, like he's following a definite pattern. Sometimes I think I'm getting a sense of him, then he does something totally out of character." The room lit up as he snapped a close-up of Perry's neck. "Every murder's been the same -- I mean as far as the pattern goes, but there's something different about each of them."

"What do you mean?"

Geist walked to the other side of the bed. "Can't put my finger on it. The missing body parts make it hard to do a thorough analysis, but I get the feeling that each murder is unique. Each girl's been killed in a different way. It's not so much something I get from evidence. It's well -- it's my gut." He stopped and studied Max. "Speaking from a purely circumstantial standpoint, I don't have a leg to stand on, but I can't shake the feeling..." He threw his hands in the air. "I know you're going to think I'm crazy, but if I didn't know better, I'd think it wasn't the same guy."

"A group?"

Geist leaned in close to the body and snapped another picture. "I wondered about that too, but my findings on the first two indicate only one set of foreign prints at each crime scene. Granted, we don't have the final results, but I studied them with a magnifying glass. We've verified all of them on the Brice and Ford cases. At each of those crime scenes we have only one set of fingerprints unaccounted for. I'll bet you dollars to doughnuts we come up with the same thing here."

"Hopefully we'll get the reports this afternoon. Who knows? Maybe we'll get a match on someone with a prior."

"I wouldn't hold my breath." Geist snapped a couple more pictures and put the camera away. "This guy's in a class all his own." He frowned. "I have a feeling the mutilation comes after they're dead." He nodded toward the bed. "This is the first time I've seen signs of struggle."

O'Grady breezed into the room. "Charlestown has the complete fingerprints and blood workup on the Ford case. The Brice workup will be at District Eleven by this afternoon. We can go to Charlestown now. It'll speed things up if we get them ourselves. Otherwise we won't have them 'til tomorrow."

"Great." Max rubbed his hands together. "Finally, we can get somewhere."

"I'll be done here in a few minutes," Geist said. "I'll meet you over at Eleven with my preliminaries this afternoon. Then we'll bang heads and see what we have."

"Good enough." Max gestured toward the door. "Let's get this show on the road."

Half an hour later he and O'Grady pulled up in front of the Charlestown station.

"Maybe we'll see Flynn," Max said.

"No way," Colleen said. "I don't want you two near each other. I'll deal with him. You stay here in the car. I'll get the report. It'll only take a minute."

Max grabbed the door handle. "Come on, O'Grady, you don't think..."

"I don't think anything." She put her hand on his arm. "You don't know him like I do. Stay here. I don't want any trouble."

She's serious, Max thought. If I didn't know better, I'd think she was protecting me. What the hell, I don't want to see her upset. We don't need any distractions. He threw his hands up. "Okay, okay, you win."

She held on a moment longer as if to drive home the point, then went into the station. Max slouched back and watched the comings and goings out front, sitting straight up when two men in rumpled suits come out. His adrenaline kicked in. One of them limped slightly, the other wore a trench coat.

He recognized the one with the limp. The "drunk" at Savin Hill station. Max didn't have to guess about the one in the trench coat. His build matched that of the piece of shit who sucker punched him. Max slid down again and watched them walk to a car across the street. The limper slid into the driver's seat. Max eyed the ignition. Shit, no keys. O'Grady had them.

The man wearing the trench coat stopped and patted his pockets as if he forgot something, then turned and went back into the station.
There was a God.

As soon as the door closed behind him, Max left the car and walked up the street, keeping his head down. When he reached the driver's side of the other car, he leaned against the door with his back to the man and tapped on the window. It rolled down.

"The fuck you want?"

Max turned and smiled. "Hi, remember me?" The man's eyes widened and his mouth dropped open.

"Tell Flynn he can have his present back." Max grabbed the limper by the tie. In one motion he pulled him toward the window while driving his fist into the man's face, knocking him across the seat. He slumped unconscious.

Max looked around, yanked the door open, then patted him down. He found a gold detective's shield and I.D. identifying him as Sgt. Hubbard, Charlestown Homicide. Max found a set of handcuffs on Hubbard and a bag of ty-wraps in the glove compartment. He cuffed Hubbard's hands to the steering wheel, went around to the passenger side and opened the door.

"What the fu..." Hubbard shook his head. Max hit him again. Hubbard went out. Max found a pad and paper and jotted a quick note:

HERE'S A PRESENT FOR **YOU**, FLYNN. HOPE

YOU LIKE THE GIFT WRAP.

A SECRET ADMIRER

He ty-wrapped Hubbard's ankles to the passenger door arm rest, then pinned the note to his lapel with his shield. Trotting across the street, Max stepped inside the station and walked down the hall in search of Trenchcoat.

He'd only gone two steps before O'Grady came out of a side hallway. Max ducked into an office.

A pot-bellied cop in uniform rose from behind a desk. "Where you think you're going?"

Max flashed his shield and put his finger to his lips. The cop took the shield, examined his I.D. and frowned. Max watched O'Grady walk by.

"Thanks," he said, stepping back into the hallway. He saw O'Grady heading out the front door and Trenchcoat crossing the hall ahead of him, going into the men's room. Perfect. The door opened and a plainclothes cop brushed past him. Max looked up and down the hallway. O'Grady came back in the front door. He stepped into the men's room before she spotted him.

Except for a pair of legs in one of the stalls with the pants down around the man's ankles, the room was empty. Max went into the next stall, climbed up on the toilet and peered over the divider. The trench coat hung on the door of the stall. Its owner sat on the toilet reading a newspaper.

Stepping down, Max walked to the outer door, opened and closed it.

"Evacuate!" he yelled. "Fire!"

The newspaper rustled. "Jesus Christ!" Max recognized the voice from the other night.

"Hurry up!" He banged on the stall door. "Get out or you're dead!" He heard the jingle of a belt buckle and more rustling of newspaper.

"Open up!"

The latch slid and the door opened. Max saw the man fumbling with his zipper. He looked up, recognition flashing in his eyes, and raised his hands. "Hey, man. No, man, it wasn't..."

Max smiled when he saw the scar on his nose. "Looks like I caught you with your pants down, slick." He kicked at the half opened door, sending Trenchcoat flying back against the wall. His hands flew up and his pants fell. "Tell Flynn he has lousy taste in gifts."

Max stepped back, crossed his arms and waited for the man to stumble to his feet. When he was halfway out of the stall, Max opened the door. The man frowned, took another step and Max slammed the door into his face, sending him sprawling backward and backed out of the stall as a bevy of officers burst into the room.

"What's going on?" the first cop shouted.

"He needs help." Max pointed to the stall. "I think he fell."

The cop looked at Max with a puzzled expression. Max pushed past him and addressed the rest of the cops. "Man's sick in there." He jerked his thumb over his shoulder. "Better go help him." He cut through the crowd and went out into the hall.

O'Grady stormed up to him. "Broderick, what the hell's..."

Max took her by the arm and walked toward the front door. "You got the files?"

She held up a folder. "Where've you been? What's happening?"

Outside, they saw a crowd gathered around Hubbard's car.

"What's happening over there?" she said.

Max guided her toward their car. "We better get going. We have work to do."

Once inside their unmarked, O'Grady gave him a sideways glance. "I don't want to know what's going on."

As they drove past the other car Max saw Hubbard, still secured to the door and steering wheel.

"What are you staring at?" Hubbard yelled at the crowd. "Somebody go get help."

Max rolled down the window. "What happened?" Hubbard's eyes met his and Max saluted. When he turned back to face O'Grady, he saw the corner of her mouth turned up in a smile.

CHAPTER EIGHTEEN

Nick listened for the voice, but his mind remained silent. Unable to sleep after his nightmare, he dressed and went out before anyone else woke up. He had no idea of where to go, but his feet carried him forward, seeming to know where to take him.

The morning cold refreshed him. He liked this time of day. Like his thoughts, things were quiet. The drunks, freaks and night people had all gone into hiding for the day and the working stiffs hadn't stirred yet.

He knew he should be going to work himself, but the last few days had rattled him. Particularly his nightmare. Who could he talk to about it? Who would understand? There was nothing he could do but figure this one out himself.

He rounded a corner and saw Town Field, then Saint Augustine's rescue mission; the only place he might find answers. He was glad it was early. He didn't want to see the magician.

Maybe he could talk to Father Derlen, then again, maybe not. The priest would give him a few kind words, then he might call the cops. No, the only thing that made sense was to find the bearded man and try to talk to him without being seen by the magician.

A few bums slept in the doorway of St. Augustine's. The bearded man wasn't among them. Nick wanted to see if he had slept in the mission or showed up at the door, but he didn't want to be seen by anyone, so he crossed the street, shinnied up the drainpipe of the Town Field clubhouse and found a comfortable spot on the roof where he could watch.

Ten minutes after the mission opened, the bearded man came shuffling down the street from the direction of Field's Corner station with a Hefty bag slung over his shoulder. Nick watched him go into the mission, then peered over the other side of the clubhouse. Confident he wouldn't be seen, Nick shinnied back down the drainpipe.

More people trickled into the streets on their way to work. The smells of an awakening city filled the air; diesel exhaust from a passing bus and good old carbon monoxide from the cars. Nick sneezed and hustled across Dorchester Ave. using the bus for cover.

He stood next to the doorway of the mission with his back to the window, feeling strangely vulnerable. What would he say if he ran into Father Derlen? He was still looking for Obie?

Two winos brushed past him on their way inside. Nick followed them, once more greeted by the strange mixture of institutional food and oppressive human smells.

To his relief he didn't see Father Derlen. When he felt sure no one could see him, he walked back and forth between the rows of tables studying the faces of every person in the room. The bearded man wasn't there. He glanced at the kitchen doors on the far side of the room. He had to be back there. Where else could he have gone?

One of the doors opened. Nick turned around and slipped into the crowd, working his way to the back of the room, studying the faces he passed. Finding a seat at a corner table, he stayed low. A couple of men sitting next to him slurping over what he guessed to be oatmeal frowned and put their arms in front of their bowls in protective gestures. Nick smiled and they pulled the bowls closer as if he might steal them. No one spoke.

Father Derlen appeared from the kitchen. Shit. Nick lowered his head while the priest moved about talking to people, sharing laughs and giving reassuring pats on shoulders. Nick moved his head out of Derlen's line of sight and peered out from behind the man he kept between himself and Derlen. When the priest turned his back, Nick started toward the door. When he got within a few feet of it he made a dash.

His hand clutched the knob, he opened the door and did a double-take. Sully stepped out of a car and came toward him. In that first instant, Nick recognized his gaunt, pockmarked face, but he almost went into the street anyway because he'd never seen Sully in plain clothes.

Spinning away from the door, Nick looked across the room. Derlen still hadn't seen him. He turned his back to the two men and heard the door open behind him. Screwed, blued, and tattooed. He slumped into an empty seat.

"What the fuck you want?" a gravelly voice said beside him.

Nick looked into a pair of bloodshot eyes in a weathered face framed by scraggly, silver-gray hair. Sour breath enveloped him.

"I don't want nothing," Nick said speaking low.

"Then what the fuck you sitting next to me for?"

Just what he needed -- to be the center of attention. He half expected Sully's hand to clamp down on his shoulder.

Nick stared back. "Shut the fuck up and go back to your chow," he rasped. "Or I'll use your face to wipe the table."

The fire behind the bloodshot eyes went out and the man went back to his meal. Nick let out a slow sigh. No hand came down to claim him. Thank God. He waited a few more seconds to be sure, then peeked over his shoulder and saw Sully and Derlen hugging. Talk about the Odd Couple. What was a nice guy like Derlen doing with an asshole like Sully? Derlen put an arm over the cop's shoulder and the two disappeared into the kitchen.

Nick bolted for the door, not daring to look back.

Once outside, he ran toward Field's Corner station. What the hell was going on? What was he doing? The next thought struck him like a brick hitting a wall. He was losing it. The certainty of it shot through him. He couldn't catch his breath. Jesus Christ. He was going crazy. His breath came in short, uneven bursts. Every part of him, his mind, his breath, his heart, all spun out of control as if the fear drove the life and sanity from his being.

He forced a deep breath.

Another.

He bit down hard on his lower lip, letting the pain jerk him back and forced the panic from his mind. No time for thoughts like that.

Instead of going to work, Nick went to the mission early every morning for the next three days in search of the bearded man who responded to the voice in his head. He didn't bother calling in sick. He knew he'd lost his job, besides, he wouldn't have been able to keep his mind on work. He had to find out what was happening.

Each morning he tried in vain to tune in to the voice as he had the day he found the man in the graveyard, but it remained silent. Before the mission opened each morning, he climbed onto the roof of the Town Field clubhouse to watch the building and the field. The bearded man never showed. Neither did the magician.

In the afternoons he went to the Cedar Grove Cemetery, hoping he might see the man there, but all he saw were the same conspicuous dicks trying their damnedest to look inconspicuous. He made sure they didn't see him.

The magician showed up on the morning of the fourth day, his bag at his side, his cape fluttering behind him like Dracula. Nick flashed on the man in his dream who grabbed for him. He hadn't heard the voice for almost a week. Where the hell had he been? What had he been doing? What did he do with the bearded man? What if he sees me?

Nick waited until a crowd gathered before sliding down the drainpipe on the far side of the clubhouse and running in the opposite direction. He didn't stop until he entered Field's Corner station. The headline on that morning's Globe jumped out at him from a newspaper rack, making his stomach twist.

SERIAL KILLER TERRORIZES BOSTON
Third Ritual Murder in Roxbury

The headless body of Yvonne Perry, a twenty-six year old cocktail waitress was found in her Roxbury apartment yesterday afternoon. Perry is the third victim of a man Lt. Jerome Flynn of Charlestown Homicide has dubbed the Headless Horseman.

Flynn claims that: "We have several leads and we're closing in on our suspect. We expect to have him in custody soon."

Lynn Ford, a Cambridge college student and Barbara Brice, a Charlestown resident have also been victimized by the Horseman. Other than Brice, their heads have still not been recovered.

See Horseman page A-2.

Nick felt lightheaded as the details of his nightmare rushed into his mind.

That's where the magician had been.

Grabbing the newsstand, he doubled over and vomited.

CHAPTER NINETEEN

Max closed his office door and spread the contents of the files from the Boston Police Department in front of him and compared them with the Justice Department reports, The National Center for the Analysis of Violent Crime reports, and the Violent Criminal Apprehension Program reports he had just received. Four separate files on the Ford case and two on Brice. He looked from one to the next and back again, scrutinizing the details.

Christ, he thought. Looks like more than one murderer, but the signatures are too similar. What's worse, there's no record of these guys anywhere. NSA, FBI, NCAVC, VICAP, Interpol, and Boston P.D.. No rap sheets, no driver's licenses, no birth certificates. Maybe Geist was right about more than one murderer. It would be interesting to see what he came up with on the Perry killing.

He went through the files again, then called the Justice Department in Washington. A familiar, gruff voice came on the line.

"Gibbs."

"Tony, it's Max. Just got the reports from the Boston P.D. and the workup you guys did."

"Strange shit, isn't it?"

"Now I know why it took you so long. The Boston P.D.'s results match yours. Different fingerprints and different blood samplings on the Brice and Ford workups. The fingerprints from the crime scenes don't match. Neither do the DNA profiles from the hair and tissue samples."

"We're still checking, but to date there are still no matchups to any known criminals or any kind of public records. It's as if these people don't exist."

"Or they're already dead."

"Already dead?"

"It's an idea I'm considering based on another case. In the meantime we just had another one. Black girl this time. This new evidence indicates that it isn't a serial, but I have a few more leads to check out. I'll be sending you a file this afternoon. Have Hart give me a new behavioral analysis. Does he know about the different prints?"

"No."

"Don't tell him. I want to see what he comes up with on his own."

"No problem. How you getting along with the locals?"

Max rubbed the scab over his eye. "A few minor disagreements, but we're working them out. The administration here is getting a lot of heat from the press. My partner says there's talk about a task force. That's all I need; all those hotshot detectives going in a million directions, muddying the waters. I'll never get it solved."

"They start screwing with you, we'll see that the reins stay in your hands."

"You might get some resistance. There're a few hardheads up here."

Gibbs chuckled. "You kidding? All I have to do is mention the possibility of losing a couple of social service grants to the right people. You need help from us, just give me the word. I'll have some people up to you in a few hours."

"Not yet. I have a good partner and a solid forensics man on my team. I think the three of us can crack it."

"You're calling the shots."

Max picked up one of the files. "Thanks. Put top priority on the Perry case. Run it through the same channels and see if you can get someone to do a comparison of all three."

Max smelled O'Grady's perfume and looked up from the file to see her come into the office, her movements quiet and graceful. He nodded as she took a seat across from him, her green eyes intent on him. He looked down, not wanting her to see the way she affected him.

"You got it," Gibbs said. "Keep me posted. I'm due to make my monthly report to the president on Friday. This thing gets any bigger, he'll want to know what we're doing."

"Okay, Tony, thanks a lot. My partner's here now. I'll touch bases with you soon."

"Keep up the good work, Max."

Max hung up and held out the folder to Colleen. "I'm not sure what's going on here, but I just got my reports from Washington. They match the Boston P.D.'s findings."

She shook her head. "None of the prints and none of the DNA samplings match. What about priors?"

"Nada."

She pursed her lips and looked at him thoughtfully.

"I have some ideas," he said, "but I want to wait until Geist gets here with the preliminary on Perry. Did you find anything on Derlen or the soup kitchen?"

She reached into her bag and produced a notebook. "Guy's squeaky clean and well connected. Listen to this. Appointee to the Mayor's Council on the Homeless; Board Member of the Massachusetts Council for Homeless Women and Children; Boston Committee for the Training and Education of the Learning Disabled; Troop Committeeman for Boy Scout Troop Thirty-One of Dorchester; National Delegate to Big Brothers of America; State Committee for Drug Abuse..." She flipped a page.

Max waved his hand. "Enough."

"You don't want to hear about his political friends?"

"The committees say it all. With all his connections he no doubt has lots of local clout. Last thing I want is to get in a pissing match with the mayor's office over bad press for Derlen and his shelter. That weirdo cop, what was his name?"

Colleen grimaced. "Sullivan."

"Yeah, Sully. He's probably already opened his mouth, but my cover's still good. If our man's hanging around Derlen's mission, no one needs to know about it, certainly not the media."

Colleen flipped her notebook shut and tossed it into her bag. "Any progress on your surveillance?"

"I've seen Sully there a few times, and the usual assortment of down on their luck people, but no one's made me. Yet."

She crossed her legs. Max fought to keep from looking. "Nothing else out of the ordinary?"

Max spun a pen between his fingers. "It's probably nothing, but I've seen this kid a few times. He acted pretty strange. I don't think he's a suspect, but all the same, I have my eye on him. Other than that…" He threw his hands in the air. "Our druid…"

"Or druids."

He nodded. "Somehow they tie into the mission. I feel it in my gut. They may all be transients or posing as transients. I'm starting to recognize the regulars. If I have to, I'll put tails on all of them, but I don't want to waste our resources or arouse suspicion and I don't want to spook anybody."

Someone knocked on the door. Max opened it and Geist stepped in carrying a battered leather briefcase. He had on a pair of faded corduroy pants and a chambray work shirt. Opening his case, he pulled out a file. "You were right about the sickle." He handed Max the file on Yvonne Perry, pulled up a chair and sat down next to O'Grady. "How'd you know?"

"We're dealing with a druid -- or druids."

"You're kidding."

"I wish I were." Max handed him a copy of his research. "I think your hunch about each murder being different and Perry being killed before the mutilation is right."

Geist looked up from the papers. "Yeah?"

"It's my bet that Perry was smothered. Remember the word Teutates?"

Geist nodded.

"Get this. Teutates is a druid god. The method of offering sacrifice to Teutates is by suffocation."

Geist's eyes widened.

Max continued. "Cromm Cruaich, sacrifice of the first born. Ford was an only child.

"And the way we found Brice is a classic sacrifice to the druid goddess Andrasta," O'Grady said.

Max pointed to the papers he gave Geist. "It's all in there."

"Holy shit."

"More like unholy shit," O'Grady added

"Go ahead and read while I scan what you have on Perry." Max took half the papers from the file Geist gave him and handed them to O'Grady. "Let's take a few minutes to digest, then we'll talk."

The three sat in silence reading reports and studies. When Max finished his half of the report he traded with O'Grady. Geist flipped through the pages of Max's study, punctuating his reading with an occasional "Wow", "Holy shit", and "Un-fucking-believable."

"I'd like you to do an in depth forensic study of all three cases," Max said. "I want to link all the commonalities with a revised profile I'm expecting back from Washington. Use the research I've given you to track down the knowns; the sickle, mistletoe, and oak. Use your own judgment. You've been on the crime scenes, and you're getting a sense of this guy."

"Or guys," O'Grady added.

Max nodded. "It might be more than one, but I'm not going to rule out the possibility of a single perp."

"Why not?" O'Grady said. "We have different prints for each murder."

Max leaned back in his chair. "Let me tell you a little story."

O'Grady and Geist both leaned forward.

"I had a case," Max said. "Three or four years ago. These two guys, brothers, in Louisiana. They'd kill a man, cut off his hands, freeze them and toss his body in the bayou." He looked from O'Grady to Geist. "Every time they murdered someone, they wore gloves. Then they took the thawed-out hands and put prints all over the room."

Geist whistled. "Talk about giving a guy a hand."

Max let himself smile. "Every time we investigated we came up with great prints, but no suspects. After six months of investigation we finally realized we were hunting dead men. By the time we nailed the Laroquette brothers, they'd committed thirty-three murders."

Geist sat back and scratched his head. "It would fit the meticulous care that went into planning these killings, but I still have an uneasy feeling that different people are doing these."

"Maybe in light of the research I've given you, your study'll help break it loose."

"Might, but your hand job theory... Oops." He put his hand to his mouth and shot a glance at O'Grady. "Sorry, officer."

"Don't worry about it," she said with a dismissive gesture. "Let's cut the formality. Call me Colleen." She pointed at Max. "He's Broderick -- Max if he thinks you're cute."

Geist looked from one to the other and shrugged. "Anyway, your -- er hand theory. I think it's worth checking out."

"Can you check the M.E.'s office?" Max said to Colleen.

"What do you need?"

"Check the coroner's reports, particularly any John Does. Find out if there've been any murders in the past six months - no, make it a year -- where the corpses' hands were missing."

"Anything else?"

Max thought a moment. "Yeah, check my body snatchings. See if there's any record of hands being removed on any of the recently buried. In the mean time I have a stakeout to resume."

CHAPTER TWENTY

Nick heard no voices and no whispers in the week following Yvonne Perry's murder and the only person who might be able to help make sense of the mysterious voice in his head had vanished after going into Saint Augustine's. Sully's unexpected appearance ruined any chances of talking to him.

Nick felt sure the magician caused the girl's death, especially after his four day absence from Town Field and the new murder. His reappearance convinced Nick of his worst fears. He had to find a way to expose him.

Saint Augustine's held twin fascinations of terror and curiosity for Nick. He dreaded the thought of going there, yet he couldn't stay away. He knew he could find the answers to what haunted him there. In spite of the threat from Sully and the magician, Nick felt compelled to go, but as soon as he caught sight of either of them, he left.

Even though he hadn't heard the voice in over a week, the lucid dream of that night in the closet still haunted him. At the first thought of it, the sights, sounds, and smells of it rushed in, flooding his mind like water from a burst dam. At the end of the flood came a rush of shame, followed by anger.

One morning after seeing the magician and running from Saint Augustine's, Nick stopped halfway up Park Street, sat on the curb and put his head in his hands. Now that the bearded man was gone, maybe the voice was too, but even if that were so, it would only be a matter of time before the magician did it again. Guys like that didn't stop.

Then there was the question of Obie. Where had he gone? Same place as the bearded man? Had Obie been in someone's closet? Nick had the crazy thought that *he* would be the one doing the next murder. He would go to bed one night, start hearing the voice and black out, waking up in some closet like a mindless killer robot, like in his dream...

Whoa, dude. He caught himself. Ain't gonna happen. Dammit, Powers, you got no balls. What are you going to do? Keep running every time you see Sully or that magician? He smacked his fist into his palm. "Fuck no! I'm going to do something."

During the day he kept watch on the magician and Saint Augustine's from the far side of Town Field with a pair of small binoculars. At night the cover of darkness let him climb to his vantage point on top of the Town Field clubhouse where he could watch unnoticed for hours.

Every night he saw two dicks in their standard Boston cop unmarked parked half a block up the street from the mission. He never saw any cops during the day other than Sully visiting the priest, but as far as Nick was concerned Sully didn't count as a member of the human race, let alone the police department.

As out of place as he seemed, the street magician became a standard fixture at Town Field, and in spite of his fear, Nick felt a certain familiarity with him. Every hour or so he went through his routine. His tricks weren't very good, but his audience was usually a small group of parents and little kids. Easy to fool. At the end of each act he passed his hat. When he wasn't doing his act, he sat and watched the mission.

After a week of what became an unchanging routine, Nick grew impatient. The cops knew something. Otherwise they wouldn't be parking up the street, but they weren't doing shit. Chances are they didn't know shit. It's a wonder they could do anything right with assholes like Sully on the force. How else could they catch the magician? Why didn't they come during the day when he was here?

Slipping down the drainpipe, he ran through the darkness of Town Field and made his way home through the shadows to think things through.

He smelled stale beer when he crept through the back door. The trash overflowed with Bud cans. The sound of Mike's snores filled the apartment. He looked up at the clock above the stove. Twelve-fifteen.

In the living room he saw Mike passed out on the couch, mouth hanging open in a vigorous snore. More Bud cans littered the coffee table. Nick shook his head. Ignorance is bliss. He went back to the kitchen, grabbed a notepad, pen and an envelope from one of the drawers and started down the hall to his room.

"Nicky, that you?" his mother called softly from her room.

He felt a sudden rush of warmth for her. She never slept good until she knew he was home. "Yeah, Ma, it's me."

"Everything all right?"

"I'm okay, mom. I'm gonna crash. Get your beauty rest."

"Goodnight, hon."

"Night."

He closed his bedroom door and climbed into bed. Propping the notepad up on his knees, he began to write.

Dear Detectives,

I feel it's my duty to come forth as a citizen. I know why you've been watching the Cedar Grove Cemetery and St. Augustine's Rescue Mission. You're close to the killer, but you're looking in the wrong place. I've overheard conversations and seen things that others have missed. The guy who's killing these girls is hiding in closets. He's using a sickle and he has something to do with an old religion that sacrifices people in a place like Stonehenge. You're wasting your time watching the mission at night. You need to watch Town Field during the day. The street magician who's been there in the past few weeks is the man you need to watch. He leads the sacrifices. He's the one behind the murders.

Sincerely,

A Concerned Citizen

Nick re-read the letter, folded it and put it into an envelope which he addressed to the District Eleven Station. He shut off the light and lay awake with his hands behind his head. A shudder passed through him as he remembered the nightmare of the sacrifice, the magician, and the experience of being in the mind of the murderer watching Yvonne

Perry's death struggle. He hoped his letter would help put an end to the craziness. As soon as morning came, he'd put it in the mail.

Closing his eyes, he waited for sleep to take him, but it didn't come. Only the letter filled his mind. He wouldn't be able to sleep until he knew it was in the mail – it was as simple as that. He swung his feet over the edge of the bed, stood and pulled on his pants. Five minutes later he was out the door.

A light fog had rolled in off the ocean, giving the streetlights a misty halo. Nick saw two shadowy figures standing beneath one of the lights in front of Shawmut station, then they disappeared into the mist. Had they seen him?

Confusion swept over him in the moment before the mists swirled and darkened in front of him. Two ethereal black-robed masses swooped down out of the fog, flapping like dark, suffocating bat wings. Emptiness and despair pressed down on him; a palpable, malevolent, intelligence that choked the life from him. As his world dimmed, all he could think about was the letter. When the fog rolled out, they would find it on his cold, stiff body.

The thought of the magician snuffing him out like this enraged Nick, flushing the fear from him with hot anger. A chilled, wet breeze gusted, sending the dark mist swirling in front of him and the pressure relented.

Gasping for breath, Nick launched himself down an alley. After vaulting a fence and running down the middle of the next street, he stopped two blocks later to drop the letter in a mailbox and ran the rest of the way home, locking the door behind him when he got there.

CHAPTER TWENTY ONE

The door to Max's office flew open and O'Grady stormed in, tossing her purse onto a chair. "Goddamn Flynn! I knew he'd pull something like this."

Never seen her this mad, Max thought. Bet old Flynn knows how to push the buttons. Knowing him it's probably more like turning the screws.

She dropped into the chair across from him. "We have trouble."

"What's up?"

"Our favorite cooperative detective leaked information about the Brice and Ford murders to the press."

Max bit back his own rising anger. "He what?"

Colleen chewed on her lower lip and nodded. "Then he went to the commissioner's office and told the old man your investigation has stalled. He's convinced the commissioner to reassign him to the murders."

"Even after direct orders from the governor's office to yank him?"

"He persuaded the media to pressure the mayor's office, making the brass confirm rumors that they started a task force. Officially he's still off the Brice case. Technically he's been reassigned to the task force, not the murder."

"And they announced that they started the task force?"

"Led by Flynn."

"When?"

She glanced at her watch. "They're holding a press conference in about an hour."

Max felt something let loose inside him. Flynn and his monkeys never learned their lesson. Only language a hardass understands is force. He made a fist. "Fine with me," he said. "They want to play hardball, we'll play hardball. They don't know it yet, but they're going to play by my rules." He grabbed his jacket and took Colleen by the arm. "Come on, partner, we have a shitstorm to start. If they think they're going to have their soiree without inviting us, they're in for a surprise."

She grabbed her purse. "I think it's too late, Max."

"I'll call in a few favors and pull a few strings." He rubbed his chin. "Where to?"

She looked sideways at him and one corner of her mouth went up into a smile. "The press conference is downtown. Outside the commissioner's office. What are you going to do?"

He led her into the hall, then turned back. "I need to make a couple of quick calls. Get the car and meet me out front."

She snapped to attention and gave him a salute.

"Funny O'Grady. Real funny."

Forty five minutes later, Max hustled down the hall outside the commissioner's office, Colleen at his side. Ahead he saw a bevy of reporters, three minicams and a glare of lights. As he and Colleen worked their way to the front of the crowd, the office door opened and a tall balding man with feathery white sideburns stepped into the hall, flanked by Flynn and another uniformed official. The crowd converged on the three men, cameras flashing, microphones pushed forward, questions flying.

Max took Colleen's hand, pulled out his shield and held it in front of his face, pushing reporters aside. "Federal emergency," he said, keeping his back to the crowd while stepping between them and the commissioner. "No comment at this time."

"What?" someone said behind him. "What are you talking about? Who are you?"

"A public servant," Max said without turning.
The commissioner blinked. "Who the hell?" Max pushed him gently back into the office.

Flynn's jaw dropped. "Broderick," he growled. "You got balls pulling this shit."

"What the hell do you think you're doing?" the commissioner said indignantly. His face flushed red and his cheeks puffed out. "You fucking feds have no jurisdiction here. I shouldn't have let this go on as long as it has. I need results and I need them now."

Max pulled Colleen in behind him and closed the door. Plainclothes detectives and uniforms filled the room. Max recognized Hubbard and Trenchcoat who both stared at him. Max nodded and handed his shield to the commissioner. "Special Agent Broderick, U. S. Justice Department." He jerked his thumb over his shoulder. "Sorry about crashing your party out there, but I had to stop you before you ruined my investigation."

The commissioner frowned. "You're the guy who pulled the strings to make me yank Flynn off the Brice murder. I'm not impressed by your friends in Washington." He gestured impatiently. "Those people out there represent the public. They want answers. Action. Now get out of my way, I have a press conference to give before I launch Sgt. Flynn's task force."

Max looked over at Flynn, who stared back, arms crossed, rocking back and forth on his heels. Something resembling a smile curled the corners of his mouth.

Max shook his head. "Flynn, Flynn, Flynn. You know what, commissioner? Flynn wouldn't recognize a ritual murder if he were the one being sacrificed."

"Whoa," someone said from among the cops gathered at the back of the room. Flynn blinked and uncrossed his arms. Max caught O'Grady's smile out of the corner of his eye.

"Hey, Flynn, you gonna take this shit?" someone said from the crowd. Flynn grunted and stepped toward Max. The commissioner put out his arm and stopped him.

"Good move," Max said. "Saved him from getting hurt -- and embarrassed."

"We'll see who gets hurt," Flynn growled.

"Yeah, we'll see all right, won't we, Hubbard?" Max nodded toward the crowd.

"Listen." The commissioner jabbed his finger at Max. "There's nothing you can do. This thing's already been set in motion. Doesn't matter who you know in Washington. You feds are going to have to learn you're not running the whole damn country. You can't go walking in anywhere you damn well please."

"Besides, you ain't getting shit solved," Flynn added.

The commissioner waved his hand at Max. "Now step aside. You're out of your jurisdiction."

Max's anger surged. "Fuck jurisdiction! No matter what your pet gorilla says, I have my own team and we're onto something. We need secrecy or it'll blow my cover and our investigation. Last thing I need is a bunch of hotshots muddying up the waters."

The commissioner started to say something when a young blonde woman in a short teal dress stepped up beside him and tapped him on the shoulder. He turned and glared. "What do you want?"

Her head jerked back. "I'm sorry to bother you, sir, but the governor's on the phone. Says it's urgent."

He stared at Max, a frown deepening the lines on his face.

"You can still save face and avoid a lot of explaining and embarrassment later," Max said.

The frown softened into a puzzled expression. The secretary waited. Flynn looked from the commissioner to Max and back again. Colleen's gaze remained on the commissioner. No sound came from the rear of the room, then someone coughed.

Max folded his arms. "Governor's waiting."

The commissioner stared down at the floor, then back at Flynn. "Come with me." They followed the secretary out of the room.

Max and O'Grady stood apart from the rest of the detectives who stayed at the other side of the room talking in low voices. Except for an occasional glance, no one acknowledged their presence. Max stuck his hands in his pockets and leaned against the wall. "Friendly bunch."

Five minutes later, a door opened and the commissioner poked his head out. "Agent Broderick, Lieutenant O'Grady, could you come into my office, please?"

Max and Colleen eyed each other, then Max leaned toward her. "Ready for the fast shuffle?" He held out his hand. "Ladies first." Max followed her, acutely aware of the way she moved and the scent of Dare trailing behind her.

They stepped into a thick carpeted office. The commissioner waited behind a huge mahogany desk. A gold framed oil painting of Faneuil Hall graced one wall. Above the desk hung a similarly framed picture of the state house. Flynn stood beside the desk. The commissioner nodded toward two chairs. Max pulled one out for O'Grady, then took one himself.

"I don't know who the hell you are, or who you work for," the commissioner said, shaking his head. "But whoever it is, they have weight." He nodded toward the phone. "That was the governor. I'm to give you full cooperation. No questions asked. My entire department is at your disposal. You're in charge of the task force, but I'm telling you something, Mr. Hotshot." He shook his finger at Max. "I want results and I want them fast."

Max held up his hand. "I don't want a task force. You have other crimes that need to be solved and you're not exactly overstaffed. No sense wasting your manpower."

"You don't seem to understand," the commissioner said evenly. "We're getting pressure from the public."

"Public pressure doesn't solve crimes. A good cooperative investigative team does. Good people." He gestured toward Colleen. "Like Lieutenant O'Grady here. I'd like to commend your choice of her as your department's liaison. She's done a superb job." He looked at Flynn. "You need more people like her and your man Geist from the M.E.'s office. They're all I need for the time being."

The commissioner moved uneasily, then glared at Flynn. "Yes, well -- um, very good, but -- well you see, I'm caught between a rock and a hard spot." The older man leaned forward, putting his elbows on the desk. Tiny beads of sweat formed on his forehead. "The press is waiting out in the hall. They want a statement. I told them there's going to be a task force."

"Tell them it's already been formed. Tell them Flynn's running it. I don't give a shit, only don't fuck with what I've already got going."

The commissioner pulled out a handkerchief and wiped his forehead. "Will you go out with me? Make a statement?"

Max shook his head. "Sorry, I can't be seen on the tube. Can't compromise my cover. You and Flynn can give them the dog-and-pony show they expect. Tell them there's a task force investigating the murders, nothing more."

His eyes widened. "That's it?"

Max pursed his lips. "No, one more thing. Tell them, detectives Flynn, Hubbard, and Hubbard's partner with the trench coat have been assigned to the task force. The rest of its members are to remain anonymous."

Flynn's eyes widened. "Hey, wait a minute..."

"Shut up, Flynn!" the commissioner snapped. "That's fine, Broderick. If there's anything else you need, come straight to me. You have my complete cooperation -- and the cooperation of detective Flynn and his squad. Isn't that right, Detective?"

Flynn stared at the floor. "Yeah," he muttered.

"I can't hear you, Detective."

"Yes, sir."

"That's better. Now let's go out and give the media the tap dance they're expecting." He rose from behind his desk.

Max stood and shook the commissioner's hand. "Thank you commissioner."

"Any problems, you call me direct. I want a fucking report three times a day." His voice rose again. "I want fucking results, Goddammit!"

"Flynn will give you the reports," Max said. He caught O'Grady's eye and motioned toward a side door.

"Are you crazy?" O'Grady whispered after she and Max closed the door. "Flynn's going to foul everything up. What on earth are you thinking Max?"

"Keep your friends close and your enemies closer. I can keep those three monkeys on a leash by keeping them busy."

"How? If anyone can muddy up the waters of the investigation, those three can. They'll try their best to sabotage everything you do."

"Not if I keep them busy enough."

"Doing what?"

"Staking out Barbara Brice's grave."

"Brice's grave? There's nothing happening over there. The focus of the investigation is in Dorchester."

Max smiled. "I know."

CHAPTER TWENTY TWO

Nick's eyes snapped open. Gray morning light filtered into his room from beneath the window shade. He sat up, rotated his shoulders and moved his head in a slow circle. He felt tense and the beginnings of a headache hung at the back of his skull.

Raised voices came from the kitchen. Mike and his mother. He couldn't make out the words, but the tone told him all he needed to know.

Another argument.

Shit. He laid back down, put his pillow over his head and his mind drifted back to the previous night. A cold tremor passed through his chest as if someone stroked him with an icy claw.

Shaking himself, he pushed the fear aside, wondering what the cops would do after reading his note. He hoped they'd arrest the magician, but he wasn't going to hold his breath. With people like Sully counted as one of Boston's finest, it was a wonder they could direct traffic. He couldn't depend on them to do anything right. He had to keep an eye on things and maybe give them another shove until he could make the craziness stop.

After last night, it didn't matter that it had been awhile since he heard the voice.

He rolled over onto his side and pulled the pillow away from his head. Another volley of muffled shouts came through the wall. Climbing out of bed, Nick pulled on his jeans and a shirt, then went to the bathroom to wash up.

When he closed the bathroom door, Mike and his mother lowered their voices, but he still heard their heated exchange. What were they fighting about? He studied himself in the mirror a moment and knew. Me. What else? The thought fueled his headache, making his head throb. He didn't need this shit.

After taking two Excedrin and brushing his teeth, he grabbed his jacket and steeled himself for the uncomfortable scene awaiting him. Tension hung in the air like smoke from the aftermath of an explosion when he stepped into the kitchen. "Morning," he said keeping his back to them as he took a cup from the cupboard. He poured coffee and turned to face them.

"Morning, Nicky," his mother said, staring down at her coffee. Mike looked up, his bloodshot bug eyes reminding Nick of the soulless, glassy-eyed gaze of a shark. "What the hell you doing up so early? How do you manage to stay out all night and keep your job?"

Nick's mother put a hand on Mike's arm. "Mike…" He waved her away. "Mike nothing. Face it, the kid's a loser. And a liar."

The throbbing in Nick's head increased. So that was it. Mike knew he had lost his job. "Where do you get off calling me a liar?"

"I should've known you were a little shitbum. A mooch. Living off me."

Nick's mother slammed her palm on the table. "That's enough!" Mike blinked.

"Listen here, buster." She jabbed her finger toward his face. "You haven't spent one red cent on Nick. You barely give me enough to feed you, let alone make the rent. All your money goes to your ex. How dare you imply that you've ever given anything to Nick."

Mike glared at the finger wagging in front of his face. "If you know what's good for you, Louise, you'll put that finger away before you lose it."

"You better be ready to lose your face, then." The words flew out of Nick's mouth. He set his cup down and took a step toward Mike. "You lay one hand on my mother and you'll wish your sorry, lard-ass was never born." The pounding in his skull felt like someone dropped a steady stream of cinder blocks on his head.

Mike leveled his gaze at Nick. "Izzat so?" He pushed back his chair and stood.

Nick stepped closer, adrenaline racing through him. His mother stepped between them, her back to Nick. "The nerve of you," she said, face close to Mike's. "How dare you threaten me. Or my son." She pointed toward the back door. "Get out of my house!"

"What?" Mike drew back as if he'd been slapped.

"You heard her."

Mike looked from Louise to Nick and the rage in his eyes faded. "Two against one, huh?" He stood a moment longer, defying them, then his shoulders slumped. He shook his head. "Fine. It ain't worth it." He grabbed his work shirt from the back of a chair and left.

Nick rubbed his temples. His mother dropped into her chair and put her head in her hands.

"What brought that on?" Nick said, joining her at the table.

His mother spoke without looking up. "Jimmy's Harborside called looking for you. Mike answered. They wanted to know where you've been, wanted to make sure you were all right. They said you stopped showing up for work. Oh, Nicky." She gazed at him, her eyes red-rimmed. "Don't be mad at Mike. He means well -- I mean you should have heard him. He was so proud of you, holding onto that job."

Nick's anger left as suddenly as it came. He remembered the night Mike saved him from Sully and felt a twinge of shame, and for the first time since he'd known Mike, he understood his anger. Nick had risen to some new status and respect in Mike's view because of the job. The phone call from Jimmy's had popped the bubble. In his own strange set of morals, Mike was rooting for Nick and Nick disappointed him. What could he tell Mike? Or his mother for that matter? He was hearing voices? That he knew who the serial killer was?

"What's going on, Nicky?" his mother said, breaking in on his thoughts. "Are you in some kind of trouble? Where have you been going? What have you been doing?"

"I'm sorry, mom. I know why Mike's mad. He's disappointed. I didn't mean to let him down. Tell him I'm sorry."

"What is it?"

He sighed. "Ma, I'm a big boy. This is something I have to work out for myself. Don't worry, it's nothing bad."

She studied him a long moment, then put her hand over his. "My little boy really is growing up, isn't he? If you need help, you'll come to me?"

"Course I will, ma. You know that. It's just that -- well this time   I have to be on my own."

"I understand." She rose from the table and kissed him on the forehead. "I'd better get ready for work, or I'll be losing *my* job."

Nick stood and gave her a hug. "Thanks, mom. What about Mike? You just threw him out."

She smiled. "You kidding? He'll come crawling back tonight on his hands and knees. I might even get some flowers out of it."

Twenty minutes later, Nick stood out in front of the house, zipping his jacket against the cold wind. He started walking toward Field's Corner with hopes that the cops would be onto the magician. While walking, he tried to figure out what happened to his life. Ever since he took a ride in that hot box with Joey, his whole world had turned inside out and backward.

The worst of it was, there was no one he could talk to. Who would understand? It seemed as if every part his life strained at the seams, threatening to fly apart at any moment. Sully, Mike, the magician, the priest and the voice. Any one of them could send him over the edge, *especially* the voice. After last night, he didn't know what he would do if he heard it again. Didn't know if he had the strength to deal with it. The memory of it booming through his head made him shudder.

He made a wide circle around Town Field and found a hidden spot on the far side behind a fence where he could watch the magician unseen.

Nick's heartbeat jumped at the sight of the man when he appeared half an hour later. A cold hollow, feeling sank into the pit of his stomach. He started toward the mission, keeping close to the far fence and out of sight of the magician. When he saw a break in traffic, he darted across Dorchester Ave. and ducked behind a parked car.

You are the divine instrument of his will! The voice exploded in his head like a shattering bottle. Nick clapped his hands over his ears and stood up to see the magician staring at him from across the street.

CHAPTER TWENTY THREE

Max watched the street and the mission, smiling to himself as the events of the previous day played themselves out in his mind. He and O'Grady stood outside the commissioner's office watching the group of detectives waiting to join the task force file out a side door while Flynn and the commissioner took the door to the outer hall. Hubbard and Trenchcoat stayed behind.

"I'll be back in a few minutes," O'Grady said, slinging her purse onto her shoulder. "Have to make a pit stop."

"Meet you back here," Max said. "I need to talk to Hubbard and his buddy."

"Hope you're still not holding a grudge about Savin Hill," Hubbard said when the door closed behind O'Grady. "Nothing personal. We only did what Flynn told us." He gave his friend a sideways glance. Trenchcoat nodded.

"Forget about it," Max said. "To be honest, I don't have time for this silly shit. There's a nutcase running around out there who needs to be stopped, so if you two are done fucking around, we can work together and do some real police work." He allowed himself a tight-lipped smile. "I've had the chance to get to know you, Detective Hubbard, but my meetings with your partner have been brief." He gestured toward Trenchcoat. "We never did get introduced. I'm Special Agent Broderick, U.S. Justice Department."

"Detective Thompson. Listen, um…" He tugged at his ear. "Flynn's not really a bad guy, it's just that…"

"Flynn and I can work things out for ourselves."

Thompson stared at the floor. "Yeah, sure."

"I need you two to find out where Barbara Brice is buried, then I want you to stake out her grave."

Hubbard cleared his throat. "Her grave?"

"Three shifts. You, Thompson, and Flynn. Decide between yourselves who gets what shift, but I want the grave covered and a report on my desk every morning."

"You want us to stake out a grave?" Thompson said. His Adam's apple bobbed. "At night?"

"I do it all the time," Max said. "You Beantown badasses aren't afraid, are you?"

Thompson scowled. "Of course not."

Flynn and the commissioner came in from the outer hallway. The commissioner glanced at Max and went straight to his office without speaking. Flynn joined Max and the two detectives.

"I was just giving Hubbard and Thompson their assignments," Max said. "You're in charge of the stakeout, Flynn."

"Stakeout?"

"Of a graveyard," Hubbard said.

"What?" Flynn's brow furrowed. "Say it ain't so, Broderick."

"I wish I could, but I can't. You're in charge of the commissioner's report too."

Flynn's eyes narrowed. He stuck his hands in his pockets and kept his gaze on Max. "Okay, Thompson and Hubbard," he said without looking at them. "You know what to do, so get on it." He jabbed his thumb over his shoulder. "I'll be in touch. Broderick and I need to discuss the case."

The two detectives left.

Flynn continued staring at Max, then became animated. "Listen." He put a meaty hand on Max's shoulder. Max smelled gin on his breath. "I'm sorry things didn't get off to such a great start between us. I didn't think they'd go so far."

"No shit, Flynn. You probably thought they'd end at Savin Hill. You're lucky they didn't go any further than they did."

Flynn patted him on the back and pulled out a cigar. "But I want you to know I'm willing to let bygones be bygones. Way I see it we've got common interests."

"And what are they?"

"Catching this killer and watching out for the safety of my ex. What do you say we cut the bullshit and work together."

"That's what I'm doing."

Flynn ran the cigar under his nose, then stuck it in the corner of his mouth. "Between you and me, Broderick, this is a man's thing. I don't like to see Colleen exposed to this shit. I've done my best to keep her out of it, but when it comes to the shit, she's like a fly, if you know what I mean."

"Nobody's forcing her into anything. She wants to do this."

"Yeah, I know, but face it Broderick, she's a broad."

Max stiffened.

"Don't put me on this stakeout," Flynn continued. "It'll drive me batshit. Let me do some of the digging for you. That's what I do. Stick Colleen on a desk where she belongs. Give her a job filing. She don't belong on the streets."

Max rubbed his chin as if considering Flynn's proposition. "You think she should be a desk jockey?"

"Absolutely." Flynn jabbed at the air with his cigar. "Let me do the investigating. I'll do it right."

"Let me get this straight. You think I should put O'Grady on a desk and put you on the investigation in her place because she's a broad and doesn't have what it takes to do a good job."

An expansive smile filled Flynn's face. He patted Max on the shoulder. "You're a pretty sharp guy. I knew I liked you, Broderick." He lowered his voice. "Like I said, sorry we got off on the wrong foot, but I know she turned you against me from the get go."

"What makes you say that?"

"It was obvious when you had me yanked from the Brice case."

Max felt his anger rising. What a snake. The more he talks the more he puts his foot in his mouth.

"You and me, Broderick. We'll put a lid on this case. Reassign Colleen for her own good. All this blood and gore is messing her up and she's screwed up already." He lowered his voice. "I'm telling you, Broderick. I've always done my best to protect her."

"This is a man's thing, isn't it? Women don't belong. We men have to straighten this out, right?"

Another smile. Flynn gestured with his cigar as he talked. "I was good to her, kept the shit off her. She didn't appreciate it. She left me because she couldn't hang. Now all the bitch does is talk shit about me. Colleen's one hell of a good looker, but up here in the cabeza." He pointed to his head. "She's just another whacky broad."

Max stifled the urge to jam Flynn's cigar down his throat. "Let me tell you something," he said between clenched teeth. "You better treat that lady with the respect she deserves."

Flynn's mouth dropped and his eyes grew wide.

Max jammed a finger into his chest. "Quit while you're ahead. You've gotten off easy so far. I hear you bad mouthing her any more, especially in front of any other cops, you're going to get more than a beating in a subway station." He grabbed Flynn by the lapels and put his face inches from Flynn's. "Colleen has more class and more smarts than you…"

Max looked past Flynn and saw her coming. His face flushed.

Letting go, he waved Flynn away. "You'd better get going. You have a stakeout to oversee." He nodded toward Colleen. "Come on *partner*, let's get out of here."

They left Flynn staring as the door closed behind them.

While O'Grady drove them back to Dorchester, Max stared out the window. "Tell me about you and Flynn," he said without turning from the window.

"What do you want to know?"

"I don't get it." He shrugged and turned to her. "I'm not kidding when I say you're a good cop and I respect you. Aside from that you're smart and good looking. A class act. How'd you ever get involved with a slob like him?"

She gave him a sideways glance, then looked ahead, concentrating on her driving. "I was young when I joined the force. Twenty-two, starry-eyed, and impressionable. Flynn was in his prime. You should have seen him back then." She shook her head. "He was a rugged, hard core homicide dick with a reputation for tenacity. He has one of the highest arrest and conviction records in the city."

"He'd be really good if he wasn't so busy being petty."

"I realize now that I saw him as a father image. To a young girl of twenty-two a man fifteen years older is very exciting. A take-charge kind of a guy. Problem was he wanted to take complete charge."

"How long did it last?"

"Two years. It wouldn't have lasted that long, except that we both worked strange shifts and sometimes wouldn't lay eyes on each other for days. I didn't see it at first, but even then he had a drinking problem. The stuff he's had to put up with in homicide, the things he's seen…"

"Explains why he doesn't like you working with me."

She nodded. "That's a big part of it. Flynn cares in his own way, but I suspect his bigger motivation is jealousy."

"Of me?"

"For the most part, but he's also jealous of me."

"Do tell."

"I stayed in the administrative section of the department, but I wanted to get out into the action. All my requests for transfers were denied. I can't prove it, but I'm sure Flynn was responsible." She bit her lower lip. "In spite of his manipulations I went to school and rose in rank. He went nowhere. His drinking got worse. So did the violence."

Max's gut tightened. "He hit you?"

"It was more mental than physical. He smashed things and yes, he smashed me a few times, but the mental part was the worst."

"Why didn't you leave him sooner?"

"It's hard to explain, but I felt sorry for him. I don't know if you've ever had the experience of watching someone self-destruct. It's not pretty."

"He's been smoldering all these years."

"You kidding? It's not easy for someone with an ego as big as Flynn's to deal with rejection."

Neither one spoke for awhile. Max kept stealing glances at her, wondering what it would be like to be with her. The thought of his lonely hotel room made his desire all the more poignant. The idea of a relationship developing outside of working hours flitted through his brain, but he didn't want to complicate things any more than they were. He was too emotionally fucked-up as it was.

He looked up and down Dorchester Ave., then at the mission again, thinking about Lieutenant Colleen O'Grady. Striking green eyes and red hair. A beautiful Boston cop with a model's figure and some of the greatest legs he'd ever seen who also happened to be his efficient and more than competent partner in the investigation of a series of grisly ritual murders. With all she had been through and all she saw, she still retained her dignity. No, more than dignity, she had class. Max understood why Flynn tried to keep her away from the shit. Not that it was right. It wasn't. But he understood.

Best thing he could do now was to keep an eye on things here. He did another scan of Town Field and the mission, recognizing the kid he saw hanging around earlier running across the street.

CHAPTER TWENTY FOUR

The voice rang in Nick's ears like the aftermath of an explosion. The magician continued to stare, as if his eyes drove the words deeper into Nick's mind. Ducking behind a car, Nick crouched low, then bolted up Dorchester Ave., putting distance between himself and the magician. Half a block away, he darted into an alley and watched the street from behind the front steps of an apartment house.

You have been chosen as the instrument of his will, the voice said. Though not as loud as the first admonishment, its closeness made Nick's scalp tingle as if thousands of tiny spiders scurried across it. His whole body shook and a rush of panic flashed through him.

Peering above the steps, Nick watched the magician pack his bag and trot across Dorchester Ave., cape flapping behind him like a bat wing. He circled the car Nick had hidden behind and looked up and down the street in both directions. Nick slumped down beside the steps to avoid being seen. Jesus, what was he going to do? He peered over the steps again and saw the magician two houses away checking alleys.

Coming toward him.

You cannot escape your destiny. A burst of adrenaline propelled Nick down the alley. He ran around the back of the house and saw a pot bellied man in a greasy t-shirt coming out the back door carrying a bag of garbage. A cigarette hung from the corner of his mouth. He stared at Nick from the top of the steps. Nick waved and kept running around the back of the house and up an adjoining alley, slowing when he reached Dorchester Ave. Now he would be behind the magician.

Nick poked his head from around a bush and watched him continue up the street checking alleyways. *It is your duty. His will must be appeased.* Nick shook his head. The voice sounded softer, no longer demanding; trying to persuade. Nick forced himself to breathe slow. He had no choice but to follow the magician and see where he went.

He pictured himself staggering through the streets, pissing his pants, holding his head, and talking to himself like the bums he saw almost every day of his life. He cringed at the thought of people laughing at him and kids hassling him. If the voice won out, he would become a non-person, reduced to a life of shopping carts, trash picking, and soup kitchens. The thought frightened him more than the threat from the magician and the possibility of witnessing another murder.

Great, he thought. I can go off the deep end or I can watch another poor girl get turned into hamburger. Some choice.

He waited until the magician turned the corner, then followed, dodging in and out of alleys and stooping behind cars to avoid being seen, always keeping a half a block behind. The magician eventually stopped looking into alleys, but kept a brisk pace, periodically scanning both sides of the street.

The voice still came into Nick's head, sometimes admonishing, sometimes cajoling, sometimes in a steady hypnotic patter that droned like bees on a warm spring day, lulling him.

They turned another corner and headed back toward Town Field. Nick concentrated on the voice to see if he could hear anything that might hint at another murder.

Come to me, my son. Let me help you to cleanse your soul and purify you for your divine mission.

"I don't think I can go through with it," a slurred voice said. "I'm not strong enough."

Nick jumped when he heard the second voice. Outside of him. He stopped and faded back into the shadow of a three-decker apartment house.

Of course you are, otherwise you would not have been chosen. Don't fight it. The only way to put your mind at peace is to submit to my will.

The last sentence slithered into Nick's mind, wrapping itself around his thoughts. He shook off a chill. He understood this last admonition all too well. He had no doubt that the voice's relentless persistence could wear a man down, particularly if they were susceptible to begin with -- like a homeless person.

"Please, don't make me do it."

Nick heard it from across the street, but couldn't see its owner. He watched the magician continuing his stroll like some psychic pied piper, never turning back to see if the rats still followed.

Shit, who do I follow? Nick wondered. If I lose the magician, I won't know where he comes from. If I lose the bum, I won't be able to stop him from killing someone else.

The voice in his head made the decision for him. *I won't make you do anything. You will give yourself over to me willingly.*

The homeless guy would be doing the killing.

Nick darted across the street and listened. At first he didn't hear any response, then he heard a muffled sob. He started toward the voice, checking over his shoulder from time to time to see if the magician looked back, but he didn't. With a sinking feeling in the pit of his stomach, Nick knew he was about to lose him.

He spotted a shopping cart next to a dumpster in an alley. Beside it a man wearing a ragged navy pea coat and a blue wool watch cap slumped with his back to the bin, rocking back and forth, head clutched between his knees. Tangled blond hair jutted out from the sides of his hat.

The anguish in the man's cries touched something in Nick. His throat tightened and his eyes burned. He couldn't believe he was going to crack like a sissy -- and he didn't even know the guy.

As if sensing Nick's thoughts, the man looked up with ice-blue, bloodshot eyes. The whites around the irises held a startled look, like blown fuses. His face had the raw, reddish-brown tint that came from continual exposure to the elements. His cheeks glistened from tears. He eyed Nick, twin pinpoints of blue accusing, as though Nick were the source of his misery.

"Just fucking leave me alone!" the man yelled, pressing his hands to his ears. "I don't want to kill anybody."

Nick backed away while the voice in his head continued, unruffled by the outburst. *There can be no peace until you have given your soul to me. Only I have the power to grant you serenity.*

The man shook his head as he rose and grabbed his cart. "You won't let me rest until I do it, will you?"

Such a complete rest. The voice flowed velvety and seductive. *Never have you felt such comfort.* Its promises sounded enticing. The thought of giving in flitted through Nick's mind.

The man pushed his shopping cart out of the alley, then stopped and stared as if seeing it for the first time. A puzzled look twisted his face, then he walked on, leaving the cart and his belongings. Nick pictured Obie abandoning his cart the same way.

Keeping his distance, Nick shadowed the man the way he'd followed the magician while the voice continued its gentle cajoling. Nick heard muttered replies while the man shuffled down the street toward Field's Corner, oblivious to his surroundings. Nick wasn't surprised when the man turned on Dorchester Ave. and headed for Saint Augustine's.

Afraid of being spotted by the magician, Nick hung back when he reached the corner. The homeless man stopped outside the mission and stood motionless for a few minutes before going in. The moment he went in the voice in Nick's head stopped.

Had the building cut off the connection? Maybe it was a holy place that kept the dark voice out. He looked up and down the street, hesitating. All he had to do was watch out for Sully, the priest, and the magician. If he stayed where he was he'd lose the guy. If he went in -- fuck it! He shoved his hands into his pockets and strode toward the storefront.

He didn't see Father Derlen or Sully anywhere. After one last look over his shoulder to check for the magician, Nick stepped through the door into a room laden with the now familiar smells of cooked cabbage, institutional food, and unwashed bodies.

People hunched over their meals at most of the seats at the tables. Nick searched the room for the man he was following, then watched the slow moving line of people beside serving tables at the far end of the room. Two haggard looking men ladled out soup in front of the kitchen. He saw movement and recognized the watch cap and the pea coat a moment before the man disappeared behind one of the kitchen doors.

Shit. What should he do now? What if the guy was talking to the priest? What if Sully was back there? Nick headed in the direction of the kitchen, feeling that the bigger part of the mission lay behind those doors, but he didn't know how he could see behind them without getting busted.

"Hey, boy." A raspy voice. Someone tugged at his sleeve.

Nick jerked his arm away and looked down. A grizzled older man with thick lips, an unshaven gray stubble, and yellowed teeth smiled up at him. The bushy eyebrows on his protruding forehead made his eyes look as if they sat deeper in their sockets. Dark eyes glittered in the fluorescent lights; twin caves harboring vicious little creatures.

Nick felt a flash of impatience. "What do you want?"

"Come here, boy, sit down." He grabbed Nick by the arm and pulled him toward the table. Nick struggled, looking around to see if anyone watched. A few men stared indifferently. Not wanting to draw attention, he dropped into the seat next to the man.

"What do you want?" he asked again.

"What's a nice looking young boy like you doing in a place like this?" Fetid breath assaulted Nick.

"Looking for someone." He edged away.

"Maybe I can help you." The man put his hand on the inside of Nick's thigh. "Then you can help me. I can think of a lot of things a nice young boy like you could do for a lonely old man like me."

The closeness of the man and the stench of his breath turned Nick's stomach. He pushed the man's hand off his thigh. "Keep your fucking hands to yourself."

The man leaned in closer. "Don't play hard to get with me. I've had lots of boys like you. I'll bet you can make me happy and I know I can put a smile on your face." His hand slid down over Nick's crotch.

Nick's elbow shot out catching the man in the ribs and the man let go. "I told you to keep your hands to yourself, you fucking queer!" His frustration of the last few weeks came to the surface, focusing itself on the stinking man who fondled him and exploded, following the elbow with a right hook that caught the man squarely in the side of the head.

People pressed in from the surrounding tables. Nick didn't care any more. He hit the man twice more in the face, then pummeled him about the head. All he could see were shocked wild eyes looking up at him. Blood ran from the man's nose.

Hands grabbed at him. Nick pulled away, punching again and again. A flash of white. Something hit him on the back of the head, stunning him. He fell forward shaking his head. Everything went fuzzy.

"Fucking Powers." The familiar voice shook him.

Two hands grabbed him by the shoulders and jerked him backward, sending him sprawling to the floor. He looked up into Sully's pockmarked face and saw a smile on his lips. Malevolence glittered in his eyes. "You're mine now." He raised his billy club.

Shit.

The smile widened. Sully brought the end of the billy club down into

Nick's stomach, sending a hot explosion shooting through his gut. He gasped, unable to catch his breath. He fought back the urge to vomit while struggling for breath.

Darkness closed in. Nick forced himself to stay conscious and tried to pull more air into his lungs. His world grayed. Sully's smile seemed to go up into his eyes. He raised the club again.

Someone else's hand shot out, grabbing it.

"I'll have no violence in my mission."

Nick thought it was the voice in his head until Father Derlen's concerned face swam into view.

"But, Father, he beat up that poor old man." Sully pointed. Two men from the serving line lifted the man with the bloodied nose into a chair.

Nick tasted bile in the back of his throat, but his breath came a little easier. He clutched his stomach.

"So you think that gives you the right to use violence?"

Sully stared at the floor. "But, Father..."

"I'm ashamed of you, Richard." Derlen knelt down over Nick and gently lifted his head from the floor. "I would expect you of all people to set a proper example in front of these poor souls." He gestured toward the crowd.

Nick sat up and saw that the smile had gone from Sully's face. He glared at Nick.

"Are you all right, son?" Derlen said.

"I'll be okay," Nick gasped. His mouth felt dry and his body trembled.

"I'm sorry, father," Sully mumbled. "You're right. I got carried away."

"Let's put it behind us," Derlen said. He looked into Nick's eyes. Nick felt safe with the priest beside him and grateful that he stepped in when he did.

Sully slid his billy club back into his belt. "Let me take him down to the station and book him for assault. Keep this from happening again."

A scowl stole across Derlen's face, then passed. He took a deep breath. "You'll do no such thing, Richard. I think it's best that you leave, you're trying my patience."

"But."

"Now."

Sully left without another word.

"Now the rest of you get back to your business," Derlen said, shooing the crowd away. "And someone get him cleaned up." He pointed at the man Nick had beaten. One of the men from the serving line took the older man away.

Father Derlen helped Nick into a chair. "Someone get a cup of tea for this young man."

Nick breathed in slow, shaky breaths, happy that his lungs had resumed their normal functioning. The side of his head throbbed. Reaching back he felt tender stickiness and a bump. Someone handed him a hot cup of tea.

"Thanks."

"Now what's this all about?" Derlen said, kneeling next to him. "You're still not looking for your Obie, are you?"

What am I going to tell him? Nick thought. I followed a man who was hearing the same voices I heard? He cleared his throat. "I didn't mean to cause trouble. That old guy, he grabbed me."

"Grabbed you?"

"My privates."

Derlen's eyebrows shot up. "Your privates?"

Nick sipped his tea. Now that things were calmer, Derlen's Irish brogue had a sing-song, melodic quality. Nick found himself pondering the change from the tone he used with Sully a few minutes ago.

"I didn't mean to cause a scene. When he touched me, something let loose inside. Next thing you know I was all over him like stink on shi -- like a new suit."

"All right, son." Derlen clapped Nick on the shoulder. "Old Bernie's got an eye for younger men. I intend to have a word with him, but I'm sure I don't have to tell you to steer clear." He looked over his shoulder and chuckled softly. "Although, judging from the job you did on him, I'd wager he'll be steering clear of you."

Nick took another sip of tea.

"For that matter, it's not a good idea for you to be coming around here. We tend to get some unsavory types from time to time. It's not a place for a young man like you."

"You're right, Father. I promise I'll keep my distance."

Derlen smiled and ruffled Nick's hair, barely missing the bump. "Good lad. Feeling better now?"

Nick's stomach settled into a dull ache, but the throbbing at the back of his head increased. He gingerly touched the lump. "Yes, I am." He drained his cup. "Thanks for the tea."

"Think nothing of it. I have duties to tend to, so if you're sure you're all right." He stood.

Nick had an urge to tell the priest everything about the voices, his dreams, the magician, and the murders. He might understand. "Um, Father?"

"Yes, my son?"

"There's..." Something made him stop. What the hell was he thinking? He couldn't tell anybody. "Forget it. It's nothing."

"You sure?"

"Thanks for the tea and everything. I'd better get going."

Father Derlen stared at him a moment, then shrugged. "God bless." He turned and walked back toward the kitchen.

Nick stood and the pounding in his head came harder. Better get my ass home. He took one last look around for the man in the pea coat, then stepped out the front door onto Dorchester Ave. and started walking toward Field's Corner station.

At the end of the block he heard foot steps running up the street behind him. He turned around and saw the magician coming after him, cape flapping in the breeze the same way it had in his nightmare. The same way those things in the fog had.

CHAPTER TWENTY FIVE

Not wanting Sully or any other neighborhood cops to see his disguise, Max made a quick change at his hotel room, then drove over to District Eleven to meet O'Grady and Geist. Halfway down the hall to his office, he spotted the two plainclothes detectives who had been assigned to stake out Saint Augustine's at night.

"Hey, guys, how's it going? Anything new to report?"

The two men stopped and waited for Max. Both young, one had big shoulders straining the seams of his shirt, crew cut black hair that made his head look like a brush, and thick eyebrows. Small and wiry, the second man had quick, nervous movements, and sharp features that reminded Max of a rat.

"Place is deader than a morgue," brush head said.

"Nothing else?"

"Oh, yeah. Almost forgot." The smaller one reached into his pocket, pulled out a crumpled envelope and handed it to Max. "This came in the mail the other day."

Max opened the envelope and scanned its contents, his incredulity growing with each line. It was all there. The stakeout at Cedar Grove, the mission, the closets, the sickle.

He re-read the last few lines.

The street magician who's been there in the past few weeks is the man you need to watch. He leads the sacrifices. He's the one behind the murders.

He looked up at the two detectives. "Why didn't I get this sooner?" The big one shrugged.

"We meant to give it to you sooner," the smaller one said, "but you know, night stakeout and all. It's not like we see you every day."

No one knew all the details about the crimes written in the note except Geist, O'Grady, and himself, and neither one of them would have pulled a stunt like this. He studied the last part of the note again. The magician! "Okay," he said. "Anybody else know about this?"

"We told Sully," brush head said. "He donates a lot of time to the mission."

"Did he see the note?"

"He was real interested. Wanted us to give it to him. Said he'd take care of it."

"Tell him you gave it to me and I threw it out."

A perplexed look passed over the smaller man's face. "Sure. What's this all about?"

"Nothing. It's probably a crank letter, but I have to follow through. You know, procedure."

"Yeah, we know the drill," brush head said.

"Anything funny happens around there, I mean anything. Someone farts, shits, or sneezes, I want to know about it."

Two nods. "We'll call it in."

"Thanks." Max went past them toward his office, puzzling over the note. Who the hell could have -- it hit him when he stepped into his office. "The kid!" he said aloud.

O'Grady looked up from his desk. Her long red hair, perfume and pretty features brightened the otherwise lifeless room. "What?"

"The kid." Max handed her the note.

Colleen took it and scanned it, her green eyes devouring each line. "Where did you get this?"

Max took off his jacket and flung it over a chair. "Came in the mail." He pulled up another chair and straddled it, resting his arms on the backrest. "There's this kid I've seen around the mission. Not really a kid, probably around twenty. He's been acting strange. Sticks out like a sore thumb."

"You talked to him?"

"I couldn't risk compromising my cover, but when I saw the way he was acting, I tried tailing him." He shrugged. "I lost him. Twice. But get this." Max looked over his shoulder, then stood and closed the door before returning to the chair. "Remember that weirdo cop?"

She frowned and handed him back the note. "Sully."

"Yeah." Max folded the note. "Spends a lot of time down at the mission. The other day the kid got into an altercation with one of the transients. Sully showed up out of nowhere and started beating the shit out of him, but the priest stopped it." Max shook his head. "That son-of-a-bitch has a mean streak in him."

Colleen wrinkled her nose. "Somehow that doesn't surprise me."

"I want to talk to the kid."

"Sully probably knows who he is. Maybe we should ask him?"

"Sully knows all right. I think he knows too much. According to the guys I had watching the mission, Sully was very interested in this." He held up the note. "He asked them to give it to him. Said he'd take care of it."

"Smells funny."

"I have a bad feeling about him. Might explain his attitude toward the kid." Max stuck the note into his pocket. "The kid knows something and I'm thinking that Sully knows more than he's letting on."

Colleen's eyes grew wide. "You think he's a suspect?"

"Something down at that mission stinks. I think he knows what it is. Derlen probably has no idea."

"Should we tell him?"

"As far as I know my cover's still good. If anything gets out in the open, who knows what the priest might say or do. Chances are, he'd say something to Sully, then my cover will be blown. We have to get to the kid. He knows too much already and if *he* knows, there's a good chance that whoever's behind the murders knows. If that's the case, we'd better find the kid before they do. Otherwise we're liable to find him gutted."

Geist poked his head in the door. "This a private party, or can anyone join?"

"Come on in," Max said. "Pull up a chair. Anything new?"

Geist pulled an envelope from under his arm and handed it to Max. "I picked it up from the desk sergeant on the way in."

Max opened the envelope and studied its contents while Geist took a chair from against the wall. "It's a revised behavioral profile from my man Hart," Max said. "And the DNA study from the Perry murder." He looked up. "I didn't tell Hart about the separate prints at each scene.

Wanted to see what he'd come up with on his own."

O'Grady leaned forward, green eyes intent on Max. "What does he say?"

Geist opened his briefcase and began stacking files on the desk. "We can compare notes."

Max flipped through the profile. "For starters we have a third set of DNA and fingerprints, completely different from the first two." He paused. "And again we have no records, no priors, no rap sheet, social security, welfare -- nothing. Like three separate ghosts have gone on killing sprees."

Geist held up a file. "Fits in with my findings. Three sets of prints. No matchups. What about the psych profile?"

O'Grady flipped through her notes. "I'm still following up your missing hand angle." She glanced over at Geist. "Hand job theory, right Geist?"

Rick smiled and shrugged. "Different strokes for different folks."

She shook her head. "I've only come up with two handless corpses in the past six months. In both cases the hands were recovered, one of them too mangled to be of any use."

"That's what I figured," Geist said.

"Probably a dead end," Max said, "but keep digging. Things are falling into place. Where they'll end up I don't know, but we're getting closer. I can feel it. Anything else?"

"Not until I hear what's in that profile," Geist said.

"Okay, let's see," Max said, reading from the report. "He finds the intraracial angle unique. Puts a kink in his serial killer theory, but the pattern intrigues him. He thinks the sloppiness is the killer's way of wanting to be caught."

He flipped through a few more pages. "The religious overtones, attention to detail, arrangement of the organs, methodical dismemberment, and the ensuing lack of neatness confirms his belief that our suspect or suspects are in a disorganized mental state. One moment sociopathic. The next, totally psychotic."

He stopped and looked up. "Get this. Because of the religious aspects, the perpetrator probably frequents a church, rescue mission, or some other kind of religious institution. Consider concentrating the investigation in that area."

"Sounds like a hit," O'Grady said.

Max continued. "Probably stays on the fringes of society, unable to function within normal social constructs. This reinforces Hart's feelings about watching the mission. He thinks our killer's a transient."

"A transient." Geist rubbed his chin. "That would explain some things, but different prints?"

"Transients." O'Grady slapped the desk with the palm of her hand and stood, her voice rising with excitement. "That's it! Transients. More than one. That's why we have different prints that can't be made. There's hardly any public record of transients. How can we run a make on them if there's nothing to look at?"

Max flipped the file closed. "That would explain the different prints, but it doesn't explain the similarities of the murders."

"Unless our perp is killing the transients too," Geist added. "Cutting off their hands, and giving the murder scenes a hand job."

"Intentional sloppiness," Max said, feeling a twinge in his gut. "If that's the case, this is one cunning son-of-a-bitch we're dealing with, not some poor bastard crying for help."

Colleen sat back down. "He must be hiding the bodies, because we haven't found any. I've been focusing most of my attention on the John Does."

Geist held up a file of his own. "All the consistencies match up on the Perry murder along with the inconsistencies. Same neatness in some areas. Same sloppiness in others."

Max handed Geist his file. "Keep at it. Cross reference. Cross-check. Keep looking for the things in common. Anything new comes up, call me right away." He turned to O'Grady. "Stay on your hand hunt, but I might need you to help me corral this kid. We have to talk to him."

"What kid's that?" Geist said.

"A kid I've seen hanging around the rescue mission. I'm convinced he knows something. One other thing." He turned to O'Grady. "We'd better keep a close eye on our boy Sully."

CHAPTER TWENTY SIX

Midnight.
Nick sat alone at the kitchen table drinking his third cup of coffee, watching his hands shake as he raised the cup to his lips. He kept his jaw clamped, gritting his teeth while his mind raced, keeping time with the pulse throbbing in his temples.

Noticing the pot was empty, he stood, took a fresh filter from the cupboard and pulled the used one from the coffee machine. When he opened the kitchen closet and dumped the old filter into the trash, his stomach did a slow roll. The mixed smells of coffee grounds and garbage brought the image of the magician swooping into his mind. He stared at the plastic bag of his stinking clothes half-buried in the trash and remembered the footsteps running up the street behind him. The magician, cape flapping like in his nightmare, like those things in the fog – if they had been real.

Nick played it back in his mind. Running down Park Street, past the library, hearing the man yelling, not making out the words. Cutting into an alley behind Lucky Strike Lanes where he saw an open dumpster. He slid to a stop and made a beeline for it, grabbing the cold, greasy top. The slimy feel of the metal and the stench of the dumpster revolted him, but fear overcame his disgust. Fuck it, he thought pulling himself over the top.

Something cold and slimy slapped against his face as he tumbled into the dumpster. Nick brushed it away and pulled the lid down, wrapping himself in darkness. Stale beer, coffee grounds and sour, rotting food assaulted him. His breathing came hard, drawing the stench deeper into his lungs. Sweat soaked his body. He grabbed a few loose newspapers and covered himself.

Footsteps came running into the alley, then slowed. As they came closer, the voice drifted to him, each word hitting his brain like the first chilling flakes of snow driven by an icy New England wind. Whispering.

Come now, my child, you mustn't be shy. None but one of the chosen can bring happiness to those who rule. Only by performing the miracle can the chosen one find peace.

Nick shivered.

The footsteps came closer, stopping outside the dumpster. Nick let his breath out slowly.

Don't resist. Pleading. Soft. Intimate. *You cannot escape my will. It is an extension of the great ones. Give yourself to me. Allow yourself to become an instrument of the divine.*

Still no sound.

Nick pictured the magician outside the dumpster, sending his thoughts into Nick's brain from the other side of the cold metal. He wanted to press his hands to his ears, but it wouldn't stop the voice. The idea of giving in slithered into his mind, followed by the seductive possibility of quiet.

Fuck that! I'll go nuts first.

He pushed the voice to the back of his mind when he heard the sound of gravel grinding under a shoe, then the footsteps went back the way they came. When he figured the magician was close to the end of the alley, Nick eased the lid up. His eyes rose above the lip of the dumpster in time to see a black cape disappearing around the corner.

His first instinct was to run, but the magician might be hiding around the corner, so he lowered the lid and plopped down into the garbage again. Something cold and wet soaked through the seat of his pants, then he heard footsteps again and froze.

He crouched in an awkward position that made his knees ache. The steps echoed down the alley, stopping outside the dumpster. Nick held his breath.

Time stretched. There in the cold rotting darkness the world became one eternal suffocating moment until the lid flew up.

Nick gasped and fell backward, banging his head on scummy metal, falling into a ripped bag of trash. He felt a flash of pain, but stayed conscious.

A dark-faced man wearing thick-rimmed glasses with one lens missing peered over the top of the dumpster. The left side of his unshaven face twitched. His graying dreadlocks spewed out like mop strings.

"Hey, mon," he said in a sing-song voice. He shook his head slowly. "What you doing in dere? Dis is my pickin's."

Nick stood and brushed himself off. "You can have it, brother." He vaulted over the side of the dumpster and made his way to the end of the alley, keeping close to the wall.

As dusk settled over the city, shadows lengthened and street lights winked on. Nick looked up and down Park Street and saw a few passing cars, but no other sign of activity. He waited until the darkness grew complete, then made a wide berth around Field's Corner and started toward home, keeping to side streets.

An icy wind gusted through tree branches, sounding eerily like whispers. He had a hard time distinguishing those sounds from the voice, which had diminished to hushed tones hovering in the peripheral of his mind like phantom butterflies. He kept looking over his shoulder, half expecting to see the magician stalking him.

When the wind shifted, the stench that clung to him made him gag. The spasms in his chest sent stabs of pain shooting through his gut where Sully hit him with the billy club. His hands, hair and clothes all felt greasy, as if the stink of the dumpster had become a permanent part of him.

Christ, I'm becoming one of them, he thought with rising panic. The voice is wearing me down. He shuddered and pulled his jacket tighter. Ain't going to let it get to me.

To his surprise and relief, he made it home before Mike and his mother. He stripped, sealing his stinking clothes in a plastic bag, then took a long hot shower, lathering his hair and body three times to make sure he washed all the stink from himself.

Now he wanted to sleep, but didn't dare.

Staring at the half-buried bag of clothes, he finished emptying the coffee filter and closed the kitchen closet door.

No way was he going to allow himself the luxury of sleep tonight.

CHAPTER TWENTY SEVEN

Midnight.

Hands behind his head, Max stared up at the empty ceiling of the hotel room, his loneliness threatening to swallow him. He pushed his feelings aside and turned his thoughts to the kid he saw hanging around Saint Augustine's and the scuffle he witnessed. His urge had been to break things up, but it would have blown his cover. Good thing the priest stepped in when he did. Sully could have done serious damage. Max had to find that kid before Sully did. Before the murderer or murderers got to him. Murderers? O'Grady was right. More than one. How many? Was Sully involved? He didn't strike Max as smart enough to pull off what had happened, but he was one cunning son-of-a-bitch. Good chance he was in it, but he definitely wasn't the brains behind it. Either way, he couldn't be trusted.

Max rolled onto his side, pulled the covers to his chin and closed his eyes. Ten minutes later, he was on his back again staring at the ceiling. He hated these times alone. Life came to a complete stop, leaving him to face the emptiness of what he had become -- one of the highest paid investigators in the country with the freedom to run his investigations the way he saw fit. A position many envied, but success had taken its toll. Outside of his work, he had no life of his own.

He remembered his mother's gentle scolding. He didn't remember her as a whole. She came to him in a series of sensations and images; the way she cuddled him, the warmth of her body, loving hands, soft smells, soap and perfume, sparkling blue eyes and long blonde hair. Those were the memories he kept. Not the body lying in the coffin or the cloying smell of flowers.

His anger had saved him. Kept the pain at bay.

The woman they said was his mother didn't look like her. Mommy didn't wear thick makeup. Her skin was soft and natural. The way the body in the coffin wore her hair was not the way mommy wore it either, yet he recognized her cheekbones, small nose, and delicate hands.

Max remembered kneeling in front of the coffin next to his father and putting his hand on the cold fingers of the shell that had been his mother. I'll get them, he vowed. I promise Mom, wherever you are.

"It's okay, Max," his father said in a hoarse whisper. Max smelled cigarettes and booze on his breath. "There's nothing to be afraid of."

Max clenched his hand into a fist. His father didn't understand. He wasn't afraid. I promise you Mom. I'll never stop going after the bad guys.

His father patted him on the back and left him alone with his mother. Longing for one last touch, Max clasped the unresponsive hand, wishing it was warm. Wishing the life would come back.

How long had it been since he felt the tenderness of a woman's love? There had been girls in college and hard-edged woman cops, but none had shown him true affection and none lasted. His obsession always overtook and ruled his life.

Of all the policewomen he'd met, O'Grady stood out. He pictured the way her face hardened when confronted with something unpleasant. Sure, she had the veneer that all cops wore to protect themselves, but Max knew that beneath Colleen's lay tenderness.

He would give a lot to know the real Colleen.

Reaching into his nightstand drawer he pulled out the kerchief she gave him the night Hubbard and Trenchcoat worked him over. Though spotted with his blood, the scent of her perfume remained. He held it to his nose, closed his eyes and inhaled, then put the kerchief back in the drawer, wishing she were beside him. Someone warm to share his feelings with. Someone to hold. Someone to talk to.

He thought of the unholy parade of lifeless bodies that had become his work; some dismembered, some old and rotting, most dead from lunatic violence. The concept of tenderness in a world of bloody, impersonal police procedure seemed distant and foreign. Could he lower his walls? He wasn't sure he could relate to someone as his real self. Was there anything left of the real Max? Shit, for that matter, who was the real Max?

He swung his legs over the edge of the bed, went to his briefcase and dug out O'Grady's phone number and address. 698 East Broadway in South Boston. He picked up the phone and started to call, stopping at the third number. He paced the hotel room until he couldn't stand it any longer, then dressed, grabbed the keys to his rental car and went out.

He found himself driving past South Station heading into South Boston. The streets in Southie were deserted, except for the few lone figures Max saw bundled against the cold, moving furtively through the streets, hands in pockets, heads covered, breaths coming in white plumes. Max wondered where they could possibly be going at this hour.

A few minutes later he turned onto East Broadway. Cars crammed both sides of the street. He drove past block after block of three and four story brick and wooden buildings joined together with little or no space between them. Corner stores, bakeries, pizza shops, funeral parlors, insurance agencies, and apartments all vied for sidewalk access. He smiled at the names on the signs. O'Connor. O'Reilly. Murphy. O'Shaughnessy. Businesses had most of the frontage, but an occasional apartment hallway had steps leading up off the street, two and three floors above the businesses.

698 East Broadway had a small apartment doorway wedged between the O'Hara Brother's funeral parlor and Sullivan's Insurance agency. Max squeezed into a parking spot, then stepped into the cold pre-dawn darkness and hustled across the street. He looked up at the building a moment before climbing the wooden stairs.

The mailbox and doorbell with O'Grady's name told him she lived on the third floor. Max stared at the name, wanting to ring the doorbell, then wondered what he would say.

"Hi Colleen. What am I doing here at this hour? See, I'm lonely as hell and I wanted some company. Someone to talk to. Aside from being the only person I really know in this town, I can't stop thinking about you."

He went back to his car, turned the heat on low, slouched back in his seat and gazed up at the third floor apartment wondering what she looked like sleeping.

The wind gusted, blowing a few scraps of trash up the empty street. Upstairs in that apartment slept a caring person who deserved to be loved. How many other women had been robbed of the chance to love and be loved, their lives literally cut short by a madman with a sickle?

The thought sickened him.

It was up to him to put an end to the madness. He had to stop whoever it was from turning warm living beings into cold lifeless husks.

He looked up at O'Grady's apartment again, wishing he could explain his obsession. His heart felt heavy. The weight and responsibility of the lives that might or might not continue because of his actions seemed to push him down further into the seat.

Sighing, Max closed his eyes and dozed.

CHAPTER TWENTY EIGHT

Nick poured another cup of coffee and rubbed his burning eyes. The sound of Mike's snores came to him from the living room. Mike could sleep through a nuclear attack. Nick wished *he* could. To be able to sleep without dreams. Without voices. Even if only for a couple of hours.

His mind raced. He had to stay awake 'til daylight. His eyelids felt heavy. Though he couldn't quite hear the whispers, if he closed his eyes, he sensed their presence hovering beyond the reach of his consciousness like vultures moving closer with his diminishing awareness.

He forced his eyes open, sat up straight and stared at the kitchen clock. Two-thirty. Four or five more hours. He thought that if he could stay awake he might be able to stop another murder from happening, but what was he going to do when daylight came? He took a sip of coffee. Its bitter taste made the bile rise in his throat. There didn't seem to be any choice. The answer was at the mission, but it was dangerous to go near there again. If the magician didn't get him, Sully would. Maybe he *should* tell the priest what was happening.

He stared into the black of his coffee and imagined himself sitting with Father Derlen in a corner of Saint Augustine's.

"Hey, Father, I'm hearing voices, seeing murders." Yeah right.

Putting his elbows on the table, he propped his head on his fists and shut his eyes a moment.

Esus.

The whisper caressed his mind with featherlike softness, comforting him. He gave in and drifted...

Images flashed in his mind. A bare leg shaking and twitching. Smooth calves. Sleek curves. A cinnamon patch of pubic hair. Small breasts jiggling. Arms flopping in a spastic dance, then a noose and a tortured expression distorting pretty features...

Esus. Louder.

His eyes flew open and his breath stabbed in his chest. "Son-of-a-bitch!"

Nick pushed himself away from the table and looked up at the clock. Three-twenty-two. Talk about a nightmare. He shook his head, grabbed a jacket from the back hall and went downstairs onto the street.

The sky looked crystal clear, each star a pinpoint of frost. No fucking spooks tonight. A chilled breeze blew, cutting through him. He shivered, glad for once to feel the wind stinging his face and ears. Shoving his hands in his pockets he started toward Field's Corner, then changed direction and headed toward Lower Mills.

That shit with the hanging was just a nightmare, he thought. He had only been out for a few minutes. No way anything could happen that fast. He expected comfort from the thought, but his unease overshadowed any solace they might have brought. When you cut away the bullshit, making sense didn't count anymore. Nothing that had gone down in the past few weeks made sense.

The cold, clear air sweeping through Boston's pre-dawn streets had a cleansing effect on his tortured mind. The voice stayed silent. Either it had accomplished its purpose or given up.

An inhuman screech pierced the silence. Nick stopped short, his hair bristling on the back of his neck. Trash cans rattled in an alley, then a rat darted across the sidewalk heading toward a sewer on the far side of the street, a cat pouncing after it. A blur, another high-pitched squeal and the cat trotted back across the street, the lifeless rodent hanging from its mouth.

The magician and those things had swooped on *him* that way, first in his dreams, then in real life. So far he escaped, but he felt jammed into a corner and the walls were closing in.

He shuddered at the memory of the rodent's last squeal, swallowed up in darkness. It was only a matter of time before the magician...

Fear flashed into anger. Why should he sit around waiting for that scumbag to make oatmeal out of his brain and hamburger out of all those girls? He thought of his father when the bigger kids had picked on him at school. Fourth grade.

The big kids blamed him for telling the teacher they were smoking, but Nick hadn't snitched. He had heard Helen Culhane telling the teacher, but he wasn't about to get her in trouble. He liked her.

"You, know, big man," his father said squatting down beside him. "I can go have a talk with your teachers, but it's not gonna do you any good in the long run."

"Why not?"

"'Cuz those kids'll catch up to you sooner or later when there's no one around."

"We can go to the police."

His father snorted. "The cops won't do shit. Besides, those punks'll be looking to get even with you for ratting them off."

Nick's chest tightened. "Then what do I do?" He wondered if his father heard his voice shaking.

Big Nick patted his son on the back. "You gotta take things into your own hands. Take the fight to the other guy. It's the only way."

"But how?"

His father lowered his voice. "Next time they fuck with you, go after the biggest one." He crouched low into a boxer's stance. "Take all that scared feeling and put it into your fists." He jabbed. "Hit him with everything you've got and don't stop until he stops moving, you stop moving, or someone breaks it up. Give him your best fight and they'll respect you. That's what it's all about on the streets, Nicky. Respect."

"What if he's bigger and he hurts me?"

"Then you need an equalizer. Two by four, rock, a pipe. Whatever it takes, Nicky. There's no such thing as a fair fight. It's him or you."

One more confrontation and that had been the end of it. Nick came out of it with a bloody nose, but the bigger kid lost a tooth.

It's him or you.

The old man was right. Take the fight to the other guy. He stopped. This prick was inside his head. He couldn't cold-cock him, but he needed to be stopped. This magician with his radio brain was different. Real dangerous. A knife or a club wouldn't be enough. Nick couldn't let the bastard get that close. He needed something to do damage at a distance. Something he could ditch -- like a Saturday Night Special.

Shit. He didn't think he had the balls to take someone's life. He thought of all the people who died, both the victims of the sacrifices and the missing bums that the cops didn't know about. Nick felt sure that they weren't alive.

It's him or me, he thought. I don't have any choice unless I want to die. But can I do it?

When the sky grew lighter, Nick turned and started back toward Field's Corner. A Saturday Night Special was the only way. Whack him and throw it off the Malibu bridge. Cops would never find it.

He walked down Dot Ave. running scenarios through his mind. He could steal a car and do a drive-by, that way he'd have a quick get-away and be able to ditch the car over in Southie. Maybe he could take a shot from a rooftop. He needed a rifle for that and he'd have a hard time ditching it. Maybe the best bet was to follow the magician and take a shot from an alley.

Darkness and shadow still shrouded Town Field when he cut across to his spot by the corner of the fence to watch the mission. He thought of sneaking over to the clubhouse and climbing to the roof, but he didn't want to get too close.

Darkness turned to gray. He saw a purple shimmer on the horizon. The unmarked sat up the street from Saint Augustine's. Two winos wrapped in blankets and newspapers slept in the doorway, waiting to be first in line for chow. A few cars drove by, white plumes trailing from their exhausts.

Nick huddled close to the fence. His feet, ears and legs had gone numb from the cold, but he didn't care. At least he had stayed awake and didn't give in. He remembered his brief nightmare.

Out of the corner of his eye he spotted a dark figure shuffling toward the mission, carrying a bag over his shoulder. Keeping next to the fence, Nick stayed low and moved toward the street until he recognized the man in the pea-coat moving as if in a trance.

A moment later the front door of Saint Augustine's opened. The man stepped over the two people sleeping in the doorway and disappeared inside.

CHAPTER TWENTY NINE

"Hey, what the hell you doing in there?"
The muffled voice sounded like it came through a padded wall.

"You all right?" A slight accent. Irish? What did he want? Why didn't he go away?

A rap on the window jolted Max awake. He grabbed for his gun. A heavy set, red-faced man holding a nightstick looked through the windshield, his broad face showing concern. Max froze, seeing the badge and black leather jacket.

"I'm okay." He held his hands up slowly, so as not to alarm the cop. "Fell asleep, that's all." He made a show of withdrawing his wallet, then flipped out his shield and rolled down the window. A cold blast of air hit him, sharpening his senses. His neck and legs felt stiff.

"What the hell you doing in there, Bucko?" The cop took his wallet. "Had me worried. Thought you might be a stiff. That's all I'd need, come on shift and find a stiff on my beat. Fucking paperwork'd take a week."

Max looked up at the leaden sky. Rose colored dawn shimmered over the upper half of the buildings on his side of the street. A bus roared by, filling the car with the smell of diesel. People spilled onto the sidewalks, waking up with the city.

"Been on a stakeout," Max said. "Must've dozed off."

The cop studied Max's shield a moment longer, then handed it back.

"You're the fed working the Headless Horsemen murders?"

"That's right."

"Good. Nail that son-of-a-bitch quick, will ya? My old lady's going bugfuck. She thinks he's another DeSalvo."

"We'll get him."

"Mind a bit of advice?"

Max put his wallet away. "Sure."

"This is the wrong neighborhood to fall asleep in. You might wake up without your pants." He chuckled, his breath coming out in tiny wisps. "But at least it ain't Roxbury. Fall asleep there and you'll wake up without your balls."

"Good advice," Max said. "Thanks."

"My pleasure." The cop tipped his hat and went off down the sidewalk.

Max checked his watch. Six-fifteen. He glanced up at O'Grady's apartment. The idea of paying her a visit crossed his mind. Bad idea. He put his foot on the brake pedal, grabbed the shift lever and stopped when he saw the front door to O'Grady's apartment open. He slid down in his seat when he saw red hair.

Shit.

She came down the stairs dressed in powder blue sweats. Max slouched lower in his seat and waited while she did a few stretches, before raising his head in time to see a flash of powder blue and red disappear around the corner.

He made a U-turn and drove back to his hotel where he showered, changed, and ordered coffee. After scanning his notes, he drove over to District Eleven to see if anything new had come in from Washington.

Hustling down the corridor to his office, he turned the corner and caught a whiff of perfume. Two more steps and he saw O'Grady behind his desk smiling, her searching green eyes lingering on his for a moment that felt a little too long. He looked away, thinking that she saw him in front of her apartment. He groped for something to say and came up empty.

"I tried to catch you at your hotel," she said. "Call came in from the morgue. Beat cop over in District Three found a body wrapped in a trash bag stuffed in a shopping cart. River street near Mattapan station. They think it might be one of ours."

He took a deep breath, let it out slowly and turned to face her. In the stark fluorescent of the dingy office, the natural color in her cheeks made her look fresh and vibrant. "Why do they think it's one of ours?"

"No head."

"You call Geist?"

"He's already at the morgue."

"Ready to check it out?"

She pushed back from the desk. "Been waiting on you."

The phone rang. Max snatched it up. "Broderick."

"Hey, Broderick, Flynn here."

Max put his hand over the mouthpiece. "It's our favorite detective. Why don't you sign out an unmarked? I'll meet you out front in five."

"You got it." She went out, leaving behind the lingering scent of her perfume.

"What's up, Flynn?"

"I heard about the stiff at the morgue. Mind if I take a look see? Who knows, maybe I'll come up with something?"

"You're on surveillance."

"C'mon Broderick, don't bust my balls. The stakeout's covered. I'm climbing the fucking wall here while this asshole's having a field day. I just want to take a look at the stiff. See if anything clicks. Give me something to think about on those long days and nights. Have a heart, will ya?"

Maybe Flynn had a point. O'Grady said he had been one of the best. It might keep him busy. Besides, Max knew he'd go anyway. "Tell you what, Flynn. I'll make a deal."

"Talk to me."

"You go over later this afternoon. I'll see you get a copy of the forensics report. You can get copies of the rest of the stuff on your own. You get any ideas, I want to see them in writing. Understand?"

"In writing. Yeah."

"No bullshit. Unless you're actually seeing a crime being committed, I don't want to hear one word out of you. Don't call me. Don't bother me. Send me your thoughts on paper."

"You got it."

"I mean it, Flynn. You cross me on this and I won't cut you any slack next time."

Flynn thanked him again and hung up.

"What did Flynn want?" O'Grady said when Max climbed into the car.

"To see the body."

She pulled onto Gibson street and headed toward the morgue. "What did you tell him?"

"I told him he could see it later and I'd give him a copy of Geist's report."

"He would've gone anyway."

Max smiled. "I knew that. This way, he has his fingers in the pie. Who knows, maybe he'll come up with something. Besides, idle minds are the devil's playground."

"When it comes to Flynn, it's more like Disneyland."

"Lots of open space, huh?"

She laughed. "Something like that."

They found Geist under glaring fluorescents in the coroner's examining room bent over a headless female torso on a steel table. The corpse's skin shone white and pasty under the lights, as if it were made of something other than human tissue. A pale, pink-lined slit ran between the breasts down to the pubic area. Max saw the blue and white of internal organs lying below the surface of the wound. A brown tag was tied to a toe. The smells of formaldehyde, rubber, and alcohol hung heavy in the air.

Geist, wearing latex gloves, a surgical mask and a black rubber apron, looked up from his work and nodded toward a tray of tools, instruments, evidence bags, and a camera. Max stepped toward it, instantly recognizing the sprigs of mistletoe Geist had collected. He grabbed two pairs of gloves from a box, handed one set to O'Grady and donned the other.

"Different M.O., but she's definitely one of ours," Geist's muffled voice said from behind his mask. "Give me a few more minutes. Couple more things I want to check."

Max eyed the camera sitting on the edge of the cart. "Mind if we look?"

"By the time you finish, I should be done."

Max picked up the camera and scanned the pictures with O'Grady. Shots of a shopping cart stuffed with a black plastic bag. A headless corpse laid out on a steel table taken at different angles. Closeups of the hands, neck and torso. The word "Esus" was scrawled in blood across the back and on the inside of a thigh. The wrists and part of the neck had welts.

O'Grady pointed at the display. "Ligature marks. She must've been tied."

"Hung." Geist lifted one of the corpse's arms. It moved as if it were made of a single piece of wood. Leaning close to the body, he scrutinized the hip area, then moved slowly up the torso toward the armpit.

"She was most likely dead before she was decapitated," O'Grady said.

"That's right." Geist pulled out a magnifying glass and examined the armpit. "Well, well, looks like we might have something. Colleen, grab the camera."

Max stepped closer. "What is it?"

"Looks like a hitchhiker who's going to tell us a few things."

Colleen frowned. "Hitchhiker?"

"Yeah." He held the arm further away from the body and pointed to a small dark spot with a pointed instrument. "Can you snap some closeups?"

Colleen gave Max a quick sideways glance and her now familiar stoic look hardened. "Sure, Rick." She leaned close and snapped while Geist held the arm out. "Yuck, that's disgusting. It's a bug and it's still moving."

"That's not just any old bug," Geist said. "Get a few more shots, will you?"

O'Grady obliged.

"That should be enough," Geist said. "Thanks. Hey, Max, can I get you to hold this for a minute?" He shook the arm.

Max took the proffered hand, acutely aware of the cold, stiffened fingers. He flashed on an image of his mother lying in her coffin. "What kind of bug is it?"

Geist leaned forward with a pair of tweezers, lit a match and blew it out, then touched the glowing end to the bug while grasping it with tweezers. A moment later he stood examining what looked like a tiny bean with moving black hairs. Geist picked up his magnifying glass and studied it. "Wood tick." He grabbed a jar from the cart and dropped the squirming tick into it. "This little dude's going to tell us where and when."

Colleen looked puzzled.

"When someone dies," Max said, "hundreds of bugs flock to the corpse. They're attracted by what scientists think might be a universal death scent. Flies, beetles and who knows what else migrate to the corpse to either eat the flesh or lay eggs."

Geist set the jar on the cart. "If the weather were warmer we'd have had more than a tick, which would tell us even more, but I'll settle for our buddy here."

Colleen bent over the jar and studied the tick. "How do you determine where and when?"

Geist removed his gloves, mask, and apron. "Death triggers predictable patterns of insect activity that can be traced backward through time." He rolled up his sleeves and washed his hands. Max and Colleen removed their gloves.

"In warm weather in the open air, blowflies and flesh flies lay thousands of eggs in a body's mouth, nose, and ears within minutes of death. The eggs hatch into maggots that feed on tissue. When they finish, they move away from the body and cocoon in the nearby soil, then a second wave of beetles and other critters come to chow down on the drying skin."

He pulled paper towels from the dispenser and dried his hands while Colleen scrubbed hers.

"After that come spiders, mites, and millipedes." He threw the paper towels into a waste basket. "All their life cycles are fixed and precise. They can give an accurate method of estimating time of death." He picked up the jar. "By studying the amount of blood our little vampire's gorged himself on, we can get a better fix on the time of death."

Geist opened the door, pushed his instrument cart out into the hall and motioned for Max and O'Grady to follow. "I have to do further analysis on my samples, but so far we have a Jane Doe. No clothes, no I.D.. Looks like the same M.O., sloppy prints, mistletoe, missing head and all, but judging from the evidence, it's safe to assume our boy's on the move and it looks like he might have accomplices."

They stopped beside a small glass-walled office where a short, dark-haired man in a white lab smock sat with his feet on a desk. "Hey, Frank," Geist said. "I'm done with the lady down in twelve. Can you put her back on ice?"

He turned back to Max and O'Grady. "Let's borrow an office. I'll fill you in." They followed him down a series of institutional green corridors until they came to a tiny off-white office at the end of a shorter hall. Though weaker, the smell of formaldehyde still lingered. Geist waved them in, pushed the cart against a gray enamel desk and closed the door.

"Here's what we have. I found coarse fibers embedded in the neck and wrists. Too coarse for hair or clothing. I'm sure it's hemp from rope. Even though the head was removed, there are signs of trauma around the neck. The depth of the fiber impressions convince me she was hung."

O'Grady looked from Geist to Max. "Sacrifice to another druid god?"

Max nodded. "I'll bet that's what the Esus is all about. I'll look it up when I get back to my office."

"I found wood fibers and dirt," Geist said pointing toward his evidence bags. "The soil's loamy. Not something you'd find in the inner city. She was definitely moved from a wooded area."

"And I'll bet the wood fibers are oak," O'Grady added.

Geist nodded. "That's what I think. I managed to lift a few prints off the shopping cart handle, but I bet we come up empty on a comparison."

CHAPTER THIRTY

Nick spent all day watching a steady stream of homeless people shuffle in and out of Saint Augustine's, but the man in the peacoat never re-emerged and the magician never made an appearance. By late afternoon he had the dawning realization that his brief flash of a nightmare might have been more than he wanted to accept.

When afternoon passed into evening and lights came on, Saint Augustine's began closing for the night. Nick's experience of the previous day kept him from following his impulse to sneak in and take a quick look around. For all he knew, the magician lay in wait for him at the end of some dark alley; a cat waiting to end the rat's miserable existence, unless this Dot Rat could do something, like get a piece and blow the cat away.

Cold and exhausted from his long vigil, Nick went home. The first warmth he felt all day greeted him as he climbed the back stairs, following the smell of his mother's meatloaf. He hadn't eaten all day.

Shaking off the cold, he hung his jacket in the hall and went in the back door. Mike sat at the kitchen table, stocking feet stretched out, face behind the newspaper, Budweiser in hand. Nick's mother leaned over the stove stirring something in a pot.

"Hi, honey, you're just in time for supper. Hungry?"

"Starving."

"Why don't you set the table?"

"Yeah," Mike added without looking up from his paper. "It's the least you can do to earn your keep around here."

Don't see you getting up off your fat ass to help, Nick thought, but didn't voice it. His mother looked like she was in a good mood and he didn't want to spoil it. Ignoring Mike's jab, he set the table, working around Mike's beer and elbows. As soon as he finished, his mother served.

"Come on." She slid a plate in front of Mike. "No reading at the table." Mike grunted and lay the paper aside.

Nick gorged himself and listened to his mother while tuning out Mike's ramblings about the Celtics and the Bruins. He listened and nodded at the appropriate times, but his thoughts were preoccupied with finding a gun.

Taking a bite of broccoli, he chewed and started to swallow when he glimpsed the word "Headless" on the front page. He inhaled sharp and the broccoli went down the wrong passage. Panic shot through him and the newspaper rustled.

"What the hell's wrong with you?" Mike said.

His mother jumped out of her chair and pounded him on the back. Two more wheezy coughs erupted followed by the bitter taste of bile, then the broccoli jarred loose.

"Jesus." He cleared his throat and took a drink of water.

His mother brushed the hair out of his face. "You all right, honey?"

He took a deep breath and another sip of water. "Yeah, Ma, I'm okay. Went down the wrong pipe. Thanks."

She hovered a moment longer, then sat down again. Mike shook his head and went back to his paper. Nick stared at the headline.

HEADLESS HORSEMAN CLAIMS FOURTH VICTIM

His stomach went sour. The thought of finishing dinner made the bile rise again in the back of his throat. He wiped the tears from his eyes with the palm of his hand. "Hey, Mike, can I see the front page?"

Mike tossed the paper at him. Nick stuck it under his arm and went to his room, listening to their voices drifting to him from the kitchen. "I'm telling ya, babe, the kid's on bennies."

"You don't know what you're talking about."

"Christ, Louise, I'm a goddamn trucker. I've seen lots of guys popping 'em to make good time on cross-country runs. Did you get a good look at him? Bags under his eyes, and you have to admit, he's been acting pretty strange lately."

Nick closed the door to his room, making the voices indistinguishable. He heard it all before. Kicking off his shoes, he dropped onto his bed, opened the paper and read.

> Early this morning, the Boston Police discovered the headless body of an unidentified woman in a trash bag stuffed into a shopping cart on River Street in Dorchester. The murder is believed to be the work of a killer sources have dubbed the "Headless Horseman".
>
> Enraged citizen's groups have stepped up the pressure and petitioned the mayor's office for increased police action. Their efforts have resulted in a special task force assigned to investigate the grisly murders of four Boston women in the past few weeks.

Nick folded the paper and dropped it on the floor beside his bed. They were freaking out because four people were murdered. What about the homeless guys? Why didn't anyone give a shit about them? Four of them missing and no one noticed. He was willing to bet that the shopping cart on River Street belonged to the guy in the pea-coat. No doubt he was history too. Twice as many people were getting snuffed than the cops knew about and those assholes were chasing their tails.

He listened and realized the argument had subsided. Good. Now that he ate, the intensity of the last two days weighed on him. His eyelids fluttered. How long had it been since he slept? Thirty-six hours? He rolled over and closed his eyes. The cops hadn't done anything. Now it was up to him. He had to get a piece. Sleep crept up, swallowing him.

His eyes popped open at ten the next morning with no recollection of any dreams. His first thought was of how to get a gun. He didn't know how he would get one, but he thought he knew someone who did.

Late that afternoon, he spotted a short, wiry, older man wearing a black leather jacket and a fedora stopping outside Layden's Tavern on Dot. Ave.. He looked up and down the street twice before flicking his cigarette onto the sidewalk. One more scan of Dot. Ave. and he stepped into the bar. Nick waited a minute, then crossed the street and followed him in.

The sour-smelling odor of old beer met him at the door. The bartender had his back to the bar, ringing up a sale on the cash register. Two men at the far end of the bar looked up, then went back to their discussion. Three more sat at a table. The older man Nick spotted stood talking on a cell phone next to the men's room. Nick took a seat at the end of the bar closest to the door.

The bartender, a dark-haired, burly man with hairy arms turned from the register. "What'll it be?"

"Club soda," Nick said.

The bartender studied him a moment, eyes narrowing. Nick thought he was going to get carded, then the man shrugged, poured a club soda and set it down on a napkin in front of Nick. "Seventy-five cents."

Nick fumbled a dollar from his pocket and handed it to the bartender. "Keep the change."

Sipping his drink, Nick spun around on the barstool to watch the man on the phone. He couldn't hear his words, but he knew the conversation. Nick had known Hot Ticket for as long as he could remember. He smiled at the memory of his father telling him that Hot Ticket was a numbers runner when *he* had been a kid. If anyone in the neighborhood had connections, Hot Ticket did.

The older man finished reading his numbers, then touched a lighter to the paper and held it out. Nick admired the way he let it burn almost to his fingertips before dropping the tiny flaming corner. By the time it hit the floor, the flame consumed it completely, leaving nothing but ash. A grind of his shoe left no trace of his transaction.

Hot Ticket pocketed his phone and his eyes took in the bar, flashing recognition when he saw Nick. He smiled and nodded, then came over holding out his hand. "Nicky Powers, how are ya?"

Hot Ticket looked impeccable. A man of angles, he had sharp creases in his pants and shiny shoes with pointed toes. His weathered face had an aquiline nose, jutting chin, and narrow eyes. He wore his fedora slanted down over his forehead.

Nick shook his hand. "Doing okay. How 'bout you?"

"No complaints. How's your mom? She still with that big dummy?"

Nick laughed. "Unfortunately." He lowered his voice. "Listen. I need a favor."

"Your old man and I go back a long way. You need some money?" He reached into his pocket, pulled out a wad of bills and peeled back a few twenties.

Nick held up his hand. "No, not that. I need to find out where I can get a piece."

The old man frowned, put the money back, and slid onto the stool next to Nick's. "A piece?" He spoke lower. "You in some kind of trouble? If you are, I have friends. You know, a few words to the right people, a coupla broken legs."

"No trouble."

His face showed concern. "Then what do you want a piece for, Nick? You ain't going to start pulling that armed robbery shit, are you? You got more class than that."

Nick shook his head. "Nothing like that. It's personal, that's all. Some business I have to take care of."

Hot Ticket looked around, then put his arm around Nick and pulled him closer. "You're serious about this, aren't you?"

Nick pulled out a small roll of bills. "Serious as a heart attack."

"Wait here a minute." Hot Ticket stood, and made another survey of the bar before going back to the spot by the men's room. After a brief conversation on his cell he came back.

"Okay." He glanced at his watch. "Three hours. Parking lot on Park Street across from Town Field. Guy will be driving a beat-up brown Eldorado. Name's Willie McKnight. Tall slinky black dude, six-two, six-three. Still has one of those Afros." He made a motion with his hand. "You tell him Hot Ticket sent you, said to do you right."

"Thanks."

"No problem. I don't want to hear nothing bad about you and the heater. I shouldn't be doing this, but your old man was family to me and you ain't no kid any more. I figure you must know what you're doing."

"You got it."

Hot Ticket started toward the door, then stopped. "Anybody asks, you didn't talk to me. You don't even know me."

"You don't have to tell me that."

Hot Ticket smiled and did one last scan of the bar. "Keep your nose clean, Nicky." He stepped out onto the street. Nick waited a few minutes before leaving.

Two hours and forty-five minutes later a beat-up, brown Eldorado with a white vinyl top rolled into the Supreme lot and pulled into the last row near Park Street. A tall, lanky black man emerged, wearing a black beret tilted to one side, a brown leather jacket and camouflage fatigue pants. Nick walked across the parking lot, slowing as he approached the car. The black man leaned against the back fender studying him.

"You a friend of Hot Ticket's?" Nick said.

The man crossed his arms. "Who wants to know?"

"Nick Powers. Hot Ticket said to tell you to do me right."

"Well, my man, you come to the right place." He pulled his right hand from his pocket and slapped Nick five. "Willie McKnight's my name and packing heat's my game. Step into my office and we can talk a little biz." He pulled open the passenger door and went around to the driver's side. Nick climbed in, feeling uneasy. McKnight slid in beside him and gave him a lopsided grin, then started the car.

"Where we going?"

"Doing biz where the man can see you is bad biz."

Nick pictured McKnight pulling into a dark alley somewhere in Roxbury, jabbing a knife or a gun into his ribs and taking his money, but Hot Ticket had set things up and his connections were solid. He settled back into the seat.

McKnight turned up the volume on the car's CD, filling the interior with Bob Marley, then he pulled off his hat and produced a joint from the recesses of his Afro. "Good shit, man. You want a taste?"

Nick's heart hammered. Maybe a couple of hits would relax him. Maybe that's what McKnight wanted. "Yeah, sure." He hoped he sounded relaxed.

McKnight flashed him another lopsided grin, then pushed in the car's cigarette lighter and touched it to the end of the reefer. They drove down to Morrissey Boulevard, passing the joint back and forth, then past the Dorchester gas tanks and over the Malibu Beach drawbridge toward South Boston. With each inhale, Nick felt himself relaxing. Nothing to worry about. Hot Ticket's connections were good.

McKnight made a U-turn near Boston College and the Kennedy Library, then doubled back toward Dorchester on Morrissey Boulevard, all the while checking the rear view mirror. He pulled into a deserted parking lot near Malibu beach. Across the bay, Nick saw a few boats moored near the Dorchester Yacht club and behind it, the traffic on the Southeast Expressway.

McKnight pinched the coal off the end of the joint and popped the remains into his mouth. "Let's get down to biz." He motioned backward with his head and hopped out of the car. Nick followed. A gentle breeze blew across the water making tiny whitecaps. He turned his collar up. McKnight did a quick check of the parking lot, reminding Nick of the way Hot Ticket checked out places, then he opened the trunk. A huge suitcase lay on the bottom of it.

"How much you wanna spend?"

"Sixty bucks?"

McKnight smiled. "Got just the thing for you, brother." He opened up the suitcase. Guns of different shapes and sizes lay on top of a ribbed piece of gray foam. McKnight reached into his pockets and pulled out a pair of black leather gloves. Slipping them on, he reached in and picked out a smaller gun. "Don't know what you want it for. Don't want to know what you want it for, but it's clean." He flipped open the cylinder and spun it. "Smith and Wesson .38 Military and Police, model 12. Six shot, two inch barrel. Eighteen ounces." He handed it to Nick and tapped his finger on its side. "Serial numbers been filed."

Nick took the gun and turned it over in his hand, amazed at its weight and coldness. For its size, eighteen ounces felt unusually heavy. He looked at the barrel the way he saw guys do in the movies, then spun the cylinder like McKnight had. "Fifty bucks?"

"Yeah, and don't forget, the man catch you with that little gem, it's one year in the slammer minimum."

"Can you throw in some ammo?"

McNight's hand dove into his pocket and came out with a baggie with six bullets in it.

Nick took out three twenties. All the money he had. "I'll take it." He handed McKnight the cash, snapped the cylinder shut on the .38 and stuffed the pistol into his waistband. Its metal felt cool pressing against his stomach and the weight of it jammed into his belt felt unnatural.

"One more thing," McKnight said, handing him the bullets. "Anybody asks…"

"I didn't talk to you. I don't even know you."

McKnight's grin spread across his face. "Git down with your bad self, Homes. Hot Ticket said you were smart."

In his mind Nick had passed some barrier. The gun in his waistband put him into the big time. He didn't like the feeling.

CHAPTER THIRTY ONE

O'Grady stayed behind at the morgue, helping Geist correlate evidence, while Max took a cab back to District Eleven to sort through what they already had. Geist seemed sure there was more than one perp, and that they were on the move, which meant that his cut-off-hand theory was probably a dead end. If there was a cult they were well organized. A Druid cult here in Boston would mean that it wasn't some random psycho.

Instead it would be someone sophisticated and methodical. This last girl had been hung, then moved. What the hell was going on? Then there was the kid in the leather jacket. How did he fit in? What did he know?

As they drove past an alleyway, Max spotted a shopping cart and a spindly man in a long, ragged overcoat emerging from a dumpster clutching a bag of cans to his chest. The cart and the plastic bag stayed in Max's mind. The body found that morning had been in a plastic bag in a shopping cart. Were transients involved? The idea of a homeless Druid cult didn't make sense unless the perps were posing as transients. Maybe the kid knew.

The cabbie pulled up in front of the District Eleven Station. Max paid his fare and climbed out. After a little research, his first priority would be to track down the kid.

He hurried to his office and found his books stacked on top of his desk. Pulling out one on medieval religions, he looked up Esus in the index and found the name under Druid gods. He quickly flipped back through the book until he found the page with Esus on it.

> Divination with the bodies of human victims was recorded by the Roman Tacitus who said: "the Druids consult the gods in the palpitating entrails of men..." Strabo described the striking of the victim with a sword and the predicting of the future from his convulsive movements.

Max turned the page, studying rows of grotesque lithographs, each portraying a different sacrifice, then he read the text at the bottom.

> Human victims were offered to different gods, using different methods. Sacrifice could be slaughter by sword, spear, hanging, impaling, dismembering, drowning, or some combination. Some gods were propitiated by one particular mode of sacrifice -- Teutates by suffocation, Taranis by burning and the god Esus, thought by some to be a tree-god was appeased by hanging on a tree.

Max marked the page and closed the book. Esus by hanging. Had to be from an oak tree. That's why they moved the body. He pulled a map of Boston from one of his desk drawers and spread it on top of the book. He found River Street in Dorchester and noted open areas of the Blue Hills out near Milton and Canton. If they found her on River Street, they probably hung her from an oak tree somewhere in the Blue Hills.

He opened the book again. Okay, we've had Cromm Cruaich, sacrifice of the first born, cut off breasts to the goddess Andrasta, Teutates by suffocation, and now Esus by hanging. That left Taranis.
The phone rang. He picked it up, resenting the interruption. "Broderick."

"Hey, Broderick. Flynn here."

"This isn't what I call writing, Flynn. This better be good."

"I went and checked out the stiff, then I got copies of the reports of the three other stiffs and I ran into Coll -- I mean O'Grady. We compared notes and she told me what you've come up with. I think you're getting close…"

Max's impatience grew. "You didn't call to blow sunshine up my ass. What's on your mind?"

"I was looking through this stuff after talking to O'Grady and it hit me."

"Spit it out, Flynn, I have work to do."

"I think it's the priest."

"What?"

"The priest. What's his name?" Max heard shuffling papers. "Derlen."

Max flashed on his first meeting with Flynn, remembering the way he barged in, claiming with absolute certainty that the murder was done by Satanists. Now he thought a priest committed the murders. "What do you have to back this up?"

"Just a gut feeling, that's all."

"A gut feeling. That's great. You think I can waltz on in and get a warrant on your gut feeling? The guy's clean. He has more connections than the internet, Flynn. You called to tell me *this*?"

"What makes you so sure it isn't?"

"I've had the mission staked out. Father Derlen never left it for three of the murders and has a rock-solid alibi for the fourth."

"Oh."

Max rubbed his temples, feeling a headache start to brew. "Damn it, Flynn, don't waste my time with this silly shit. You get solid evidence on something, give it to me in writing. You don't stick to that and I'm yanking those files and making god-damn sure you stay out there on stakeout. Alone."

"Sorry, I just thought…"

"I know what you thought." Max slammed the phone down. Bullheaded son-of-a-bitch. He and O'Grady must have been a real package. He smelled her perfume, looked up and saw her coming through the doorway. After draping her coat over the back of a chair, she dropped into one across from him.

Their eyes locked for a moment, then Max picked up the map again. "I've found some pretty scary shit here that fits our killers." He rubbed the back of his neck. "Can you get in touch with the Metropolitan District Commission, and check to see if any of their officers saw anything out of the ordinary in the Blue Hill area last night."

"Sure. What did you find?"

Max slid the book across the desk and pointed out the passages he'd been studying. He watched her face deepen in concentration as she turned the page, then she looked up at him wide-eyed.

"It's the real thing, isn't it?" she said softly.

"Hard to believe."

"If I didn't see it right here in front of me…" Her voice trailed off. Her face looked pale.

"Unless we come up with something quick, our next one's going to be roasted."

CHAPTER THIRTY TWO

Nick opened his eyes to the clock on his nightstand. Eight-fifteen. A thin line of daylight slipped into his bedroom from beneath the shade. He sat up, rubbed his eyes and listened. No sound. His mother and Mike had already left for work.

He slid his hand under the mattress until his fingers touched cold metal. Pulling out the gun, he hefted it, still amazed at how heavy it felt. Eighteen ounces was supposed to be light. If this was light, a full on forty-four magnum had to feel like a fucking cannon. He popped open the cylinder, emptied the six rounds into his palm and studied the copper topped bullets McKnight had given him.

"Jacketed hollow points," McKnight said. "Go in smaller than a dime, mushroom and rip up a man's insides. Hard to trace."

Nick put the bullets aside and stared at the gun. How was he going to use it? He had shot twenty-twos in Boy Scout camp, but a twenty-two was a BB gun compared to a thirty-eight. He never shot a handgun and didn't know what to expect.

He only had six bullets and didn't relish the thought of doing a year for possession of an unregistered handgun, especially one with the serial numbers filed away. He turned it over in his hand and studied the grooves on the cylinder. Who knew where it had been? What kind of crimes had it been used in? Taking the pistol by its grip, he pointed it at the wall and sighted down the barrel, imagining the magician's head above the front sight the way they showed him at summer camp. Sliding his thumb up over the hammer, he eased it back until it clicked, then wrapped his index finger over the trigger and steadied the pistol with both hands. Taking a deep breath, he let half out and squeezed.

Die, you mind-fucking piece of shit.

The snap of the hammer filled the room.

With a bullet coming out the gun would kick and he would miss at long range. He had to hit the son-of-a-bitch fast and close, getting off as many shots as he could before making a run for it and ditching the gun where it wouldn't be found -- like in the mucky water under the drawbridge at Malibu beach.

He reloaded and slid it back under his mattress, then showered and dressed. Before going out, he retrieved it and jammed it into the back of his pants. The weight of it resting in the small of his back felt more comfortable than in the front. He put on his leather jacket, then stood in front of his mother's full length mirror and turned from side to side, happy to see that the bulge of the weapon didn't show through. Facing the mirror again, he pulled the gun from behind him, widened his stance and pointed the gun with both hands at his reflection. "You're dead, freak."

The butt of the pistol slid between his palms and his arms shook. Stuffing the gun behind his back again, he wiped his hands on his pants, did one more check to see if it bulged, then went out to the kitchen. Instead of food, he settled for a quick cup of coffee, then headed for Town Field.

Out on the street cold washed out sunlight struggled to shine through a thin layer of clouds blanketing the sky. A light breeze blew carrying with it the promise of winter. Nick turned up his collar and walked toward Field's Corner running different scenarios through his mind. Maybe he could steal a car and stash it for a quick get-away? If anybody saw him and took down the license number the trace would end up nowhere. In one sense it added to his chances of getting busted, in another it helped cover his tracks.

He pictured himself getting busted by Sully with a stolen car and an illegal gun. Shit. Sully would shoot him in a heartbeat. Maybe it wasn't worth it. His nightmares of the last few weeks flashed through his mind, followed by the faces of the murdered girls. He shuddered at the memory of the voice crashing through his head and thought about Obie and the rest of the homeless who disappeared.

Yeah, it was worth it.

When Nick reached Town Field, he kept to the far side, away from Dot Ave.. Other than three winos sharing a bottle near the bleachers, the field looked deserted. A few bums wearing hooded sweatshirts and ragged jackets lingered outside Saint Augustine's. Nick saw activity behind the front windows, but the reflections off the glass made it impossible to see clearly. He wondered if the magician would come. His pattern had been to stay out of sight for a few days after each murder.

Forty-five minutes after Nick's arrival, the magician turned the corner of Gibson Street, crossed Dorchester Ave. and took his usual spot next to the Town Field clubhouse. On seeing him, Nick's awareness of the gun pressing into his back became acute, as if urging him toward the inevitable act it had been bought for. He vacillated, then thought of the voice. His heart thudded in his chest. He took a deep breath and forced it out.

Maybe he should do it now and get it over with? Looking up and down the street, he realized that he took on the habits of Hot Ticket and McKnight. In spite of the tension, he smiled. Shady business brought shady habits.

When he was sure no one saw him, he slid his hand behind his back and gripped the pistol. Covering it with his hand, he pulled it from his waist and slipped it into his jacket pocket.

Circling the block, he walked fast along Dot. Ave., head down, gun in his pocket, barrel forward, finger on the trigger. Halfway up the block he saw the magician facing partly away.

Nick's resolve grew with each step. Walk up fast and do him point blank. Three quick shots in the chest and get the fuck out of there. If he made it to Field's Corner Station he could catch a train to Savin Hill, make a beeline for the beach, and throw the gun into the bay.

Quarter of a block.

No turning back. He tightened his hand, feeling the grip of the pistol slick against his palm. His breath came short and fast.

Closer.

The sweaty crook of his finger slid over the trigger, then stopped and started to squeeze. He did one last check of the street and faltered when he spotted the blue-and-white of a Boston Police cruiser pulling into Nanina's parking lot.

Miraculously, the magician hadn't seen him. Without stopping, Nick veered to the right and darted across the street. When he stepped up on the opposite curb, a young cop climbed out of the cruiser. Nick turned and went up the street the way he came. He felt the cop's eyes on him. A moment later, fear became reality.

"Hey, you!"

Shit. His shoulders stiffened. Don't panic. Don't run. Maybe he was talking to someone else.

"Hey, you in the leather. I'm talking to you!"

Nick wanted to run, but knew he wouldn't make it. He had to be cool. No way the cop knew he was packing. If he didn't piss the prick off he wouldn't get patted down. Play stupid. He stopped and looked over his shoulder. The cop stood in the middle of the sidewalk pointing at him.

"Come here a minute."

Keeping his hand on the gun, Nick approached the cop who had his arms crossed. He stood tall and lanky in a new uniform with sharp creases, shiny badge, shoes and mirrored sunglasses. A rookie prick. Nick hated it when they wore the mirrors, especially the rookies. Not being able to see their eyes seemed unfair. You couldn't read their expression. "Something wrong?"

"Yeah, you fucked up."

"Huh?"

"Cutting across the street in the middle of traffic like that. That's what crosswalks are made for."

Nick maneuvered himself so the cop stood between him and the magician. His legs shook. "Sorry, I was just..."

"Don't give me that sorry shit. I ought to write you up for jaywalking."

What a punk, Nick thought, struggling to keep his anger contained. If he wasn't wearing that uniform, I'd slap him. "Sorry, officer, I didn't mean..."

"You on drugs or something? You're acting awfully funny."

"It's my mother," Nick said making his voice low.

"Your mother?" The cop frowned.

"She died. This morning."

His mouth dropped. Nick would have given anything to see the expression behind the shades.

"I've been taking care of her, but she couldn't hang on. I have to go to Carney Hospital. I've been walking around for hours trying to get up the nerve." He looked up, imagining what was going on behind the mirrors.

"I -- I'm sorry. I didn't realize..." The cop flushed. "You'd better get going."

"Yeah, you're right. Can't put it off any longer." *Asshole.* Nick hurried off the way he came.

Once out of sight of the cop, he crossed the street, turned up Melville Ave. and circled back to the far side of Town Field where he took deep breaths to stop shaking. Eventually he relaxed and spent the rest of the day watching the magician and Saint Augustine's. The usual collection of bums passed through the mission doors and littered the sidewalk. The magician went through his routines, but his patrons had dwindled.

At dusk, the magician crossed Dot Ave. and went down Gibson Street. Enough of this screwing around, Nick thought. He had watched, planned, and thought about it long enough. The longer he waited the harder it would be. Tomorrow he would go early and find an alley off Gibson to wait in. When the magician came walking by, he'd jump out and do him, then leave a note on his body, telling the cops the killings were over.

CHAPTER THIRTY THREE

"The M.D.C. says they haven't seen anything out of the ordinary, but they'll put the word out to their patrols and keep a closer watch on things, particularly around Houghton's Pond and Unquity Road." O'Grady sat straight, purse on her lap, notebook in hand. All business. She wore a conservative light blue skirt, her hair pulled back, her frilly blouse open at the neck.

Max picked up a file. "We have quite a bit but it hasn't led us anywhere. All we know is that we're dealing with more than one perp and whoever they are, they're somehow tied to the mission. From what we've gathered there's a possibly we're dealing with transients."

Colleen nodded, her eyes meeting his. "I was thinking the same thing. Untraceable fingerprints and DNA. The fact that none of them match makes me think it could be a group posing as transients."

"Especially when you consider how organized they are," Max added, pulling out his book on medieval religions. He opened it to the page he marked and slid it across the desk. "You can tell from the paragraphs I've marked that each of the sacrifices have been to different Druid gods."

She tapped the page. "The only one we haven't come across is Taranis."

"Who is appeased by burning."

"Unless we can stop it."

"If our friends are going to have a barbecue, it'll be outside and if it is a burning it'll probably be in the Blue Hills. They'll be looking for an oak grove."

Max ran his fingers through his hair. "Our investigation's stalling. The pressure's been turned up and people are still dying. Something has to break."

"You getting anything out of your surveillance?"

He sighed. "That's another thing. Don't know how much longer I can keep it." He rose and checked the hallway outside his office, then closed the door and sat back in his chair. "If I change my cover, there's a greater risk of Sully making me."

O'Grady's eyes narrowed. "You think he's a suspect?"

"I don't know if I'd go that far. I don't think he's smart enough to organize something like this." He rubbed his chin. "What I really need is to find the kid."

"Maybe I can get out on the streets and ask around."

"Maybe we better do it as a team. You can smooth the way and we can do a Mutt and Jeff."

"Where do you want to start?"

"I think it's time to talk to the priest. We'll go in officially after the mission closes so we won't arouse suspicion. He could be in danger."

"He might be able to help us." Colleen pulled out her cell phone. "I'll give him a call and make an appointment."

"Don't mention Sully. We don't want to alarm him."

O'Grady set up a meeting for seven that night. After agreeing to meet at six-thirty, Max sent her to the morgue to pick up the latest reports from Geist on the Jane Doe found on River Street.

She came back at six-thirty, precisely. Her features looked softer and her skirt showed more of her legs, yet she still appeared composed and professional. Max recognized the familiar scent of Dare. He grabbed his coat from the rack. "Geist give you anything new?"

She slung her purse over the back of a chair and fished out her notebook. "Between his tick, his calculator, and the body temperature, he figures the girl was killed less than three hours before they found her."

After O'Grady gave him a rundown of the forensic details, Max deliberated a moment. "Okay, here's what I figure," he said, rubbing the stubble on his chin. "A guy pushes a shopping cart, top speed two miles an hour, so if the girl was dead less than three hours, we should be able to get a map and draw a circle with a six mile radius. Knowing she was most likely killed in the Blue Hills should narrow down geographics considerably."

"I'll get my hands on a map and pinpoint an area after we talk to the priest."

They drove to Saint Augustine's in silence, each lost in their own thoughts. Another murder was in the offing which would take place outdoors. Neither wanted to see another mutilated body.

O'Grady pulled the car to the curb in front of the mission. Under the cover of night its two darkened front windows reflecting the streetlights gave it the glassy-eyed gaze of some sorrowful, Kafkaesque character.

Four transients who could have been mistaken for discarded bundles huddled in the doorway. Max looked from the storefront to Colleen. "You ready for this?"

She slung her purse over her arm. "Ready as I'll ever be."

"Let's do it." As they stepped out of the car he looked up at a single light shining from a window above the storefront. "He knows we're coming, right?"

"Said he'd be expecting us. Cheery place, isn't it?"

"Looks brighter during the day."

"I'm not so sure that's good." They stepped over the sleepers and Max banged on the door. One of the men opened his eyes, saw O'Grady and sat up, shaking his head. "Must be dreaming. What a piece of work."

She glanced down, then turned away, ignoring him. The man reached out until his fingertips caressed her calf.

She pulled her leg back, poised to kick him. "Screw with me, buddy and your dream'll turn into a nightmare real fast."

"You'll stay down if you know what's good for you," Max growled. He knocked again and saw a light come on from somewhere in the back of the mission, then the door opened, flooding the inner darkness with a skewed rectangle of yellow. A solitary figure emerged. Crossing the hall, he came to the outer door and peered through the smeared glass. Max took out his shield and held it up. The man nodded and unlatched the door.

Warm air, thick with disinfectant and the smell of something vague and institutional greeted them as they stepped in from the street. Sawdust was scattered over the old wooden floor. A small stage and a pulpit loomed in the shadows at one end of the room. Tables stood at the far side and took up the space in the middle of the floor.

The man extended his hand. "I'm Father Derlen, welcome to my humble establishment. Though poor in substance it is full in spirit." His voice sounded mellow, its tone soft and reassuring with a slight brogue.

Max took the priest's hand and shook it, noting its warmth. He felt at ease in his presence. "Max Broderick." He stepped aside. "And my partner, Colleen O'Grady. Thanks for taking the time to see us."
When Derlen saw Colleen, he smiled and took her hand. "So pleased to meet you in person. You're prettier than I imagined."

Colleen blushed. "Pleasure's mine."

"Please, come upstairs where we can talk. I was just putting on some tea." He gestured toward the door. O'Grady took the lead with Max and Derlen following. A narrow set of wooden stairs brought them to a second floor apartment. Its walls had yellowing, flowered wallpaper. The smell up here above the mission spoke of old books. Max felt as if he stepped back into a time warp.

They walked through a small sitting room with spartan furnishings into a tiny kitchen boasting a 1950's vintage gas stove and refrigerator that looked showroom new and an old metal dinette set. The only luxury was a flat screen T.V.. In spite of its appearance, the apartment looked spotless. Monastic. Max admired the fact that a man with as many connections as Derlen lived so frugally. This guy was no Oral Roberts. He was more like Mother Theresa. His money really did go to help the poor.

"Please, have a seat." Derlen busied himself with a teapot. "I'm afraid I don't have much to offer in the way of refreshment. I don't often have visitors. I usually eat downstairs with the hungry souls who come to me. Is tea acceptable?"

"Tea would be fine, thank you," Colleen said, taking a chair in the corner.

Max studied the priest as he set out cups and tea bags. He had a broad, open face, an aquiline nose and deep blue eyes. Thick eyebrows danced beneath a shock of salt and pepper hair. His movements seemed quick and agile for a man of his years. He finished his preparations and sat across from them at the table. "Now what can I do for you?" he said, his gaze locked on Max.

Max felt drawn by the combination of Derlen's melodic voice and the depth in the old priest's eyes. He wondered if O'Grady felt the same.

"I wish we were here on more agreeable business," Colleen said, "but I'm afraid what we have to discuss isn't very pleasant."

Derlen looked puzzled. When he spoke his voice sounded strained. "What is it?"

"Have you been following the news about the Headless Horseman killings?"

His eyebrows raised. "Yes."

"Well." O'Grady took a deep breath. "Our evidence suggests that the killers may be frequenting your mission."

The priest's eyes grew wide and his hand flew to his chest. "My God! Saint Augustine's? I can't believe -- are you sure there hasn't been some mistake?"

The tea kettle whistled. "We've been very thorough," Max said. "Sorry to have to break it to you like this."

"Do you have any names? Descriptions?"

"Fraid not."

The whistling filled the kitchen. Derlen rose, lifted the kettle and poured three cups with trembling hands. Max felt guilty for burdening the old timer with the news, but the he had to know. "We're worried about your safety."

Derlen gave him a nervous glance, then put the kettle back on the stove.

"I'd like to assign you a couple of undercover men," Max continued. "Make sure you're in no danger."

Derlen sank into his chair and sighed. "Dear God!" He blessed himself. "What can I do to help?"

O'Grady pulled her notebook from her purse. "Have you seen anything suspicious? Anything out of the ordinary?"

The priest shook his head slowly. "To be honest with you, I get such a turn-over, although..."

Max nodded. "What?"

"There was that young man."

"Good looking tall kid? Dark hair, leather jacket?"

"That's him. Is he a suspect?"

Max glanced at O'Grady. Their eyes met and she nodded. "No, just a person of interest. I need to ask him a few questions, that's all."

Derlen sipped his tea. "He's been in here a couple of times. Got himself into a little trouble."

"What kind?"

Derlen shook his head. "It wasn't his fault. One of our patrons has an eye for young men. The two had a confrontation. I don't think our young friend will be coming around here again."

"You didn't by any chance get his name, did you?" O'Grady asked.

"Nick. Nick something. I don't recall his last name."

O'Grady pulled a business card from her purse. "If you remember, you'll give us a call?"

"If there's anything I can do to help, anything at all, please don't hesitate to call on me. Thank you for your offer of protection, but I'm not worried. I have friends of my own on the police force."

Sully, Max thought. Best not mention him. If the old man knew Sully might be involved that would really shake him up. Probably a good idea to send in some undercover guys from another part of the city. "Keep a sharp eye out," Max said. "If anything strikes you as out of the ordinary, get on the horn to us. Right away."

"You have my word. Nobody wants to see this madness stopped more than I do." He took a sip of tea and looked from O'Grady to Max and sighed. "Especially if it's someone who's been coming to my mission."

CHAPTER THIRTY FOUR

The numbers on the clock beside Nick's bed glowed a steady *12:17*. Except for a pool of light cast by his reading lamp, the apartment lay in darkness. Nick sat cross-legged on his bed, a pad of paper balanced on his knee and a pen in hand. He jotted a few more lines, then set the pen down and read.

Dear Detectives:

This man was the one responsible for the Headless Horseman murders. Although you were investigating the deaths of four women, what you didn't know, was that this guy was like Charlie Manson and used homeless people to do the murders, then he killed them too.

I know how crazy this sounds, but I overheard conversations between him and the street people. That's why you couldn't catch him. You'll know this is true when the butchering stops.

I don't know if I can live with having taken someone's life, but I could not have lived knowing that I allowed him to go on killing.

I hope God forgives me for what I had to do. I had no choice. It was the only way to stop him.

A Concerned Citizen

Nick tossed the pad aside, reached under his mattress and withdrew the gun, dropping it in his lap. He stared at it, then the note. Could he go through with it?

If he did, he was no better than the magician -- a murderer. If he didn't, the magician would wear him down and turn his brain to mush. Maybe even make him another killing robot. More people would die because he did nothing.

He thought of his aborted try. He might have succeeded if it hadn't been for that asshole rookie cop, then again he could have lost his nerve at the moment of truth. He would never know, but tomorrow he would have another chance.

He hadn't heard the voice for days, but he expected it to explode into his brain at any moment, robbing him of sleep until it drove him over the edge into a terrifying abyss of mental disintegration that he already felt too close to. As much as he hated the idea, there didn't seem to be any way out, except with the gun.

The worst of it was no one could help him. Ever since he got into that hot box with Joey and banged his head it had been him against the voice. He folded the note, slipped it into an envelope and tucked it and the gun beneath his mattress, then turned off his lamp to try and get some sleep.

When he opened his eyes the dim gray of an overcast day filtered into his room from beneath the shade. His clock read 10:30. He didn't remember falling asleep.

He showered, but didn't have the stomach for food. His whole being felt coiled as if one sudden move would unravel him like an overwound clock. He tucked the note into his waistband and the gun in the small of his back.

This was it.

A light breeze blew when he reached Town Field some time after one. Clouds hung dark and leaden, threatening to loose a burst of cold autumn rain. Nick pulled his jacket tighter and took up his vigil on the far side of the field. Part of him hoped the magician wouldn't show because of the weather, but no rain had fallen yet. It could threaten all day and never come. The thought of putting off his plan played on his mind, but the appearance of the magician ruined any chance he had of changing it.

Not wanting to risk anything the way he had the other day Nick kept out of sight. Out in the open there was too much of a chance of getting caught. He decided to watch, wait, and ambush him on Gibson street at dusk from the shadows.

Hours passed. Groups of homeless drifted in and out of Saint Augustine's under the magician's scrutiny while Nick watched him. To Nick's relief, he saw no sign of Sully or the old priest. Running into Sully would mean trouble and seeing the priest would mean an attack of guilt.

When the sky grew darker the magician began packing up his things. Nick circled around the back of the field and crossed Dorchester Ave. a half a block up, out of his view. Ducking into an alley off of Gibson Street he hid himself in the shadows, pulled the gun out and checked it, then crept toward the end of the alley and peered over the edge of a porch.

Nick's heart thumped when the magician started across Dot Ave.. He drew a deep breath to calm himself and stared down at the gun in his shaking hand. Did he have the balls to do it?

The magician stepped onto the curb, stopping.

His will is the ruling force of your life and the rule must be followed. The voice rammed into Nick's mind. He cried out and the gun flew from his hand when he jerked both hands up to cover his head.

A deafening blast slammed into his ears.

The percussive force of the gun's discharge cut across his legs making his knees buckle and his heart flutter like a startled bird. He looked down, amazed and relieved to see his legs intact. The smoking gun lay on the sidewalk. A quarter-sized hole was blown through the side of the porch where he was hiding. Eye level.

His ears rang and his eyes watered. Beneath the ringing, the voice continued its patter. He picked up the gun and looked around. No magician. The front door to the building he stood next to opened. Jamming the gun in his pocket, Nick ran from the alley and headed toward Dot Ave.. A reedy voice screamed behind him. He glanced back and saw an older man standing on the porch shaking his fist.

At the corner of Gibson, Nick spotted the magician hurrying up Dot Ave. toward Field's Corner Station. Nick darted through traffic. Tires screeched and a horn beeped. "Crazy son-of-a-bitch!" a man yelled. Nick reached the other side of the street and flipped the man off.

Moving up the sidewalk, Nick slowed to a trot, then a fast walk, tracking the magician from the other side of the street. He heard sirens coming from the direction of Gibson Street. Had to keep moving. The subway. Only a block.

The ringing in Nick's ears diminished and the voice grew quieter, but its insistence remained. *Peace comes with submission. Do not fight it. Obey my will and be rewarded. Taranis is all powerful.*

Nick spotted a homeless man in a tattered trench coat shaking his head as he crossed Dot Ave.. The man shambled up the ramp to Field's Corner Station as if driven by an invisible whip. A moment later Nick spotted Father Derlen. Ducking into a storefront, Nick watched him cross after the homeless man. The magician followed close behind.

It looked like the magician controlled the guy in the trench coat and Father Derlen was trying to help him. Nick waited until the magician passed, then followed, reaching the corner in time to see the magician slip into Field's Corner station.

The voice continued its urgings while Nick hustled up the ramp. Stepping into the station he saw the guy in the trench coat push through the turnstile. "Don't make me do it!" the man said, clapping his hands to his ears.

Silence! the voice hissed.

Its harsh whisper sent a chill through Nick. He thrust his hand into his pocket and clutched the gun.

You'll draw attention to yourself. Do that and you'll end up under the wheels of the train.

A train screeched in the distance from the direction of downtown, bearing down on the station. Nick stepped behind a column and watched Father Derlen go through the turnstile. He wanted to make a run for the train, but couldn't see the magician.

The screeching grew louder, then the train barreled into the station. A cold musty blast of air blew Nick's hair back from his face. The homeless guy rocked back and forth. Father Derlen stood at the other end of the platform. Nick had a horrifying revelation that the magician was trying to kill the priest. His hand tightened on the butt of the gun.

The train stopped and the doors opened. Nick stepped from behind the column in time to see the magician pass through the turnstile. The last of the people exited and the three men stepped into the subway car. Fuck it. Nick vaulted over the turnstile, but the train doors whooshed shut. "Son-of-a-bitch!"

A heavy feeling sank into his chest. He scanned the length of the train, *feeling* rather than seeing someone's gaze on him, a dark figure at the far end of one of the cars. When the train started to roll the magician's eyes connected with Nick's and flashed recognition. Fumbling for the gun, Nick yanked it from his pocket and pointed but he couldn't get a steady bead. The magician's eyes widened and the train pulled out of the station.

Nick looked up and down the empty platform. Luckily no one had seen him. He slid the gun into his pocket, went back out through the turnstile and hurried home.

Later that night he lay awake fighting sleep. The voice had diminished to a whisper that drifted in and out of his brain like billowing lace curtains, no longer loud, no longer threatening; only persistent like the steady flap of the curtains. In spite of his dread, the voice's mesmerizing drone lulled him.

Images of the day flashed through his mind, particularly the wide-eyed surprise of the magician. He had his chance to shoot and blew it again. No more advantage of surprise. The magician knew Nick was trying to kill him. Now it was a matter of survival. Who would get who first?

He drifted, shook himself and glanced at the clock.

11:45.

He struggled to stay awake, but his eyes refused to obey. His eyelids fluttered and he faded, his last conscious thought, the wide-eyed stare of the magician following him down into sleep...

...Nick flew upward while flashes and streaks of light melted his surroundings into shadows. Outlines of trees. Hills.

A still cold enveloped him.

Shivering, he made a slow circle around the area. Not a soul. He looked up into the darkness and saw crystal starlight and a gibbous moon. The smell of burning wood hung in the air. A glimmer of orange flickered over the top of a small rise.

He started toward it, curiosity urging him forward, fear slowing him. Near the top of the hill he heard voices chanting, their words incomprehensible, their rhythm mesmerizing, as if they called him.
"Ta Ra Nis. Ta Ra Nis."

He worked his way up the side of a large boulder until he could peer over the top. Below a group of men in dark hooded robes circled a flaming pyre. In the shadows outside the periphery of the circle lay a crude wooden cross that seemed to move. Something was tied to it.

A man!

The chanting stopped. The hooded men broke the circle and surrounded the cross, lifting it into the air. In the glow of the raging pyre the homeless man with the trench coat thrashed back and forth, arms and legs bound, something tied across his mouth. Wide frightened animal eyes glinted orange in the firelight. A crown of mistletoe sat on his head.

Nick reached into his pocket, expecting to find the gun, but to his dismay came up with nothing.

"Ta Ra Nis." The hooded men raised the cross higher and hurled it into the flames.

The man's hair exploded in a flash, followed by his trench coat. Flesh popped, sizzled, and peeled like blistering paint. The blackening figure writhed amid tendrils of hungry flame, and its mouth stretched in a silent scream. The sickening stench of foul inky smoke rose into the air. Nick cried out and rushed toward the fire.

The hooded men ran at him, hands outstretched. Nick turned to run but his legs wouldn't move. He tried to scream. A hoarse whisper escaped. Footsteps closed in. A hand clamped over his nose and mouth, another clutched at his ankle and an arm slipped around his neck. He choked. Stumbled. Fingers entwined themselves in his hair. More hands.

He went to his knees, swung wildly, then he was on his back looking up, momentarily glimpsing the still serenity of the night sky before hands and hoods descended, blotting out his view and drawing him down into blackness.

CHAPTER THIRTY FIVE

"Shit!" Max kicked at the ground as the priest, the transient wearing the trench coat and a third man disappeared in a late model sedan heading toward the Blue Hills. He thought he recognized the third man, but wasn't sure. "Son-of-a-bitch!" He managed a successful tail from Field's Corner to Mattapan, only to lose his quarry in the darkness of The Blue Hills Parkway.

Chances are someone would be burned tonight.

He walked the half mile back to Mattapan station and caught a cab to District Eleven. After a change of clothes, he pulled out the map of Boston O'Grady had given him. Using Geist's tick blood formula, he narrowed down the area where he suspected the murder had occurred, then drove to the Blue Hills to look for the glow of a bonfire.

After criss-crossing the hills most of the night and finding nothing, he pulled over to the side of the road. If there had been a ritual sacrifice it would be over by now. Best he could do was return in daylight to try to find the remains. Tired and frustrated, he drove back to his office.

Poring over his notes and map, Max tried to piece things together. He was close. He felt it, but his energy had dwindled. He could barely keep his eyes open. Sometime after seven, he lay his head on the map and dozed.

It seemed as if he had only closed his eyes for a second when he smelled perfume. He looked up to see Colleen standing in the doorway looking fresh and vibrant. Max scratched his itchy beard and ran his tongue over his teeth. Pasty. "How long you been standing there?"

O'Grady shook her head. "Jesus, Broderick, you look awful." Her expression softened into one of concern. Her voice lowered. "When's the last time you slept?"

He rubbed his eyes. "Never mind." He pointed at the map. "This thing's ready to blow."

She dropped her purse onto the desk and pulled a chair up beside him. The pleasant smell of her perfume filled his senses. He traced the penned-in circle on the map with his finger. "I had a good tail going and I lost it. We need to check out this area of the Blue Hills for signs of a ritual. If you can't get enough manpower from the M.D.C., put in a req. to the commissioner's office. If we need more help, let me know and I'll have some men flown up from Washington."

"You going to let me in on what set you off or are you going to banish me to the Blue Hills empty handed?"

Max smiled. "Sorry, it's been a long night. Shit hit the fan right at the end of my stakeout."

"Why didn't you call?"

"Wish I had. Believe me I could have used you but there was no time. This homeless guy started acting strange. Then get this." He tapped the desktop. "The priest showed up. I think he was trying to help the guy. Then the kid in the leather jacket came along. He had a gun."

O'Grady's mouth dropped. "What did you do?"

"The train pulled out of the station before anything happened." He shook his head. "I think the kid and the priest know who's behind the murders."

"You think Father Derlen's involved?"

"I'm not sure what to think. There was another man." He stared off into space, playing back the events of the night. Something about the third man nagged at him but the recollection hovered out of reach. The harder he tried to remember, the more the fragment receded.

"So what happened?"

"Huh?"

"Father Derlen."

"Oh yeah, sorry. I followed them to Mattapan Station. Lost 'em somewhere on the Blue Hills Parkway. They were picked up in a car." He sighed. "Focus the search around Unquity Road, past the Boy Scout camp." He looked at the map. "Camp Sayre." He glanced up at O'Grady and saw her studying him.

"Why don't you get some rest?" she said. "I'll call you if something breaks."

"I have to find the kid. He damn near blew my cover. If he doesn't screw up the investigation he's going to get himself killed. I have to talk to him before someone else gets to him and I think I know where to find him."

CHAPTER THIRTY SIX

Nick fell screaming into the blackness until his eyes flew open and his hands flailed, whacking something solid. His nightstand crashed to the floor sending his clock spinning off into the darkness. His skin felt wet and clammy. Cold. He took a long shaky breath and heard footsteps rushing up the hall outside his room.

The door and the light from the hall blinded him. His hand went to his eyes, then the wall switch clicked on, flooding the room with brightness.

"Honey, what happened? Are you all right?"

He squinted at his mother in the doorway, hair in curlers, her eyes puffy from sleep. She had on the same faded pink bathrobe he and his dad gave her for Mother's Day when he was eight. A hole had worn through the elbow.

"Sorry, ma. Had a nightmare."

She put her hand to her chest. "Jesus, Nicky, you scared the shit out of me."

"Sorry."

"Nonsense." She picked his blanket up from the floor, leaned over and kissed him on the forehead, then covered him. "Long as you're all right. That's all that matters." She put a cool hand against his cheek and studied him, her eyes full of questions. "You're sure everything's okay?"

"I'm fine, ma. Go back to bed. You have to get up early."

She gave him a faint smile, eyed the tipped over nightstand and started toward it.

"Don't worry about that," Nick said. "I'll get it in the morning. Get your beauty rest."

She stopped, turned back to the door and flicked off the light. "Sleep tight, honey."

"Thanks, mom."

"I love you."

"You too."

She stepped out into the hall, closing the door behind her, leaving him alone in the darkness. The agony in the burning man's eyes filled his mind. The same man the magician followed into the subway. All the other murders had been women. Unless you counted Obie and the rest of the missing homeless.

Maybe a woman had been killed. He could've slept through it. Maybe his dream of the man being sacrificed is what happened to all the homeless guys. Including Obie.

He stared into the darkness. Usually a woman was killed, then a homeless guy went to the rescue mission and... He sat up and rubbed his eyes. The man went to the mission never to be seen again. The magician showed up a day or two later. Someone in Saint Augustine's had to be working with him.

Nick played it through in his mind. He went to Saint Augustine's to find Obie, then followed one of the people there. Each time he tried to check it out, Sully...

Could *he* be working with the magician?

Nick remembered the way Sully's dark eyes brightened while beating him with his nightstick. Sully was no brain surgeon but he was definitely one sick dude who liked to hurt people. How far gone was he? Gone enough to butcher?

Nick shuddered at the thought of trying to shoot Sully and the magician. He didn't think he was capable and if he ever got busted. Shit. Cop killer. Dead meat for sure.

He spent the rest of the night turning things over in his mind. If he didn't get to the magician, the magician would get to him.

He waited until his mother and Mike left for work before getting up. After dressing, he pulled the gun from under his mattress and popped open the cylinder. Five bullets left. He remembered the hole in the porch on Gibson Street and the force of the revolver's discharge. He wasn't so sure he wanted to use the gun now, but he didn't dare go anywhere without it. The magician saw it. In his mind, he crossed another line. He had to carry the gun for protection.

Nick jammed it under his belt at the small of his back. What once felt foreign and malevolent became familiar and reassuring. He pulled on his jacket and left for Town Field.

The sun peeked from behind wind-blown clouds, only to be covered again by grayness. Nick hurried toward Field's Corner, arriving before the mission opened. A brisk wind blew flurries of leaves and trash in front of him as he entered the park. Except for two crackheads sitting against the back of the clubhouse getting their fix from a glass pipe and a couple of kids throwing rocks at a stray dog, no one else occupied the park.

When the mission opened Nick didn't see the man in the trench coat which didn't surprise him. Poor son-of-a-bitch was probably toast. Nick moved closer, waiting for a glimpse of Father Derlen or the magician but neither one made an appearance.

The longer he waited, the more his urgency grew. He had to warn Father Derlen even if it meant exposing himself. The urge to run gripped him but he didn't allow it to rule him. Nick Powers might be scared shitless and stupid, but he wasn't a pussy. Fuck it. He didn't care what happened anymore. He was going into the mission.

Slipping the gun from his back, he slipped it into his jacket pocket. Somehow bullets didn't seem adequate, but it was all he had. He took a deep breath, steeled himself and darted behind a passing bus, stopping in the middle of the street to let a cab pass before trotting to the far sidewalk.

His heart jumped at the sudden blast of a siren. Two more steps and he heard the screech of rubber. A paddy wagon slid around the corner of Gibson Street onto Dot Ave., skidding to a stop beside him.

What the f...

The door flew open and Sully jumped out, nightstick drawn, his glare focused on Nick. "Don't move, Powers."

Nick took two steps backward and stumbled over the curb.

Sully rushed forward brandishing his nightstick. Nick scrabbled backward, but Sully grabbed him by the collar. Nick braced himself for the pain, but it didn't come. He looked up and saw Sully glancing sideways. A heavy-set gray-haired woman pulling a two-wheeled shopping cart stood in the middle of the sidewalk watching, open-mouthed. Sully twisted Nick's shirt, popping a button as he yanked him up.

Nick tried to pull away. "Hey, man, take it easy. What's your problem?"

"Shut up, punk." Sully pushed him against a wall. "You know the drill. Put your hands against the wall and spread 'em." The end of the nightstick jabbed his ribs and a hand pushed into his back. The nightstick found its way between his knees. "I said, spread 'em." The club jerked from side to side, forcing Nick's legs apart, then Sully's hands slid up and down his chest, sides and legs, stopping at his jacket pocket.

"What's this?"

Nick felt his jacket fly up and the gun yanked from his pocket. He looked sideways and saw a horrified look on the old woman's face.

"Packing heat, eh Powers? That'll get you a year in Concord." Nick heard the rattle of cuffs, then Sully grabbed his arm and jerked it backward. Pain shot through his shoulder, followed by a sharper pain on the bone of his wrist as Sully slapped a cuff on and squeezed. Nick winced as metal bit into his skin. A moment later, Sully had his other arm, repeating the same brutal movements.

Nick glanced at the old woman who shook her head. Her previous look of horror turned to disgust.

"Nothing to worry about, ma'am." Sully pulled him backward. "It's our job to take vermin like this off the streets." The old lady stared, clucking as Sully dragged Nick toward the paddy wagon.

Opening the back door, he shoved Nick, propelling him into the truck. Nick lost his balance and banged his head against the door. "Christ, chill out, will ya?"

"Too drunk to stand, huh?" Sully pushed again.

Nick spun away and scrambled back into the dark recesses of the truck. This is it, he thought. Sully brought the meat wagon 'cuz he wants to do a number on me. Should have shot the son-of-a-bitch when I had the chance. He dropped onto one of the benches and slid back into the corner to protect as much of himself as he could.

Sully climbed in, pulled the door shut and clicked on an overhead light. Sitting across from Nick, he slapped his nightstick into his palm. The feeble illumination highlighted the dark shadows of his eyes, making his face look more skull like than human. Pinpoints of dull yellow glinted from the back of two dark sockets. A humorless smile lit his face. "Your ass is grass now, Powers and I'm the lawnmower." The nightstick shot forward catching Nick in the gut.

Pain exploded in his mid-section like a hot poker. He scrunched lower to make himself a smaller target. He couldn't catch his breath.

Sully reached into the pocket of his shirt and withdrew a baggie full of something white and waved it in front of Nick. "Yeah, you're fucked now, Powers. Possession of an unregistered handgun and a bag of crack. You have the right to remain silent. Everything you say, can and will be used against you in a court of law."

A loud bang filled the interior of the truck followed by a voice. "Hey, open up in there!"

Nick figured Sully had invited some friends to join the fun, but Sully's glare told him otherwise. Two more bangs. "I said open up!"

"Police business," Sully growled. "Take a hike."

"You'll open up if you know what's good for you," the voice said.

Sully stared at Nick. His features hardened. "Just a minute."

"Not in a minute," the voice shot back. "Now!"

"Son-of-a-bitch. Who does he think he is?" Sully put the tip of his nightstick under Nick's chin and lifted his head. "Not a peep out of you. We're not done yet." He went to the back of the truck and opened the door a crack. "What the fuck?" He lowered his voice. "You. Just a minute." The door opened wider and Sully stepped out. Nick leaned forward to try and glimpse who it was, but the door slammed shut before he could see anything.

His stomach burned, his head throbbed, and his hands had gone numb from the cuffs. A trickle of blood ran down the side of his head where he had hit the door. He thought he was going to puke. The worst was knowing that Sully wasn't done yet. No matter what happened, Sully was going to fuck him up good.

Hopelessness swept over him, then the fear in his stomach turned to anger. If Sully beat the shit out of him he wouldn't take an ass-whipping like a pussy. He'd get in one good shot. Make it count. He knew he'd pay for it later, but it didn't matter. Sully would work him over anyway. Might as well get in his best.

The voices outside the meat wagon sounded like a heated argument, but Nick couldn't make out the words. Who was out there? The priest? His luck couldn't be that good. Probably another cop. Great. If he took a shot at Sully, they'd have a Rodney King party. Fuck it. Didn't matter. He was going down anyway. He'd go out with a flash.

When the latch to the door clicked, Nick tensed and scrunched lower into the corner. A flash of daylight lit the truck, then Sully lumbered toward him. Nick looked up and their eyes met. The insane fire had gone from Sully's eyes. His face looked ashen.

Nick dropped his head, listened for another step, then drove his whole body forward with all his strength. The surprised grunt and softness told him his head found Sully's stomach. Arms flew out in a failed attempt at balance, then Sully crashed into the wall with a cry of pain.

A jolt of agony shot through Nick's shoulders and neck when they hit, but he didn't care. Far worse pain was coming. He got his shot in. That's all that mattered.

Sully groaned.

Nick heard footsteps rushing up behind him and smiled, calmly waiting for the clubs to find his head and ribs. Gloved hands grabbed him from behind and pulled him backward. He shook his head, looked up and his heart froze when his eyes met the steady gaze of the magician.

CHAPTER THIRTY SEVEN

"I t's all right," Max said. "I'm not going to hurt you." He felt the kid shaking in his grasp, eyes bigger than quarters. Blood ran down the side of his face and his wrists were chafed where the cuffs cut into them -- but he'd gone after Sully. Max could barely keep himself from smiling. Kid had heart.

Sully lay doubled over on his side, groaning. His gaze met Max's and pinched into a frown as he pulled himself to his knees. "Little bastard, I'm gonna…"

"Uncuff him."

"What?"

"I said uncuff him."

"You crazy? I just busted this maggot for possession of an unregistered handgun and a bag of crack." He glared at the kid. "And assaulting an officer."

"Let me see the evidence."

Sully pulled a small thirty-eight and a Ziploc bag from his jacket pocket. "Little Nicky Powers is going bye-bye."

Max held up the bag, then checked the gun. Serial numbers filed. He popped open the cylinder and emptied five bullets and one spent shell into his palm, then stuffed the gun, bullets and crack into his pocket. The kid's lower lip trembled. His eyes darted from Max to Sully and back again.

Sully frowned. "What are you?"

"I'll take care of it," Max said. "Now uncuff him."

"He's dangerous. He attacked..."

Max wanted so bad to hit this asshole. "You didn't do anything to provoke him, did you? Now quit fucking around, Officer Sullivan. You don't take the bracelets off, I'll be attacking you." He turned to the kid. Still shaking. "Take it easy, partner. Nothing's going to happen unless you try something stupid when we take off the cuffs."

The kid nodded.

"I'm taking you on your word."

Sully grunted and tossed the keys to Max. The kid rolled over onto his stomach, jerking when Max unlatched the cuffs. He pulled his arms in front and massaged the bloody red lines circling both his wrists. His hands were blue and swollen. He still hadn't said a word.

Max handed Sully the keys and cuffs. "I'm taking him with me."

Nick shook his head and squirmed backward. Max pulled out his shield. "This might come as a shock but I'm a cop too. Don't worry, you're in good hands."

Nick's mouth dropped. "What the fuck?"

"You *do* have a voice."

Sully grabbed Max's arm. "What about the gun? The crack?"

Max pulled away. "I hear anything else about crack or a gun, you're going to find yourself stuck on a lot of unpleasant details for a long time. You understand me, mister?"

Sully turned to Nick. "We're not through, Powers."

The kid stuck up his middle finger.

Sully's head jerked back and he started toward Nick. Max stepped between them. "Outta here, Sully. Go back to your beat or whatever your normal duty is."

A murderous glare lit Sully's eyes, then he relaxed and shrugged.

Too easy, Max thought. He stayed between Nick and the cop and pushed Sully toward the back of the paddy wagon.

"C'mon." Max waved the kid out of the truck. "You and I have a few things to talk about."

"You're a cop?"

"Who did you think I was?"

He shook his head and climbed out of the back of the paddy wagon. "You don't want to know."

Max took him by the arm. "Car's around the corner. Thanks for your assistance," he said to Sully. He pulled out a handkerchief and gave it to the kid. "Here, put this over that cut on your head."

"Thanks."

"What's all this shit about crack and the gun? Why'd you try to shoot me the other day?"

Nick looked back over his shoulder as they rounded a corner, then lowered his voice. "Look, I'll cop to the gun, but the crack was Sully's. Honest. He was setting me up."

Max glanced sideways at him. The kid didn't look or act like a crack head. Knowing Sully, the kid was probably telling the truth. A liar would've denied everything. "Nick Powers. That your real name?"

He nodded.

Max stopped next to his car and held out his hand. "Special Agent Max Broderick. U.S. Justice Department."

Nick held his hand out tentatively. "A fed? Jesus." He shook his head. "What the fuck is going on?"

"That's what I want to know." Max opened the passenger door and motioned for Nick to get in.

"You want me to sit up front? Isn't this a bust?"

"I have a feeling you got yourself into this mess because you know something. That's what I need to find out." He closed the door, went around to the driver's side and climbed in.

The kid stared straight ahead, a puzzled look creasing his brow. Max took off his magician's cape and jacket, started the car and pulled away from the curb, turning onto Dorchester. Ave. in the direction of the Blue Hills. O'Grady would be out there with the M.D.C.. Maybe she could give the kid a woman's touch. Help him relax.

Nick shook his head.

"Talk to me," Max said. "How'd you get mixed up with that asshole?"

Nick smiled. "I thought I knew what was happening. I was sure I knew."

"Knew what?"

Nick frowned. "You really a fed?"

Max held up his hand. "Scout's honor."

"Can I see your ID again?"

"Sure."

Nick studied the card and shield for a long time before handing them back. "How do I know they're not fake?"

"How do you think I got you away from Sully?"

"You could be working with him. You know, good cop, bad cop."

Kid was no dummy. "Believe me, I'm not working with that piece of shit. You and I are not going to get anywhere unless we trust each other. I don't know what you've seen or how you got involved, but I don't have time to play games. I need answers. I prove to you I am who I say I am, you going to come clean?"

"How you gonna prove it?"

Max took out his cell phone, hit speed dial, and handed it to Nick. "You're calling Lieutenant O'Grady from the Boston P.D.. Tell her who you are then ask her about me."

Nick looked at the phone, then back to Max as he put it to his ear. "Hi Lieutenant. My name is Nick Powers from Dorchester. I'm the guy this fed named Broderick was after. He just called you and put me on the phone. Okay?"

Nick handed the phone back to Max.

"Yeah, I got him. Just in time, too. Our boy Sully was just about to send him to Mass. General." A pause. "Good. We'll see you soon. Thanks!" He disconnected.

"I thought for sure it was you," Nick said, incredulous.

"Tell me what you know about the murders, how you got involved and why you've been hanging around the mission? Then I want to know why you pointed that damn gun at me. And what's with you and Sullivan?"

"You won't believe it."

"Try me."

They drove out of Dorchester toward the Blue Hills while Nick told Max how he banged his head and started hearing voices.

Max turned onto Blue Hill Ave. from River Street and passed Mattapan Station. "Sorry, partner," he said when Nick stopped. "It's not that I think you're not playing with a full deck and you don't strike me as a liar, but your story's a bit much to swallow."

"You're the only person I've told this to. How do you explain the letter I sent? And the murders. It hasn't been the same guy, has it?"

"What makes you say that?"

"Guys have been hiding in closets. Homeless guys. That's why you haven't been able to nail anybody. That's why I thought it was you."

"Yeah, yeah, I know. The voice."

Nick's mouth turned down at the corners. "You still don't believe me."

"It would make things a hell of a lot easier if I did, but hey, face it, if you were in my shoes would you buy a story like that?"

Nick shook his head and stared out the window.

"I'm trying to work with you kid, but it's obvious you're protecting your source. That's okay, I can respect that, but don't expect me to buy some bullshit story about hearing voices. If you can give me enough information to put these sick sons-of-bitches away, I won't pressure you to give up your source -- as long as they're not involved."

They turned onto Unquity road and passed the M.D.C. skating rink. Nick straightened and stared ahead, the color draining from his face. Trees lined both sides of the road.

"You all right?" Max said.

Nick shook his head, but didn't answer.

"What is it?"

He closed his eyes and sank back into the seat. "They burned him," he said. "Near here."

"Who?"

"The guy wearing the trench coat. He looked gross." Nick rubbed his temples. "They danced and chanted. Ta something. Ta Ra Nis?"

A tingle danced across Max's scalp. "Taranis. Where did you hear that?"

"I watched."

CHAPTER THIRTY EIGHT

"Okay, Nick, enough of the games. Either your source is connected to the people I'm after or they're so close they're in trouble. You may think you're protecting them but you're only making things worse."

Nick studied the trees on both sides of the road and his sense of deja vú grew stronger. What was it? The Blue Hills. Trees. They passed Camp Sayre and his stomach grew queasy. This was close to where it happened and this cop didn't believe anything about the voice. Thought it was a made up story to protect a snitch.

Nick looked over at Max. Without the magician's outfit he didn't look sinister. Didn't even look like a cop. Came across more like a yuppie except for the scar under his eye and the way he talked. Been around the block a few times, but smarter than your regular asshole on the street.

"Look," Nick said. "I thought for sure you were the one behind the voice. Why do you think I was going to shoot you?"

Max shrugged. "You don't strike me as impulsive, so I ask myself, why did this kid pull a gun on me? All I can figure is that A, you have psychological problems, or B, you're a fast-talking kid from Dorchester who's too deep in some shit." He looked Nick in the eye. "You don't strike me as a person with psychological problems."

Nick crossed his arms. "What do I have to do to convince you I'm on the level? Perform a miracle?"

"That would be a start."

"Funny." He stared out the window again. Trees. Not pines, but broad leaves. Oaks. Then mistletoe. Street people. Sickles and weird names. How did it all connect?

Max drove past the horse corrals of the Blue Hills M.D.C. station, turned into the lot and found an empty space next to an unmarked Boston Police car. "I know you don't trust me kid, but you might feel more relaxed talking to O'Grady. She's from South Boston."

The look in the cop's eyes told Nick that he was sincere. There had to be a way to make this guy see he wasn't running a game on him. "Yeah, sure. I'll talk to her. A chick cop from Southie. Probably looks like a lineman from the Patriots."

A broad grin filled Max's face. "She can be as tough as one if she wants, but I wouldn't give her a bunch of shit. She's one of the best partners I've ever had." He grabbed the door handle, then turned back to Nick and winked. "Don't tell her I said that."

"Don't worry." Nick went with Broderick into the station, leaving behind the sound of birds and a breeze that carried the smell of horse shit from the stables. Nick wasn't sure which turned him off more, that or the stuffy smell of a cop station. The sight of uniforms made him nervous. Except for some curious glances and an unfriendly stare from the cop at the front desk, no one bothered him.

Broderick flashed his shield and the desk sergeant jerked his thumb over his shoulder. "Down the hall. Second door on the right. She's waiting for you."

Broderick motioned with his head and Nick followed. Here we go, he thought. Time to meet the bull-dyke from Southie. She'll probably... He smelled perfume.

"Afternoon, O'Grady. I'd like you to meet Nick Powers." Broderick stepped aside and held out his hand.

A foxy redhead stepped out of the next office. A ponytail lay over one shoulder. Nick imagined what her hair looked like cascading over both shoulders. The cut of her outfit followed her curves, and she had legs that wouldn't quit. She wore a tailored light blue blazer, short skirt and a silk blouse. Her green eyes quickly took in all of Nick before zeroing in on his. When she smiled, his insides turned soft.

"You're the young man who spoke to me on the phone." She held out her hand. "Lieutenant Colleen O'Grady. Boston Police."

Nick took her hand. Soft skin. Firm handshake. "Hi. I'm Ni -- um,

Nick. Nick Powers." He realized he hung on too long and let go on the down shake before shoving his hands into his pockets.

Her brow furrowed. "What happened to your head?"

He reached up, touching matted hair. "Just a little cut."

"Little cut? Jesus, Broderick, why didn't you at least clean it up?"

"I gave him a handkerchief."

"I'm all right, really. Agent Broderick saved me from the worst of it, believe me."

"Nick has one hell of a story to tell," Max said. "Won't come clean with me. Maybe you'll have better luck."

She looked from Nick to Broderick and back again. Her gaze made Nick feel hot and prickly. Afraid she might see how she affected him he stared at the floor.

"What do you say, Nick? You want to talk about it?" Her voice reminded him of his mother's when she was concerned.

He looked at Broderick.

"Without him," she said, turning to Max. "The watch commander needs to speak to you about narrowing down your search."

"I'm gone." He winked at Nick and went off down the hall.

"Come on into the office," she said. "Can I get you something? Coffee? A Coke?"

"I'll take a Coke, thanks."

She ushered him into the office and sat him in the chair behind the desk. "Wait here. I'll be right back."

The sound of cops, phones, and keyboards drifted to him from outside. He didn't like being here. Enemy territory. Lieutenant O'Grady reappeared with a cold can of Coke and a small first aid kit. She closed the door behind her, blocking out the sound of cop talk and cop noises leaving him alone with her and the smell of her perfume.

He took a long sip and eyed her as she cleaned and bandaged, careful to avoid eye contact. Her closeness, soft touch, and perfume overwhelmed him. Neither one of them spoke while she worked.

"Men's room is down the hall," she said gently pressing a bandage over his cut. She closed the first aid kit and pointed. "Why don't you clean up a little? It'll make you feel better."

The combination of her attention, the Coke, and cold water splashed on his face helped. Even the uniformed M.D.C. cops didn't bother him anymore. He went back and found her waiting behind the desk.

"Have a seat." She gestured toward a chair. "And tell me what's going on."

He dropped into the chair. "What did Broderick tell you?"

"Only that you've been around the mission a lot and got yourself into a little troub -- is officer Sullivan responsible for that cut on your head?"

"How did you know?"

Her face hardened. "That no good son-of-a-..." She stopped. "Sorry. I've met him before. He's a creep." She pointed to Nick's cut and her features softened. "That proves it."

Nick wanted to tell her everything, but feared that she would think him crazy. What could he do? He had to tell her. If he didn't, Broderick would. Best do it in his own words. "I tried explaining it to Broderick, but he won't cut me any slack."

"Let's get off on the right foot. For starters I'm not Broderick, but I know how hard-headed he can be." She leaned forward and lowered her voice. "Don't let on I said this, but he's the most decent law officer I've ever come across and he's a gentleman. More important than that, he cares." Her eyes seemed to gaze at something far away, then sharpened.

If I didn't know better, I'd say they were soft on each other, Nick thought. "Broderick's going to tell you anyway, so I might as well come clean."

Nick told her about Joey, the stolen car, the voice, Obie, the rest of the homeless, Saint Augustine's, and Sully. She listened intently, stopping him only to jot a note or to clarify a point. He gave her detailed accounts of his dreams, including the most recent one of the burning and how strongly he felt that it had taken place near Camp Sayre.

When he finished he slumped in the chair and sighed, studying her for a reaction. Her face remained unchanged, just like a cop, except she was better. She didn't need shades to hide it.

"You think I'm a flake, don't you?"

She shook her head. "To be honest, I don't know what to think, but I'll tell you this. Whether it happened or not is not the issue here. What's important is that you believe it happened. That makes it real for you."

The tension drained from him and he suddenly felt tired. He let his chin drop to his chest and closed his eyes. Part of him felt relieved, the other part frustrated. If they gave him time, he'd get a chance to prove himself, but the voice could come at any moment, and when it did, he'd let them know -- no, not them. To hell with that hard-headed

Broderick. He'd tell this one. He opened his eyes and met her gaze again. Same look as his mother's. He sat up straight.

The cut on his head throbbed, his wrists burned, and his neck hurt from ramming into Sully. Whose voice told the bums to hide in closets and chop up women with a sickle? His thoughts felt like pool balls missing connections on a blown combination shot. No answers, only confusion.

"Nick?"

He jumped.

"What were you thinking about?"

He studied her. What a babe. Red hair that he wanted to bury himself in, good looks, an awesome body, brains -- and she was sympathetic. If only he were a few years older.

He looked into the endless green of her eyes and wished he could escape into them. "I'm thinking that the voice will be back and when it does, I'm going to tell you what it says, then you'll see I'm not crazy."

CHAPTER THIRTY NINE

Max peered into the office. The weak sunlight filtering in through the blinds seemed to play tricks with his eyes, but he was pretty sure he saw the kid making goo-goo eyes at O'Grady. Stepping into the stuffy room, he rubbed his burning eyes. A migraine gained momentum at the base of his skull. The last few days were catching up to him. He cleared his throat. "Excuse me. I'm not interrupting, am I?"

Colleen looked up. "Nick was just filling me in on what he's discovered."

He looked at Nick who still gazed at O'Grady. "I hope he told you more than he told me."

Nick didn't respond.

"We need to discuss some new developments," Max said. "You mind waiting here for a few minutes while I talk strategy with Lieutenant O'Grady, Nick?"

Nick leaned back in his chair and closed his eyes. "Knock yourself out. Tell her how psychotic you think I am. I don't give a shi -- damn."

Colleen came from behind the desk, rested a hand on Nick's shoulder and gave it a gentle squeeze. "We'll be back in a few."

"What do you think?" Max said when they were halfway down the hall. "Did he give you that cockamamie story about hearing voices?"

"What makes you so sure it's cockamamie?" Colleen pushed open double doors that led out to the parking lot.

"It's no different than saying a little bird told me. He's covering for someone."

"You don't think there's any truth to what he's saying?"

Max put his hand to his forehead and rubbed his temples. "You mean to tell me you're buying that shit?"

She crossed her arms and leaned against an M.D.C. squad car. A light breeze blew her hair back from her face. "What if he's telling the truth?"

"I've been around this occult, mumbo-jumbo shit for years and I have yet to see genuine psychic phenomena. All it ever turns out to be are paranoid delusions."

Her lips tightened. "You're right, but even if the kid is making it up, it won't hurt to humor him if it gets us the information we need."

Max held up a finger to argue and caught himself. He rubbed the back of his neck. "You're right. I'm sorry. I should know better. I'm too tired. Not thinking straight."

She smiled. "Now you're making sense. From what he's told me, whoever's doing this is connected to the mission, and if you ask me, that creep Sullivan is our number one suspect."

"You should have seen him getting ready to work the kid over." He stopped, realization dawning in his mind. "I'm pretty sure it was Sullivan I saw picking up Father Derlen and the transient Nick's been talking about."

"You think Derlen's part of it?"

Max held his palms up. "I'm not sure what to think. A lot of it depends on what Nick says. If that man was burned, Derlen could have been the last person to see him alive. What does that tell you?"

Colleen frowned. "Father Derlen? Involved in murder?"

"We won't know anything for sure until we talk to him. He may be in danger. Our first priority is to pump Nick some more. The second is to sweep the area for a crime site, third, infiltrate the mission."

"I can send a squad to the mission to put him under protective custody."

Max shook his head. "Let's not alarm anybody. You know what kind of connections he has. I want to be absolutely sure so when we move, it can be decisive. First Nick. You're better at handling him. I'll follow your lead."

"We're due to go out on a search party with the M.D.C. in a couple of hours. Nick says he saw someone torched up here last night and he thinks he knows where."

"He dreamed it."

"Doesn't matter. He needs a show of good faith. Let's take him out ahead of time and see what he does."

"Without the M.D.C.?"

"He gets nervous around all those uniforms. You can't blame him after the way Sullivan treated him."

Max heard an edge in her voice. She wanted to protect the kid. Maternal instinct. Best give her the tiller here. "You've been right about him so far. If that's what you want, I'm putting it in your hands. We're running out of time."

O'Grady nodded and brushed past him, trailing a faint trace of perfume which Max followed back to the office. They found Nick dozing with his feet up on the desk.

He jumped to his feet when he spotted Colleen. "Sorry. I'm falling behind on my sleep."

"You aren't the only one," Max said. "We have a favor to ask, then you and I are both going to get some sack time."

Nick frowned. "Favor?"

"The clock's running," Colleen said. "If we got you close, could you lead us to the place where you saw the man being burned?"

Nick's eyes grew wide. "You believe I saw it?"

Max sat on the edge of the desk. "Let's just say we're giving you the chance to prove it."

Nick stared down at the floor, then pressed his palms to his eyes. "I can't explain it, but I felt like we were close when we passed Camp Sayre."

"Then Camp Sayre it is." Colleen grabbed her overcoat from a rack. "Let's get moving, fellas. I'll drive." Nick and O'Grady traded smiles.

It felt to Max like they were wasting time, but Nick had warmed up to O'Grady and she had taken a shine to him. Maybe the excursion would loosen him up. He'd see that they wanted to help. Might even give up his source.

They took O'Grady's unmarked, she and Nick in front, Max in the back listening to them chatter as if he weren't there. She seemed to genuinely like the kid and opened up to him more than she ever had with anyone else and Nick definitely lowered his walls with her. She did a great job of getting him to talk. He had never seen her this relaxed around anyone.

Part way down Unquity Road, Nick stopped talking and turned his head to the side as if listening, then he sat up straight and looked quickly from side to side.

"What is it?" Colleen said.

Nick waved his hand up and down. "Slow down. We're close."

Max leaned forward, thinking that the kid knew, but was putting on an act so they didn't press him for the name of his informant. "How do you know?"

"I can feel it. Pull over. Down there." He pointed to a dirt road off to the left. "Follow it as far as you can."

"This better be good." Max looked ahead and thought he saw tire tracks, but couldn't be sure because of the leaves covering the ground. Colleen eased the car down the dirt tracks until the frame scraped on the bottom.

"This is far enough," Max said. "I'm too damned tired to have to get out and push."

"You're right." She put the car in park, cut the engine and they stepped out. Colleen popped open the trunk and traded her pumps for a pair of Reeboks. While she tied them, Max checked out the surrounding woods.

Washed out sunlight trickled through the trees and a cool breeze rattled the leaves at their feet. Except for a few pines dotting the hillsides, the woods were barren. A crow cawed off in the distance as if giving them a warning.

"This way." Nick pointed to where the road turned into a foot path. O'Grady pulled her jacket tighter and followed. Max took up the rear. No one spoke.

Nick went a few hundred yards, stopped, turned to his left and set off at a right angle to the road. Max listened and heard nothing but the unseen crow, dried leaves crunching beneath their feet, and the sound of running water.

They came to a stream at the base of a steep hill. Nick studied the water a moment, then looked up the hill.

"Far enough," Max said. "If you think I'm climbing that you *are* nuts."

"We're close," Nick said in a low voice. "I can feel it."

"That's what you've been saying all along."

Colleen turned to Max. Her expression said she wanted to push to the top of the hill.

"Okay," Max said. "Top of the hill. We don't see something by then, we turn back. Fair enough?"

Nick jumped from boulder to boulder, crossing the creek in three steps. O'Grady followed, moving gracefully from rock to rock like a dancer. Max slipped on his third hop. "Son-of-a-bitch!" Icy water filled his shoes making the bones in his feet ache. He clambered onto the far bank.

Nick and O'Grady were already halfway up the incline. Max leaned into the hill. The effort made breathing harder, aggravating the pounding in his head. His feet and shins were cold and wet, his shoes caked with mud. He crested the hill and found Nick standing motionless, both hands pressed to his head. O'Grady stood beside him frowning.

"We're wasting too much time," Max said between gritted teeth. "Let's turn back. Let the M.D.C. do their job."

Nick stiffened, then grabbed O'Grady's arm. "This is it." He pointed to a small rise. "Other side of that."

Max looked from Nick to O'Grady.

"Come on Max", she said. "A little further."

Nick had already started.

"We don't find it there, we go back," he said.

She hurried after Nick.

Max followed. The faint smell of burnt wood hung in the air. When he reached the base of the hill, he saw Nick and O'Grady next to a huge boulder near the top. When Max caught up, the three worked their way around the side of the rock.

Nick stopped short. O'Grady gasped.

Max came around behind them and looked down into a grove of oaks. The remains of a bonfire lay at its center. "Could have been campers," Max said.

The color drained from Nick's face. His eyes looked as if they would jump out of their sockets. His head went from side to side. "Not campers," he whispered. "Guys in robes. With hoods. Tied the guy to a cross. Threw him into the fire. God. His eyes. Like an animal. And mistletoe on his head." Nick's color flooded back. His breathing came short and fast. "Ta Ra Nis. That's what they chanted. His hair. It exploded. His skin bubbled." Nick dropped to his knees and grabbed his stomach. O'Grady knelt beside him with her hand on his back.

"Calm down, Nick. It's all right."

"Black." Nick gagged. "The smell." He vomited.

The wind kicked up rattling dead leaves and the crow let out a mournful cry. Colleen looked up at Max, her eyes questioning. "Believe him now?"

Max shook his head. "Could still be a campfire." He walked down toward the center of the grove. He heard O'Grady helping Nick up, then their footsteps behind him.

He hated to admit it, but the fire had been bigger than a campfire. He squatted beside it and pressed his hand to the coals. "No heat," he said. "Could've been here for days." Picking up a stick, he stirred the ashes. Nothing. "Sorry, Nick, I'm still not convinced. Do you realize how many fires…"

"Does this make a believer out of you?" O'Grady said.

Max turned back to face her. She held up a sprig of mistletoe.

CHAPTER FORTY

The smell of burnt wood mixed with the bile in the back of Nick's throat. At least he hadn't hurled on himself -- or Lieutenant O'Grady. He retched again, but nothing came up. Wiping tears from his eyes with the back of his sleeve, he took a deep breath and stared at the mistletoe O'Grady had found. Max studied it, then looked over the surrounding area before his gaze came to rest on Nick. "You going to make it, partner?"

"I'll be all right."

"Looks like we'll have to get Geist and someone from the M.D.C.'s forensics squad," Colleen said, taking her cell phone from her pocket. "I'll make the call and go wait for them."

"We'll wait here," Max said. "I want a closer look."

O'Grady disappeared over the top of the hill.

"Congratulations." Max put his hand on Nick's shoulder. "Looks like you've given us something."

Max twirled a mistletoe sprig between his thumb and forefinger, then nodded toward the blackened circle. "It has all the signs of a ritual pyre and the mistletoe is pretty damn convincing, but I don't believe a little voice told you where to find it. It would really help if you gave us your source. We'll protect them if that's what you're worried about."

After the voice, the dream, and finding this place, Nick even surprised himself, but this hard ass still didn't believe him. "I don't know how many times I have to tell you, there ain't no source. You don't believe me, that's your own tough shit. I brought you here, didn't

I?"

Max held up his hands. "Okay, okay." He pointed to a log. "Take a seat over there and relax. You still look a little pale. And be careful where you step. We don't want to disturb any evidence." He jerked his thumb back toward the woods. "I'm going to take a look around."

Nick propped himself on the edge of the log and stared at the blackened ring. His stomach still felt queasy. He studied the boulders he remembered hiding behind in his dream while the man in the trench coat burned. Being here proved that the whole thing had actually happened -- except the part where the hooded men dragged him down. What did that mean?

He put his head in his hands and rubbed his eyes. If Broderick the magician wasn't doing the killing, then who? Sully? The man -- if that's what you could call him, was twisted enough, but too stupid. Sully knew something though. Had to. He always showed up at the weirdest times, especially around Saint Augustine's.

It *had* to be someone inside the mission. Someone Nick hadn't seen yet. Sully was always there to make sure he couldn't get close, so how could he get in?

The crow cawed again as if taunting him. Nick looked up into the trees, then down at the ground, his eyes coming to rest on the fire ring. A dull glint in the dirt at the edge of the dark circle caught his attention. He crossed the clearing, knelt beside the remains of the fire and picked up a blackened piece of metal. He blew it off and turned it over in his palm. A button. He went back to his perch on the log and studied it. Probably came from the poor bastard's jacket.

Nick heard leaves rustling and looked up to see Broderick emerge from a thicket of trees.

"Find anything?" Nick said.

Broderick shook his head. "Some tire tracks, but nothing solid. Looks like there's more than one way in."

Nick held out the button. "I found this next to the fire. Looks like it came from a jacket."

Max took the button and held it up. "Trenchcoat?"

"That's what I thought."

Max stared at the fire circle, then did a slow turn while studying the bent oaks surrounding the hollow. "Classic druid ritual spot." He stared at the button again. "I've seen all I need to see. Let's go find O'Grady and let the other guys come in and do their job before we disturb it any more."

"No argument from me. This place gives me the fucking willies." Nick stood and a wave of blackness engulfed him. He swayed and grabbed at Max's arm, then his mind cleared.

"You all right?"

He shook his head. "Whew. Sorry. I'm okay. Passed out for a second there. Guess I do need some sleep."

"Amen."

When they reached the top of the hollow, Nick took one last look at the remains of the pyre. The phantom crow let out a mournful cry. Nick flashed on the silent scream and the agonized face of the man he saw burned. Shuddering, he drew his jacket closer, but it didn't stop the chill. He turned and hurried to catch up with Broderick.

Twenty minutes later, they found Lieutenant O'Grady back at the car talking with four M.D.C. cops and pointing in the direction of the oak grove. Broderick joined the discussion. Nick felt too drained to care about cop talk, so he climbed into the front seat of the car, slouched back and closed his eyes.

The sound of car doors jolted him awake. O'Grady climbed in the driver's side and gave him a smile. Broderick stretched out in the back seat. The two M.D.C. cruisers backed down the road to let them out. A handful of uniformed cops stayed behind to check out the oak grove.

Nick looked in the rearview mirror on the drive back to Dorchester. Broderick had passed out. The mistletoe and the button. Proof that they burned the guy. Proof that they probably killed Obie and other street people along with victims with families who cared about them. Cops didn't give a shit about people on the fringes. Neither did the system for that matter. Didn't even care if they existed -- unless they became an eyesore to businesses with money and political pull.

"You okay?" O'Grady said.

"Just thinking."

"Penny for your thoughts."

Nick sighed. "I was thinking that I've known Obie all my life."

"Obie?"

"The man was a neighborhood fixture as far back as I can remember. Used to buy beer for us. We'd all pitch in and give him a couple of bucks for making the run. Then one day, poof!" Nick threw his hands into the air. "Gone."

"Where?"

Nick pointed back over his shoulder. "No doubt to the same place as that poor bastard who got roasted. Sure Obie didn't pay taxes and his stink and bad breath were nothing to brag about, but he was a human being with thoughts and feelings."

She pursed her lips and nodded. "Hate to say it, but you're right. Most cops feel that way."

"Bad attitude."

"Can't argue, but we're not all that way."

"Who do you know that's different?"

"Broderick." She lowered her voice. "He can be a son-of-a-bitch but he really cares. Doesn't matter how much someone takes a bath, Max wants to save everybody. That's why he's so goddamn stubborn." She shook her head.

They pulled out of Unquity road and headed down the Blue Hills Parkway. Nick checked the rear view mirror again. Broderick hadn't moved. It sounded strange to hear O'Grady call him Max, but not as weird as hearing her say that he cared about street people. "If that's what makes him so bull-headed, more power to him."

"He wants to put the bad guys out of business."

They drove the rest of the way without talking. When they turned onto Dorchester Ave. she asked him for his address. He told her and she drove to the apartment, parking behind Mike's car. Nick hoped Mike or his mother wouldn't see him getting out of a cop car, even if Max and O'Grady were plainclothes.

"What are you guys going to do?" he said when she put the car into park. "I want to help."

"Thanks for the offer but you've done more than enough. We can't put you at risk. Stay here until we tell you otherwise." She fished through her purse and pulled out a business card. "Call the number on the back."

"You saying I'm grounded?"

"I want to make sure you're safe."

"But I want to help."

"Give us the name of your contact," Max said from the back seat. Nick looked in the rearview mirror and saw Broderick rubbing his eyes. "I liked you better when you were asleep."

Max leaned forward and squeezed Nick's shoulder. "You change your mind sport, give us a call, otherwise stay put. For what it's worth, as far as the bag of crack and the gun go, they don't exist, but I don't want you out on the streets until this thing is over. If our friends find out how much you know, it's going to be your ass on the campfire. Cabeesh?"

Nick looked from Max to O'Grady, who nodded.

"How will I know when it's over?"

"We'll give you a call," Max said.

He sighed. "Okay. Thanks for the break." He shook hands with Max. "And thank you", he said to O'Grady. "For listening and believing." He shook her hand, then let himself out of the car. Before closing the door, he popped his head back in. "One more thing."

She raised an eyebrow. "Yes?"

"I think you're beautiful." He closed the door and turned away before she could respond. His face felt hot. He heard the car pulling away from the curb but didn't dare look back.

Unlocking the door, he trudged up the steps. Right now he didn't care about anything but copping some z's. Maybe the caped crusader and his beautiful sidekick would nail the bad guys. Maybe the voice would stop?

He chuckled at the thought of Broderick and O'Grady wanting him to stay put. If the voice came again there was no way he could stick around. Whoever was behind it had to be stopped, especially after seeing his nightmare alive and well in the Blue Hills.

He paused at the apartment door and calmed himself. He wasn't ready for another exchange with Mike. He stuck the key in the lock, grabbed the knob, and let himself in. Strange, no noise from Mike or his mother. Were they asleep? Not this early in the afternoon. Maybe they were doing the wild thing? The thought of Mike grunting and sweating on top of his mother made him uneasy. He tip-toed down the hall, listening.

Nothing.

Panic rushed through him. He wished Sully hadn't taken his gun. It would have been a welcome reassurance. When he reached the kitchen he spotted Mike's keys on the table. An envelope lay beside it. Dropping into a chair, he saw a note in his mother's neat script. Underneath it he found a twenty dollar bill and a note.

Dear Nicky,

Mike and I went to New Hampshire for the weekend with the Hinchliffes. We'll be back sometime Sunday night. Here's twenty dollars for food or whatever. If you need anything call me.

Love,

Mom

Friday already? Christ, he didn't even know what day it was any more. He eyed Mike's keys. Must've taken the Hinchliffe's car.

After a glass of milk and a peanut butter and jelly sandwich, Nick climbed into bed. He closed his eyes and tried to relax. Images of the burning man and the smell of fire hung at the periphery of his mind.

He pushed them aside and replaced them with thoughts of Lieutenant O'Grady. His hand went to the bandage on his head. He remembered the soft touch of her fingers in his hair, her perfume, voice, legs, body, luscious smile and those green eyes. A twinge of arousal passed through his groin.

He tried to hold onto her memory, but the face and smell of the burning man forced itself to the forefront of his thoughts. How did a gorgeous babe like Lieutenant O'Grady get involved in crazy shit like this? And what about that hard ass Broderick? Were they more than partners? You couldn't tell when they were together, but the way they talked when they were apart said a lot. Whatever their relationship, they made a good team. He hoped they would put an end to the voice and the butchering.

He drifted. Lieutenant O'Grady, Broderick, Sully, the voice. Where had it taken him?

CHAPTER FORTY ONE

"You know he's not going to stay put," Max said from the back seat. "First chance he gets, he'll be running the streets trying to get himself killed."

Colleen nodded. "We ought to put a man on him to make sure he doesn't go anywhere." She turned onto Park Street and headed toward the Dorchester gas tanks.

"That's what I was thinking. If he does go gallivanting he might lead us to his source." Max rubbed the stubble on his cheek. "Most likely Sullivan's in the middle of this shit. There's no telling who else at District Eleven might be involved. We need someone from outside."

"If Sully found out where Nick was he might try to get to him."

"Amen to that." Max studied Colleen in the rearview mirror. Her forehead wrinkled in concentration, then her eyes brightened. She looked up at the mirror and her gaze found Max's. "How about Flynn?"

Max leaned over the front seat. "Flynn?"

"You've only seen his bad side," O'Grady said. "He might be obstinate and petty, but he's thorough and we can trust him."

"After that shit he pulled at Savin Hill?"

"Macho turf shit. You made a lot of points in his book by the way you evened the score. Even though he drinks like a fish, when it comes to taking care of business and getting the job done, no one does it better than Flynn."

Max leaned back. Maybe she was right. Flynn's reports came in as they were supposed to and he did his assignment like a trooper, and Max knew how hard that must've been. Why waste the manpower? Besides, if O'Grady said he could be trusted. "You were right about the kid and you know Flynn better than I do. If you think he's the man get on the horn. I don't want anything happening to Nick."

She made the call and put her cell on speaker phone. By the time they pulled onto the Southeast Expressway, Flynn's gravelly voice filled the car. "Flynn here."

"Hey Flynn," Colleen said. "You tired of hanging around with a bunch of stiffs?"

"Tired ain't the word."

"We got a live one for you. Can you meet me downtown in an hour?"

"I'll be there."

She hung up and glanced at the mirror. "What next?"

"Saint Augustine's."

"After you get some sleep. You're no good to me this way. I'll drop you off at your hotel, brief Flynn, and go back to the Blue Hills to see what Geist has. I'll call you if anything breaks." She pulled off the expressway and eased the unmarked into downtown traffic.

She's right, Max thought. He could get some solid rack time, then go into the mission under cover with the rest of the transients and have a look behind the scenes. "After you finish your business with Flynn and Geist, can you get two backup squads? We need good undercover men from somewhere other than Eleven, that way if anything happens you can send them after me."

"Done."

"Thanks. You've been a real asset. Picked up the slack and came through when I needed you."

She smiled. "Just doing my job."

Max closed his eyes wondering if she really knew how much he appreciated her. He was used to working solo. Having her backing him felt different. First time in a long time he had a partner he could rely on. When this thing ended she deserved dinner at the most expensive restaurant in town and he'd make sure the brass knew how efficient she was.

He felt the car slow to a stop, opened his eyes, and saw his hotel. "Call me with any new developments."

"Got you covered."

"Thanks, partner." He reached over the front seat, squeezed her shoulder, then climbed out of the car. He saw her smile in the rear view mirror as she pulled away.

He took the elevator up to his room. A heavy-set older woman with a fur jacket, too much makeup, and an overdose of perfume stepped in beside him. She glanced at his feet when the door shut, wrinkled her nose, and moved to the far side of the elevator.

What's her problem? he thought, looking down to see his mud-caked shoes and pants. He looked up again. She stared straight ahead. "You're probably wondering..."

"How they let a vagrant like you into this establishment," she snapped. "You're a disgrace."

His anger flared, but he caught himself. He was too tired to give a shit. "I had an accident with my dog," he said, feeling giddy. "I thought I had him paper-trained." He looked down at his shoes. "I guess he missed. Could I borrow a handkerchief?"

She gasped and punched at the buttons. The elevator stopped and she hurried off. "Don't suppose you know any good trainers," he said as the doors closed behind her.

The elevator took him up to his floor where he stepped out and started toward his room. Tomorrow he would go in under cover and find something solid to connect the mission to the murders, then he'd call in the troops. He had no doubt that Sully was working with someone inside the mission.

He thought of Flynn and found himself smiling. O'Grady was right to take him off that bullshit stakeout. He'd make sure Flynn got some credit and had a key part in the bust.

He rounded a corner, stepped around a maid's cart and a linen hamper. The door to his room stood open. He heard the tinny sound of the radio playing a country western station.

"Hello?" He went in and looked in the bathroom. "Almost done?"
He heard movement behind him. Before he could turn, strong arms grabbed him. Someone threw a towel over his head. "Almost."

A male voice.

Max opened his mouth and smelled chloroform. He thrashed from side to side and coughed. The sound echoed through his brain as it followed him down into oblivion.

CHAPTER FORTY TWO

Nick's heart kicked like a horse trapped in a burning stall when he opened his eyes to darkness. He took a long, trembling breath, closed his eyes and tried to pick up any traces of a dream, but nothing rose to the surface.

He listened for anything out of the ordinary. Silence. Rolling onto his side he looked at his clock. Five after four in the morning. He had slept for close to twelve hours. He put his hand to his chest and breathed in deep. Why did his heart beat so hard? Had the voice returned? He closed his eyes and braced himself for its onslaught.

Five minutes passed. His heartbeat slowed. Still no voice, but the feeling of something out of kilter persisted. He swung his feet over the edge of the bed. Sure as hell couldn't sleep anymore. He put water on for coffee, took a shower and sat at the kitchen table. As the first gray streaks of dawn filtered into the kitchen, Nick sifted through his thoughts, stifling the impulse to go to St. Augustine's. Broderick and O'Grady would be pissed if he showed up there. He didn't care if he pissed off Broderick, but he wanted to stay on the good side of O'Grady.

But if he sat here, he'd go shithouse.

The nightmare murders definitely came from inside Saint Augustine's and whoever was responsible for them had Sully as a partner. Now Sully ran wild helping some weirdo religious fanatic chop people up. What if Sully knew where he was and planned on coming after him?

His father's words answered the thought. "Someone fucks with you Nicky, don't sit on your ass waiting for them to come after you. They'll see it as weakness. Take the fight to them. It'll catch them off guard. If nothing else, you'll get their respect."

Nick didn't care about respect from Sully. That was like getting respect from a maggot. He did care about Lieutenant O'Grady. He put his head in his hands and stared at the tabletop. His sense of urgency grew. He looked at the note his mother left, the twenty dollar bill, and Mike's keys.

Okay, the mission was off limits, but he had a score to settle with Sully. He grabbed Mike's keys. Mike would have a shit fit if he knew, but the only way he'd find out is if someone snitched or took his parking space out on the street.

Nick pulled on his jacket and went to the front window. If he knew Broderick, there'd be a dick outside in an unmarked babysitting. He looked up and down the street. Sure enough, two cars away from Mike's Chevy sat a Boston Police unmarked, obvious as hell by trying so hard not to be obvious.

Nick let himself out the back door and tip-toed down the steps. When he reached the first floor he peered out the door. At first he saw nothing, then the glow of a cigarette caught his attention. He could slip by this one but if the cop in the unmarked was passed out, he'd wake up when he heard Mike's engine. Had to fake him out too. Nick eased the back door open and crawled down the porch steps, then walked to the front of the alley and looked over the top of the fence. One dick. Front seat.

Nick bolted from the alley, turned right and ran hard down the street. The car's engine started behind him followed by the sound of tires on asphalt. Nick took a few more steps, then darted into an alley. Tires squealed to a stop as he rounded the corner of the building. He jumped the back fence and ducked behind a large tree. The cop ran down the alley, stopped at the fence and cursed. Nick listened to the man's labored breathing. Had to be a fat boy. The man ran back to his car and drove away. Nick hopped the fence again and hurried back up the street to Mike's car. After pulling into the street he put a trash can in its parking place to save it and drove off.

Two minutes later he drove down Dot Ave. wondering how to track down a cop. He turned onto Gibson Street and drove past District Eleven. He glanced at the dashboard clock. Ten minutes 'til six. If Sully worked nights, he'd be getting off soon. If he worked days he'd be coming on -- unless he had a day off.

Nick made a U-Turn at the end of Gibson and drove toward the station. A car pulled away from the curb out front. Nick took the empty spot and killed the engine. He looked in the back seat and spotted an old copy of the *Globe* buried under a pile of empty Budweiser cans. He pulled it out, opened the passenger window a crack and unfolded the paper in front of him.

At seven-ten, he saw Lieutenant O'Grady heading straight for him. Shit, busted, he thought, sinking lower in the seat. She passed the car without noticing.

Twenty minutes later, Sully strutted through the front door in civvies, stopping in front of the station to laugh and joke with two other cops. When they finished, the two cops walked in Nick's direction. Sully went toward Field's Corner. Nick waited until he walked halfway up the block before starting the engine.

He knew where Sully was going.

Driving past him, Nick turned onto Dot Ave. and parked three cars up from Saint Augustine's. Sully appeared in the rear view mirror, coming around the corner heading straight for the mission.

After waiting ten minutes, Nick grew edgy. Best get out of there before Broderick and O'Grady saw him. He drove down to Park Street, locked the car, and set out on foot.

The answers to everything lay inside the mission but every time he tried to scope it out someone stopped him. So much for frontal assaults. Maybe the back door would be better. He went down an alley and hopped a couple of fences until he reached the rear of the building.

Trying to get in the boarded up first floor would be too noisy. The only other way in seemed to be a partially open third floor window within reaching distance of the fire escape.

After checking both ends of the alley, Nick pulled himself up onto the edge of a dumpster and jumped for the bottom rung of the escape ladder. Rusty iron creaked and the steps lowered with a groan that should have brought the whole neighborhood running. Nick scrambled up the steps when it touched the ground, stopping at the second floor and wiped sweat from his brow. So far, so good.

He sprinted up to the third floor and climbed over the fire escape railing. Pressing against the side of the brick building, he hung on with his left hand while stretching to reach the partially opened window. He found a firm grip on the sill and swung out so he could grab with his left hand. He didn't dare look down.

He pushed up on the window and had a moment of panic when it didn't move. His arms started to ache. He'd have no choice but to punch it out and crawl in over broken glass. He drew in a shaky breath, pulled himself up and pushed his arm into the opening until his armpit slid over the sill, then pushed with his shoulder. The edge of the window dug into him, pain flared, and the window screeched up a few inches. He could almost fit his head in, but not quite. He let his body go limp. Sweat soaked his chest and neck and his arm went numb. One more try.

Kicking with his feet, he inched his shoulder further into the opening, then pushed, using more of his back. Another screech. Damn. With this much noise they'd be all over him like stink on shit. He pushed his head through, worked his second arm in and wriggled his way onto the worn wooden floor of a tiny hallway where he sat against the wall to catch his breath.

A stairwell on his left led to the lower floors. One door stood across from him and two stood at each end of the hall. The scent of disinfectant undercut by the smell of rescue mission food, kitchen sounds, and the murmur of voices drifted to him from below.

He stood and pressed his ear to it, then tried the knob. To his surprise it clicked open into a small apartment.

The walls were decorated with yellowing, flowered wallpaper. He walked through a small sitting room with spindly furniture into a tiny kitchen with an old gas stove and a dinette set. The only thing of any value was a flat screen T.V.. If he found evidence it would have to be something solid. Didn't look like Father Derlen knew anything. Better get the hell out of here. He put his hand on the doorknob and heard someone coming up the stairs.

Shit! Where could he hide? He spotted an open closet.

The footsteps reached the top of the stairs. Nick ran for the closet and heard the apartment door open. Stepping sideways between hanging clothes, he pulled the door behind him, stopping short of closing it so it wouldn't make noise. He peered through the crack and flashed on his nightmare vision of hiding in a closet with a sickle.

The apartment door clicked shut. The footsteps stopped. Whoever it was had to be standing at the entrance. Nick wondered if they had seen or heard him. He breathed in and out slowly, half expecting the closet door to fly open.

Two steps. Toward him. Another pause. What the fuck were they doing? Straining to hear or see, he leaned toward the sliver of light between the door and the jamb.

The door slammed shut in his face, followed by the sound of a key and the click of a lock.

CHAPTER FORTY THREE

Max opened his eyes to darkness. Had he been blinded? His feet were tied to the legs of a chair, his hands bound behind its back. He shook his head. Blindfolded. Dryness hung in the back of his throat like the time he woke up in the recovery room after being shot. Ether. His head felt stuffed with cotton. Everything seemed fuzzy. Where was he? What happened?

He tried to concentrate. His hotel? Someone jumped him from behind and it wasn't Flynn and his boys playing turf games.

"Fucking magic man."

Sully. Off to his left. He snorted. "Glad you could make your final appearance. You thought you were such a hot shot. Well guess what? You ain't shit. I never told you this, but I'm a magician myself. Check this out." Max heard the rustle of clothing. "Poof! You're a bag of shit."

Pain exploded across his midsection. He struggled for air, but his breath wouldn't come.

Sully broke into a fit of giggles. Max heard others laughing behind him.

"What's the matter? You ain't got much to say now, do you tough guy?"

Max forced himself to breathe in. "Fuck you, asshole," he growled.

A hand slapped him on the side of his head. His ear rang.

"Still got a mouth. That red-headed bimbo you've been running with had a mouth too, but she was tougher than you -- and let me tell you something." He lowered his voice. "Best pussy I ever had. Best pussy *we* ever had, right boys?"

More laughter.

Max's gut tightened.

"Made me feel bad about taking her out. She was a real tiger in the sack. I don't know if she would have been as much fun without her hands and legs tied to the bedposts. What do you think, Broderick? She any good for you?"

Max's breath came hard and fast. A tidal wave of rage engulfed him. He wanted to yell, cry, and kill all in the same moment. "You're full of shit, Sully." He struggled to keep his voice from shaking. "There's no way you could've done anything with O'Grady."

"Why not?"

"You're a dickless wonder."

The room grew quiet. Max braced himself. Footsteps passed on his right, then came back. "You think so, huh?" He felt fetid breath on the side of his face. Sully's voice sounded low and strained, almost a whisper. "Let me tell you something, Mr. Hotshot Fed. Bitch had all the moves, even with her legs tied and spread-eagled, but they weren't anywhere near as exciting as the moves she had when we ran the sickle from her crotch to her neck. Talk about a twitch."

Can't give this son-of-a-bitch the pleasure of thinking he got to me. "You're so full of shit I can smell it."

"Is that right? Maybe this will make a believer out of you." A hand yanked his head back by the hair, then another jammed a piece of cloth over his nose and mouth. The scent of Dare invaded his senses. Blackness threatened to swallow him.

How could he have been so stupid? They murdered her because he took too long to figure out who they were.

The hands let go. Cool air rushed into his lungs. Traces of her perfume lingered. Colleen gone. He couldn't believe it. His throat constricted and his eyes burned. He was thankful the blindfold kept them from seeing his face.

"Hey, Sully." He sounded hoarse.

"Yesss?"

"I'm going to kill you."

A loud crack and a bright flash. His face stung and he tasted blood.

"I don't like your smart mouth, mister. I'm going to…"

A door opened.

"Father." Sully's tone shifted from antagonism to respect.

"What's going on here?"

Derlen.

"Broderick came to. We were preparing him."

"We don't have time for that now," Derlen snapped.

"Yes Father."

"I have the kid locked in. I need someone to get him out. I'm afraid it's going to take a little force."

"Yes Father."

A moment of silence, then the door closed.

"Hanson and Godin. Upstairs, Father Derlen's apartment. Take care of it."

"Okay Sully."

Max recognized the voice, but couldn't place it.

The door opened and closed again.

"Guess it's you and me now," Sully said. The malevolent tone had returned.

Max felt a sharp edge biting into his neck; no doubt a sickle. Sully leaned close, his rancid breath hot on the side of Max's face. Max could almost feel Sully's tongue touching his ear. He shuddered.

"Bye bye Broderick," Sully whispered and drew the point backward.

CHAPTER FORTY FOUR

No sound from the other side of the door. Nick stifled the impulse to yell. If they didn't know he was here, the noise would definitely bring them running.

Maybe they didn't know he had been locked in? Then again they might be listening. He couldn't wait to find out. He leaned back to kick the door down, stopping when he heard a creaking sound.

Another creak, then the sound of footsteps. The apartment door closed, followed by the latch sliding into place. Nick groped in the blackness until his hand found the doorknob. He turned it and slammed into the door with his shoulder but it didn't move. Fumbling through his pockets, he found a book of matches. Three left. Maybe he could find a spot behind him where he could dig through the plaster. He struck a match, pushed aside the hanging clothes and saw more darkness beyond the glow of the match. The closet seemed longer than it should be. He moved forward. Three, four steps. Still no back wall. The match scorched his fingers.

He let it drop and thought about lighting another, but decided against it. Holding his arm out he stepped sideways until his fingers found the wall, then started forward again keeping his hand in front while sliding one foot ahead of the other. Five more steps. Still no end. "This ain't a closet," he muttered. "More like a hall."

He saw a pale line of light on the floor about ten feet in front of him. He closed his eyes to let them adjust and opened them. The line swam into focus. Sliding forward, he reached the end of the passage and ran his fingers along the sides until he found a door jamb and a knob. He grasped it with sweaty fingers, took a breath, turned the knob and pushed.

Nothing.

He yanked toward him and the door swung open, banging him in the eye. Spots filled his vision. He put his hand over the stinging and wiped away the tears before stepping through.

In the grayness filtering through a bird-shit spattered skylight, he saw a narrow wooden staircase leading down to more darkness. Holding one hand over his eye, Nick grabbed the shaky railing and descended into the blackness.

He wiped his eye again at the bottom step and squinted into the dark, making out a strip of dim light through the crack of an open door. He moved toward it one step at a time listening for noises, hearing nothing but his own footsteps.

The door swung easily at his touch, opening into a dingy room. Washed-out light from a green painted window bathed everything in fuzzy outlines. Dark shapes hung from one wall. Shelves lined another. The musty smell of old plaster permeated the room.

Nick thought the dark shapes were long coats until he pulled one off a hook and recognized a hooded robe. It smelled of smoke. He moved down the wall fingering each one, half of him numb from his growing revelation, his other half grasping for an explanation to what was happening.

It seemed as if every detail of his nightmares had been laid out like pieces of an appalling puzzle dissected for inspection. Sickles, knives with odd, twisted blades, candles, rope, a leather harness, a sword, mistletoe, and a string of handcuffs connected by chain -- the kind cops used to move inmates from court to prison. On a bottom shelf he found an inverted skull, its jaw wired shut, its eyes, mouth and nostrils packed with something hard.

He grabbed one of the knives. If he was going down, he was going to take as many with him as he could, but he wasn't going to wait either.

Right now he was still alive.

He ran to the window, pushed and tried prying the edges with the knife, but it wouldn't give. The back of his neck tingled. He looked over his shoulder expecting to see someone, then stared back at the window. Fuck it. If they heard it break, he'd be long gone before they could catch him. He slammed the butt of the knife handle into the glass.

It shattered exposing a row of iron bars set in brick. Nick grabbed them and shook. Solid. He shoved his face against them and stared at a windowless brick wall on the other side of a narrow alley. He thought of shouting, but if someone came chances were it wasn't anyone he wanted to meet. If the breaking glass hadn't brought them running, nothing else would. Either they hadn't heard it or they knew they had him trapped.

The light from the window showed another wall lined with skulls from floor to ceiling. The skulls at floor level looked gray and weathered, the color of old sidewalks. The whiter ones near the top looked shiny like fresh bones chewed clean of their meat. A small pile of clothes lay at the base. Nick started toward them, heart pounding like a madman banging the walls of a padded cell.

Muddy shoes. He knelt down and touched the mud, crumbling it between his fingers. Still fresh. And a square, yuppie-looking jacket. He checked the pockets and pulled out a gold badge and an I.D.. Broderick's!

What the fuck was going on? The knife clattered to the floor and he dropped the jacket. His hand flew to his mouth. "No," he whispered. "Can't be."

He spotted another door. Were they waiting for him on the other side? He picked up the knife with trembling fingers. He backed away from the wall of skulls, yanked open the mystery door and stepped into the darkness, pulling the door shut behind him.

He smelled cedar. Holding his breath, he listened. Footsteps came down the stairs, into the room. He raised the knife. Someone paused outside, then the lock on the door clicked and the footsteps receded. No place to go but forward.

He inched ahead until something touched his face. A string. He grabbed it and tugged. Dim yellow light blinded him as a light bulb swung back and forth, then his vision cleared.

Obie's head swam into view.

Bile rose in his throat.

Obie's vacant eyes stared at him from behind the glass of an oil-filled jar perched on top of a stool like the frogs Nick remembered from biology class. Pink strips of tendon, muscle, and ganglia hung from his neck. Shadows cast by the light and dark of the swinging bulb made Obie's expression look as if he alternately smiled and frowned.

Nick gagged, stumbled backward, turned to run and tripped over his own feet. His arms flailed, the knife went flying and he went down, knocking the stool over.

Glass hit his face and the dark smell of cedar rushed into his senses. Oil splashed into his mouth and the head rolled toward him. He lost consciousness when Obie's wet nose came to rest against his cheek.

CHAPTER FORTY FIVE

"There is no escape."

The voice filled the darkness of Nick's mind, yet it sounded muffled as if coming from the other side of a wall. Where was he? His head felt fuzzy, his thoughts indistinct.

"You have no power to escape. What you once thought of as your own volition will soon be nothing more than an extension of my desire."

The words drew him closer to consciousness. What was that smell? Cedar. Bitter taste in his mouth. The side of his face felt slippery. Something soft and wet pushed against it.

"Your mind will belong to me!"

The last words jolted him fully awake. He opened his eyes to Obie's face pressed close to his. One vacuous eye stared directly at him, the other pointed toward the floor. Nick gagged and spit, then rolled backward and kicked at the head, sending it wobbling into a corner. Dizziness washed over him and his vision darkened.

Forcing himself to hold on to consciousness, he tried to breathe, but his breath came in short gasps. He pushed himself into the far wall and studied the floor. Yellow light glinted off shards of glass. A dark viscous puddle stained the middle where Obie's head had landed. Nick stared at the outline of its dark mass in the corner, looked higher and saw more jars. Keeping his back to the wall, he pushed himself up on shaky legs.

The heads of Lynn Ford, and Yvonne Perry swam into view

alongside other faces he didn't recognize. Every face wore its own version of mindless contemplation as if each one put every ounce of concentration into staring at nothing.

He put his head in his hands and turned away.

The voice drifted to him again. "A methodical deterioration of an already weakened will."

His scalp tingled. Definitely The Voice. No doubt about that, but it wasn't in his head. He looked at the far end of the room. Another door. Painted metal, with a large handle instead of a knob. He didn't want to think what might be behind it.

"Through sensory deprivation, trauma, drugged food and a need for acceptance which religion brings."

He pressed his ear to the wall. Derlen!

"Couple this with hypnosis and a relentless hammering of an individual's thought processes and you end up with a willing subject."

That's why he followed that poor son-of-a-bitch on the subway. *His* voice. The one responsible for the killing. What had he said? Sensory deprivation? Trauma?

Nick ran for the far door, jerked the handle, pulled the heavy door open and burst into chilled darkness. He spotted a switch behind him and flicked it. His stomach spasmed, doubling him over, then he wrapped his arms around himself and stared.

Two bodies. Side by side. Upside down. Headless. Arms cut off at the elbows. Legs spread. Meathooks through the ankles. Torsos split up the middle like sides of beef, stretched wide, exposing ribs and glistening, pinkish-white meat. He studied the smooth skin on the legs of one, then the hairy shins of the other. Male and female.

Broderick and O'Grady.

His knees buckled, then the sound of another door opening sent adrenaline flooding through him. He scrambled backward, looked around in panic and spotted the knife on the floor. He snatched it up and held it in front of him with shaking hands.

The door squeaked open and Sully strutted in, a broad smile filling his face.

A sick feeling sank in the pit of Nick's stomach.

Two men came in behind Sully. The first had huge shoulders that strained the seams of his shirt, crew cut black hair, and thick eyebrows. The other looked small and wiry, with quick, nervous movements and sharp features -- like a rat. Both had guns.

"It's all over, Powers," Sully said. "Put the blade away."

Nick waved the knife in front of him. "Come any closer, the only place this blade is going is up your ass."

Sully continued smiling. His two companions trained their guns on Nick, fanned out and started toward him. Sully came straight in.
"Come on, you son-of-a-bitch," Nick said. "You want a piece of this, come and get it."

Rat-face cocked his gun, followed by a second click. The gorilla.

Nick took a deep breath and let his arm drop to his side. Sully rushed in and Nick swung the knife with all his strength. The stroke floated up in a graceful arc. Sully's eyes widened and he staggered sideways. His hand hung out in open space for a timeless moment before the blade of the knife struck it, lopping off two fingers and nearly severing a third. Nick lost his grip and the knife clattered to the floor.

Sully's mouth stretched into a silent "O" and his face went ashen. He grabbed the damaged hand with his good one. His two smallest fingers remained intact. The middle one dangled by a string of ragged flesh.

At first it didn't look as if there would be any blood, then a rush of crimson burst from the stumps. Sully's face contorted and he let out a doglike howl that sounding like the mute button had been released on a too-loud television.

Huge arms came from behind and grabbed Nick in a bear hug, then smaller hands jammed a damp cloth over his nose and mouth.
He looked down through the growing haze and saw blood pooling beneath the two fingers on the floor. He coughed into the rag and remembered the smell from the time in the hospital when he had his tonsils out.

CHAPTER FORTY SIX

"It's quite an efficient system. Take the poor souls off the street and put an end to their suffering. When they've outlived their usefulness they become food for the others."

The voice again. Louder. As if it were both in and outside his head.

"A noble sacrifice and a realistic solution to an insurmountable problem."

It spoke with an even-tempered rationality that sounded convincing when you listened to the tone; confusing when you tried to comprehend its content. What was he saying?

Nick felt as if he became conscious in an out of control nightmare. He tried to get up, but couldn't move his arms or legs.

There is no need for fear. Soon you will be the first to honor the gods with a double offering.

Nick jumped as though shocked. Two voices. No. One voice. Two places. One in his head. The other close, but outside. He opened his eyes and stared up at the ceiling. A moment later Father Derlen's face swam into view.

"Welcome back, son. It's best for you to be conscious for the honor that awaits you." He smiled and stroked Nick's hair.

"Cut the little fucker up now! Let me do it." Sully's voice, strained and high-pitched, somewhere between a snarling animal and a screaming baby. Nick stiffened, remembering the arc of the knife and Sully's fingers thumping to the floor. He turned his head to the side.

Sully paced back and forth waving his bloody, rag-wrapped hand like a demented conductor. Spittle ran down his chin. Blood soaked his shirt. The rage in his bulging eyes scared Nick more than anything.

Sully glared at him and lunged. Derlen stepped between them. "I'll not tolerate that kind of language!" His voice had the harsh commanding tone that Nick had grown used to hearing in his head.

Remain calm, my chosen one. The voice in Nick's mind sounded soft and consoling. *No need to be upset. Your moment of glory is fast approaching.* "I told you to get medical attention for that hand." No longer harsh, the outer voice followed the inner without breaking rhythm. "You've lost a lot of blood. You're no good to me that way. Get it taken care of before it's too late." His last words sounded flat and unemotional.

Sully's gaze remained on Nick as if he stared *through* the old priest. "After I see the little bastard twitch and squirm under the sickle. I want to see inside him." Sully's words faded into a mumble. He started pacing again.

Father Derlen nodded toward a far corner. Rat-face and the Gorilla appeared on each side of Sully, who hung his head and pouted as each one took him by the arm.

"Please, Father," he cried, "let me stay." He raised his head and Nick saw tears streaming down his bloodless face.

"I'll have no more outbursts." *Yes, my chosen one. All is calm. Under control. No interruptions. Only serenity.*

Sully's lip quivered. He looked from Derlen to Nick and back again.

Someone cleared his throat. The closeness of the noise startled Nick. Someone was tied in back of him! Head to head. He strained to look behind him, but couldn't see.

"Sounds like your watchdog's having a bad day."

Nick couldn't believe what he heard. "Broderick!"

"Now we're both in deep shit. I told you to stay home."

Derlen's face hovered over Nick again. "You have no manners, Mr. Broderick. Maybe I should have let Mr. Sullivan continue with the sickle. If you insist on using that foul language, I'll have to gag you."

"Excuse me, Father, I shouldn't have been so rude. You're a man of principle, aren't you?"

Derlen's eyes flashed. *In a few short moments you will be the instrument to silence this blasphemy.* "I am that and much more."

Once more Nick had the sensation of the voice both in his mind and out, flowing in one continuous stream, like hearing music on headphones, then taking them off and hearing the same song on external speakers.

"So you drugged and hypnotized these poor bastards," Max said. "Programmed them to hide in closets and murder people. They come back, you butcher them for their troubles and feed their remains to the others. No muss, no fuss, no evidence, no traceable fingerprints. Nothing."

"You have to admit, it has a certain elegance."

The same maddening, matter-of-fact tone. Didn't this guy have any feelings? "He was talking in their heads!" Nick blurted.

Derlen stepped closer and studied Nick with narrowed eyes. "You've heard voices Mr. Powers?

"And little birdies," Max said. "If you haven't figured it out yet, the kid's not all there. Know what I mean?" He spoke faster. "Let him go. Nobody believes anything he says. He has a history of mental illness."

Derlen pursed his lips and leaned into Nick's face. "Is this true Mr. Powers?"

Nick's anger surged. "Fuck you!"

A flash of brightness and a loud crack, followed by a sharp sting on the side of his face. Sully let out a high-pitched giggle.

"I'll not have that language in my place of worship!" Derlen's nostrils flared and his face reddened. Sully's giggle stopped.

The slap stunned Nick into silence.

"Back off on the kid," Broderick said. "He doesn't know what he's talking about. I told you he has problems. I mean, come on, hearing voices?"

"You don't believe he heard voices Mr. Broderick?"

"Don't be ludicrous. He's a paranoid schizophrenic. Don't you see the signs?"

"I'm afraid I don't. Mr. Powers has a lot more on the ball than you give him credit for." Derlen stepped back. "If you understood what was happening the situation wouldn't look as bad as it appears."

Max snorted. "Human sacrifice and a kid who swears he's hearing voices and you say it's not as bad as it seems?"

"You've only touched on the real facts Mr. Broderick. The transformation is upon us. The gods have been waiting for these souls which are harbingers of the new age, setting the stage for the apocalypse. The cleansing. You are the last to make the cycle complete. These spirits that I give unto the gods are a sacrament to their power.

Take and eat of this for this is my body. The flesh of a new and everlasting covenant. It is an honor that many have died for. I have given the downtrodden immortality..." His voice trailed off. "I wouldn't expect you to understand."

Nick's cheek felt hot and tingly. His anger rose.

"What makes you so sure?" Max said. "Sully understood."

"Mr. Sullivan has been my novitiate since he came to me as an altar boy when I first started my journey with the Catholic church. We have shared a bond of love that only two men can give to one another. He understands the scope of our work and the nature of sacrifice." Derlen came close again, his voice rising in excitement. *These rituals are not for the living. They are for the dead.*

His voice reverberated both in and out of Nick's mind. As if the priest consciously addressed two levels, an inner audience and a separate outer one.

It is an honor to be given into the arms of the gods. He placed his hands together in a prayer like gesture. *Wretched souls like yours and the homeless who come to me are freed from their mortal shells to transmigrate to better places. The husks of flesh that remain behind feed the others who wait. The sacrament of flesh is a connection between the worlds.* He smiled and his eyes took on a far away look. *A perfect order, like that of the gods. Society's dross is assimilated and the homeless have a place to go.* He put his hands to his chest.

Nick studied his serene expression while the words insinuated themselves into his thoughts like burrowing worms. A shiver passed through him.

It is nature's way. Birth. Death. Rebirth. The cycle of life. The consumer becomes the consumed and new life springs forth to sustain the cycle.

The room fell silent, then Sully's high reedy whisper slithered through the quiet. "It's time Father."

Derlen looked up, lips unmoving. The voice spoke in Nick's mind. *It is time.*

Max started talking fast again. "These cops from Eleven are part of it?"

Derlen started toward the door. "We've been getting them transferred into the district for quite some time now under the guidance of Mr. Sullivan."

"Doesn't look like Sully's going to be in any condition to give anybody guidance. And Frick and Frack over there..."

The door closed. All Nick heard was the sound of breathing, his own and Broderick's. Where were Sully, the gorilla, and rat-face?

"Hey, Broderick," His voice sounded dry and raspy. "I'm scared shit."

"That's the first sane thing I've heard come out of your mouth."

"Is Lieutenant O'Grady coming with help?"

Max didn't answer.

Nick spoke louder. "I said…"

"They got to her before they got me."

The lights dimmed and darkness closed in.

"We're going down kid," Max said.

Nick heard a door open, followed by footsteps. He strained to raise his head, but could only see soft orange light dancing across the ceiling. A second glow came, then another and another. Each successive flame added to the one preceding it, until the whole room glowed. "What the fu…"

A hand clamped over his mouth and two hooded figures loomed above him. One held his head up while the other tied a gag over his mouth. Nick arched his back and tried to look behind him, glimpsing two men doing the same to Broderick.

"Be brave, Nick," Max said. "Don't give them the satisfaction of showing any fear." The last word came out muffled.

No fear, he told himself. No fear! He couldn't stop himself from shaking.

"To the goddess Andrasta, Taranis, Esus, Teutates." Derlen's voice filled the room. "We offer these lost souls unto you as a sacrament. A covenant between your world and this one." Then his voice rang through Nick's brain. *Come forth, my chosen one. The time has come to perform your sacred task.* Nick's stomach wrenched.

A chorus followed. "An-dras-ta. Ta-ra-nis. E-sus. Teu-ta-tes." Someone draped mistletoe across his chest and neck. The hoods closed in, passing a skull from one to the next, each taking a drink. Crimson ran down their fingers. The last drinker splashed the remaining contents of the skull in Nick's face. Warm stickiness covered his cheeks and forehead. His eyelids stuck together. He forced them open and stifled the urge to vomit, knowing if it let loose he'd choke. Maybe that would be better than the sickle? *Take the instrument. It is the key to your salvation.*

He saw blurry movement from the corner of his eye.

"Hear us great, great, Andrasta, hear us almighty Taranis, benevolent Esus, and sacred Teutates."

"Defend our secret enclave," came the chorus.

Take them, said the voice.

Nick's body shook with sobs.

"Revive our hopes," Derlen said. "Disperse our fears."

The blur loomed closer.

"Nor let thine altars be the interloper's spoil," came the chorus.

Nick scrunched his eyes shut.

When he opened them he saw the leering face of the man who tried to molest him, his garbage smelling breath hot on his face. The old transient's gaze locked on Nick's and softened, then his hand shot out. Nick stiffened as the man stroked his head.

Now is the time! Derlen's voice rose. *Do it! Make yourself complete.*

Nick felt the man's hand slide down over his groin. In spite of his terror, his anger surged and hate rose from his gut, burning itself into his throat and brain. How he hated the voice.

Now! Its volume made him jump.

The sickle flashed above him in the candlelight. Nick looked into the old man's eyes, then closed his and concentrated his thoughts, desperately focusing his hate and anger to the front of his head. Shaking with rage, he opened his eyes again and the sickle started to dip.

Fuck you! he screamed in his mind.

The old man staggered backward as if hit with a two by four. One of the hooded men put his hands to his ears.

Fuck you, you sick son-of-a-bitch! Nick screamed mentally. The old man swayed again, each word sending another jolt through him. He came toward Nick again. *Take him,* the voice said.

Cut the ropes! Nick yelled in his head with all his frantic emotion. *Free him and he's yours.*

"Stop," the old man growled. "Stop all the voices."

Kill him. Kill him now.

Cut the ropes!

The transient hacked at Nick's arm. The tip of the sickle slashed into him and the bonds loosened. Warm wetness flowed down his side. He wiggled and sat up. The transient stared at him, wild-eyed, the sickle still in hand.

What are you doing? The man who had covered his ears stepped forward. His hood dropped back, revealing Father Derlen's face. Nick waited for their eyes to meet. *Fuck you!*

The transient jumped.

Derlen blinked.

Get out of here!

The transient's eyes widened. He turned to Derlen.

How dare you turn from your duty. Stay!

And hack them all! Nick screamed in his thoughts. His head thumped. His arm throbbed. He cradled it in front of him. *The ones with the robes are your enemies. Stop them! They're coming for you!*

"No!" Derlen rushed forward as the man swung and the sickle caught him in the side of the neck, ripping his windpipe outward in a gush of red. He grabbed at his throat. A startled expression filled his eyes. Deep gurgling bubbled from the wound. The old man swung twice more before the robed men overwhelmed him. He cut two more before they wrestled the sickle from his grip.

Nick had forgotten about his own wound until he looked down at the pool of blood in his lap. He felt cold and lightheaded.

The transient disappeared beneath a sea of hoods, then the mob turned toward Nick. He tried to get away, but his legs were still tied. His head spun. He looked down at the blood again.

How much had he lost?

An angry horde of hands and robes rushed toward him. One of them grasped the sickle. Nick punched at them, but he had no strength. Arms and hands swarmed over him driving him backward and a deafening explosion slammed into his ears followed by the sound of splintering wood.

CHAPTER FORTY SEVEN

Max jumped at the sound of the gunshot. Its concussion in the closed room made his ears ring. He strained to look around, but his bonds kept his head immobile. He could only see the ceiling. He heard smashing wood and felt Nick slamming down above his head. The flurry of activity told him they had taken out the kid. Robed figures converged on him. Another gunshot and they scattered. Flynn's gravely baritone cut into the silence that followed. "Hit the deck or you're fucking dead!" he shouted. Footsteps followed. "Spread those arms and legs." His voice lowered. "Any one of these son-of-a-bitches even breathes funny, waste 'em."

Max never thought he'd be happy to hear Flynn's voice.

More scuffling.

His throat tightened when he saw O'Grady lean over him. Alive! His heart swelled. When she pulled off his gag he tried to speak, but no words came. She freed his arms while someone else untied his legs. He reached up and hugged her tight. Uniformed cops flooded the room. Hooded figures cowered on the floor. No sign of Derlen or Sully.

Max pulled away and saw his own blood staining her blouse. "My God, am I happy to see you. I thought you were dead."

She smiled weakly. Her face looked pale and drawn.

"Nick. Is he all right?"

"Doesn't look good."

Max turned and looked behind him. Nick lay on the blood-splattered altar, a weak spurt of blood pulsing from the wound in his arm. His eyes had glazed over. Two uniforms stared down at him wide-eyed. Max ripped off his shirt. "What the fuck are you gawking at? Do something!" He dove toward Nick, ignoring the stream of blood from the wound on his own neck.

The uniforms jumped and started untying Nick's feet.

"Radio ahead to Carney emergency," O'Grady said. "Tell them to have a trauma team ready."

Max made a tourniquet from his bloody shirt and tied it around Nick's upper arm. Nick blinked but didn't speak. His breathing came shallow. Max felt for his pulse. Irregular. He didn't like the cold and clammy feel of the kid's skin, either. As soon as the uniforms freed his feet, Max picked Nick up and ran for the door. His legs wobbled, but he pushed himself forward. O'Grady followed.

Two paramedics came in with a gurney. Max laid Nick on it and the two men strapped him in.

"The hell with that!" Max barked. "Get moving. He's lost a lot of blood."

A third medic blocked Max's way. "You need attention." He pushed a compress against the wound on Max's neck.

"Bullshit!" Max shoved the man aside and started after Nick. "Hang on, kid." He took Nick's hand and climbed into the ambulance behind the stretcher while a paramedic checked his vitals and prepared an I.V.. A second paramedic hooked up a portable E.K.G.. A weak rapid pulse shot across the screen.

"He's slipping!" the man yelled. "Pedal to the metal." The siren yelped and the ambulance jerked forward.

Max knelt beside Nick and listened to the medic calling Nick's fading vitals to the emergency room. He clutched Nick's cold hand and put his arm across his legs. "Don't quit on me, kid," he whispered.

They rode the short distance up Dorchester Ave. to Carney hospital. Max's own heart jumped each time an erratic line spiked across the screen.

At the emergency entrance they backed into the stall and the rear doors flew open. O'Grady screeched to a halt beside them in a squad car. Paramedics and nurses hustled Nick out of the ambulance. Max and Colleen followed them through the automatic doors to a waiting team of doctors and nurses who converged on Nick.

A steady tone pierced the air and a straight line showed on the

E.K.G.. "Fourteen c.c.'s of epinephrine, stat!" someone shouted. "He's gone asystole."

Max felt a rush of dizziness and staggered. His knees buckled. He sensed O'Grady catching him as the grayness turned to black.

CHAPTER FORTY EIGHT

Max stood at the rear of the crowd as the first flakes of winter snow drifted down on the hardened brown grass of Cedar Grove Cemetery. The priest's back was to him as the cleric sprinkled holy water over a bronze and copper colored coffin.

Max pulled his jacket tighter and tried not to shiver. No matter what he did, there was no warmth. He looked up at the leaden sky and remembered his mother's funeral. The weather had been the same and the landscape not all that different. Gray, barren trees, gray headstones, gray sky.

An icy wind cut through him. He shivered harder, then a sob rose in his chest. The wound on his neck ached. He glanced over at O'Grady. She looked pale and wan behind dark sunglasses. No doubt she felt as guilty as he did. They should have put the kid in protective custody.

The priest's words drifted to him on the wind. "Though I walk through the valley of the shadow of death, I shall fear no evil…"
The valley of death. He had spent more than his share of time in it and didn't think he could take any more. Especially after the kid. How had Nick sacrificed himself? What happened at the ritual?

"In the name of the Father, the Son, and the Holy Ghost."

The man's voice sounded familiar. The same somber monotone that all priests used at funerals.

Max wiped his eyes and studied the mourners, surprised that so many cops had shown up. In dress blues at that. He saw the profile of a heavy-set blonde woman clutching the arm of a lanky, dark-haired man. Must be the mother and boyfriend. How could he face them? He looked at O'Grady again. She hadn't moved.

He scanned the rest of the crowd. One of the uniformed cops stared back at him. Max squinted through the falling snow and saw a broad grin slowly filling the cop's face. What kind of a man would smile at a funeral?

The cop took off his hat and the wind gusted, driving itself into Max's chest as if a spectral hand had clamped its icy fingers into the soft flesh of his heart.

Sully.

Max rubbed his eyes and looked again. Sully came toward him, flanked by the weightlifter and his rat-faced sidekick, then the priest turned and joined them. Derlen. Max stumbled and fell. Before he could get back on his feet Derlen and Sully closed in, their hands sliding over his face and neck. His heart slammed and his breath locked in his chest. Blackness overwhelmed him. "O'Grady," he gasped. "Help me." He couldn't see her any more.

"I'm here, Max."

Hands felt soft on his forehead. His sight grew blurry, then Colleen's face filled his vision and the gray landscape of the cemetery faded into the pale white of a hospital room. She looked tired. Smiling, she gently wiped sweat from his forehead with a damp towel. "You're all right," she said. "I'm here."

A shiver wracked him. "Cold."

"Your fever's breaking."

"Nick!" The words barely came out. His throat felt dry and raspy. "Nick!" he said louder and tried to sit up.

O'Grady pushed him down. "Nick's fine."

"Alive?"

She nodded. "You both lost a lot of blood, but no permanent damage."

Max felt as if a lead blanket was lifted from him. "He made it?"

She patted his arm. He touched her hand and assured himself it was real, then closed his eyes and drifted back into the darkness.

The next time he opened his eyes the room looked dark. A dull throbbing pain pulsed in his throat. He reached up, gingerly touching a bandage, then looked through the curtains. A pink haze lined the horizon. He knew by the quiet it was dawn. He turned his head and saw

Colleen asleep in a chair beside his bed, a newspaper at her feet. Had she been there all night? More than one night? His first impulse was to wake her, but he stopped himself. She looked peaceful in sleep. He contented himself with watching her features becoming more defined in the growing light.

As the first rays of the morning sun brightened the room, he saw part of the headline.

SMASHES CULT

He flashed back on his nightmare and remembered waking to Colleen. It really had ended and Nick came through. "Thank God", he whispered.

Colleen blinked and opened her eyes.

"Good morning," he said.

She yawned and stretched. "How do you feel?"

"Better. Nick still okay?"

"He's been out of the I.C.U. for two days now and coming along like gangbusters. If you're good, they might let you see him later."

"Thanks for sticking around."

"You would've done the same."

Max studied her. "I thought they killed you."

"They tried but Flynn had one of his men covering me. When I couldn't reach you Flynn and I went in with the troops."

"None too soon."

"Amen to that. I don't know what Nick did, but he had them going after each other. Sully and Derlen are both dead. Sully from loss of blood. Two of his fingers were amputated. Derlen was nearly decapitated."

"And the rest?"

"Hospitalized under heavy guard or locked up."

Max felt a smile turning up the corners of his mouth. "You were right. Flynn came through."

"With his usual modesty." She picked up the paper, folded the page back and handed it to Max. He stared at a picture of Flynn flanked by Trenchcoat and Hubbard below the headline.

POLICE TASK FORCE SMASHES CULT

In a daring raid led by Jerome Flynn of the Boston Police Homicide Division, officers broke up a cult operating out of Saint Augustine's Rescue mission on Dorchester Ave. in the Field's Corner section of Dorchester. Flynn and members of his squad found evidence linking the mission to the Headless Horseman murders that have been plaguing authorities for the past couple of months.

"We've been working closely with the federal government on this one," Flynn said. "We couldn't have done it without their help, the assistance of the M.D.C., and the hours of undercover and surveillance put in by both city and federal agencies.

(See Task Force on page 3.)

Max tossed the paper aside.

"He's taking all the credit," O'Grady said.

Max shrugged. "I don't care. He deserves it. He told me he thought it was Derlen weeks ago. All that really matters is that the murders have stopped. I don't want any media attention. If they were to get my name and picture, my cover wouldn't be worth a damn anywhere."

He looked over at Colleen, his eyes locking on the deep green of hers. "As for you. I'll make damn sure you get the lion's share of the credit. You're the one who should be on the front page, not Flynn."

She shook her head. "Don't want the attention."

"Can't say I blame you, but as far as the brass is concerned, you can be damned sure they're going to know the truth and you will be taken care of. I'm going to push them to give you a promotion."

She made a dismissive gesture and looked away. "You're safe, that's all I care about."

Max waited for her to look back and caught her gaze again. "You did a great job, Colleen. I don't care what you say. When I'm out of here you're getting dinner at the fanciest restaurant in Boston that I can find."

She smiled. "I'm counting on it."

EPILOGUE

Max spotted Nick standing on the corner in the lightly falling snow. A thin layer of white covered everything, making the city seem clean, quiet and at peace. Max pulled the car over and parked. Nick came toward him. Max could tell by the big white flakes dusting the boy's hair and the shoulders of his leather jacket that he'd been waiting for a few minutes. His arm was still in a sling.

"How's your arm doing?" Max said, stepping out of the car.

"Doc says it'll be out of the sling in a few weeks."

"You shouldn't be standing out here. You'll catch a chill."

"Don't worry about it," Nick said. "I'm a big boy."

Max patted him on the shoulder. "That you are, my friend. Now what's so important that you risked catching your death of cold to meet me out here?"

"Come on." Nick motioned with his head and the two started up the street, stopping on the next corner. "In there," Nick said.

Max looked up at the sign.

SCOLARI'S -- FINE ITALIAN FOOD

"What is it?"

"You'd better go in and check it out."

Max started toward the door. Nick stayed in the middle of the sidewalk. Max turned. "Aren't you coming?"

Nick smirked. "In a minute."

Max shook his head and stepped into the warmth of the restaurant. The mixed scents of marinara, garlic, cheeses, and fresh bread greeted him. Candles glowed behind small red glass holders that dotted red and white checked table cloths.

"Mr. Broderick?" A small, heavy-set Italian man stepped from behind a podium.

"Who are you?"

"Antonio Scolari. Let me show you to your seat."

Confusion swept over Max. He followed Antonio around a corner to a small table in the back.

Colleen O'Grady sat holding a long white box with a red satin ribbon. She stood when she saw Max, a smile lighting her face. Her green eyes sparkled in the candle glow. The soft radiance of the candle highlighted her red hair which she wore loose over her shoulders.

"I waited until you got here before I opened it." She pulled the card from the box and read it, then dropped it on the table. Her face brightened when she undid the ribbon and gasped. "They're beautiful." She held up the box and showed him a dozen long stemmed roses. "Thank you."

Where in the hell had the flowers come from? Max groped for words, but couldn't find any. He looked down at the card on the table.

To Colleen,

From Your Not So Secret Admirer.

Max.

She took his hands and gave them a gentle squeeze, then he drew her close and they kissed. Max looked up at the window and caught a glimpse of Nick smiling as he peered in at them, then he disappeared into the snowy night.

ABOUT THE AUTHOR

Matthew J. Pallamary's works have been translated into Spanish, Portuguese, Italian, Norwegian, French, and German. His historical novel of first contact between shamans and Jesuits in 18th century South America, titled, **Land Without Evil** received rave reviews along with a San Diego Book Award for mainstream fiction. It was also adapted into a full-length stage and sky show, co-written with and directed by Agent Red and performed by Sky Candy, an Austin Texas aerial group. The making of the show was the subject of a PBS series, Arts in Context episode, which garnered an EMMY nomination.

His nonfiction book, **The Infinity Zone: A Transcendent Approach to Peak Performance** is a collaboration with professional tennis coach Paul Mayberry that offers a fascinating exploration of the phenomenon that occurs at the nexus of perfect form and motion. **The Infinity Zone** took 1st place in the International Book Awards, New Age category and was a finalist in the San Diego Book Awards.

His first book, a short story collection titled **The Small Dark Room Of The Soul** was mentioned in The Year's Best Horror and Fantasy and received praise from Ray Bradbury and has been released as an audio book.

His second collection, **A Short Walk to the Other Side** was an Award Winning Finalist in the International Book Awards, an Award Winning Finalist in the USA Best Book Awards, and an Award Winning Finalist in the San Diego Book Awards. It has been released as an audio book.

DreamLand a novel about computer generated dreaming, written with legendary DJ Ken Reeth won first place in the Independent e-Book Award in the Horror/Thriller category and was an Award Winning Finalist in the San Diego Book Awards. It has also been released as an audio book.

It's sequel, **n0thing** is titled after the main character, who in the real world is his nephew, an international Counter-Strike gaming champion. After winning what amounts to the Super Bowl of gaming, n0thing and his winning teammates, are recruited as a literal "dream team" whose mission is to go into the nightmares of battle scarred veterans and rescue them from their traumatic memories while becoming ambassadors for a gaming platform that exceeds virtual reality with an experience that pushes the boundaries of reality itself.

Eye of the Predator was an Award Winning Finalist in the Visionary Fiction category of the International Book Awards. **Eye of the Predator** is a supernatural thriller about a zoologist who discovers that he can go into the minds of animals.

CyberChrist was an Award Winning Finalist in the Thriller/Adventure category of the International Book Awards. **CyberChrist** is the story of a prize winning journalist who receives an email from a man who claims to have discovered immortality by turning off the aging gene in a 15 year old boy with an aging disorder. The forwarded email becomes the basis for an online church built around the boy, calling him CyberChrist. It has also been released as an audio book.

Phantastic Fiction – A Shamanic Approach to Story took first place in the International Book Awards Writing/Publishing category. **Phantastic Fiction** is Matt's guide to dramatic writing that grew out of his popular Phantastic Fiction Workshop.

Night Whispers was an Award Winning Finalist in the Horror category of the International Book Awards. Set in the Boston neighborhood of Dorchester, **Night Whispers** is the story of Nick Powers, who loses consciousness after crashing in a stolen car and comes to hearing whispering voices in his mind. When he sees a homeless man arguing with himself, Nick realizes that the whispers in his head are the other side of the argument.

His memoir *Spirit Matters* detailing his journeys to Peru, working with shamanic plant medicines took first place in the San Diego Book Awards Spiritual Book Category, and was an Award-Winning Finalist in the autobiography/memoir category of the National Best Book Awards.

The Center Of The Universe Is Right Between Your Eyes But Home Is Where The Heart Is was an Award Winning Finalist in the International Book Awards. Based on a lifetime of research into shamanism, visionary states, the evolution of written communication and the roots of storytelling, award-winning author, editor, and shamanic explorer Matthew J. Pallamary takes those with open minds courageous enough to question the illusions that most of us think of as real on an expansive journey that pierces the veil of reality itself.

AfterLife: The Adventures of a Lost Soul was inspired by real life events, William Peter Blatty's *The Exorcist*, and the dynamics of demonic possession.

Matt has also produced and directed *The Santa Barbara Writers Conference Scrapbook* documentary film and co-wrote the book of the same title in collaboration with Y. Armando Nieto, and conference founder Mary Conrad.

Death: (A Love Story) a first person narrative spoken by the omniscient voice of Death itself, who says, "I'm here to tell you stories and share some science, history, and myths, all of which are your creations that I want to share to help you understand me more. You have seen me as Satan, Anubis, Mot, Thanatos, God, the Devil, loving, punitive, dark, light – the list goes on and on! It is my sincerest hope that our friendly reintroduction here will change the way you think of me, and maybe in some small way reflect the depth of the love I have for you.

Picaflor is the sequel to *Spirit Matters*, a San Diego Book Award winner and an Award-Winning Finalist in the National Best Book Awards that chronicles the two decades since of Matthew (Mateo) J. Pallamary's adventures in *Spirit Matters* through the mountains, deserts, and jungles of North, Central, and South America pursuing his studies of shamanism and visionary experience working with plant medicines and shamanic plant diets, among them Ayahuasca, Peyote, San Pedro cactus, and many more.

Picaflores: The Nerve Endings of GOD was an Award Winning Finalist in the International Book Awards that details a magical, otherworldly, intimate connection with the spirit of hummingbirds that comes from two decades of visionary journeys experienced within the context of shamanic plant diets in the Peruvian Amazon. It also contains a treasure trove of pre-Columbian myths about hummingbirds and an in-depth collection of amazing facts and figures about these magical creatures.

Holographicosmic Man: The Holographic Heart of the Golden Mean is an amalgam of quantum physics, mathematics, geometry, ancient texts, current research, ancient architecture, beliefs, and myths, astronomy, anthropology, human anatomy, brain structure, shamanism, neuroscience, neuropsychology, indigenous wisdom, biology, astrophysics, neurophysiology, holography, cosmology, neuroanatomy, neurocardiology, cosmometry, and more.

I Am Consciousness Incarnate is an in-depth analysis of consciousness which includes scientific and philosophical theories and studies, examinations of unconscious, subconscious, and awareness, spiritual beliefs, mindfulness concepts, plant, animal, and artificial intelligence, as well as history and mythologies surrounding this age old enigma.

The Thinning Veil: 13 Twisted Tales is an Award Winning Finalist in the International Book Awards and Matt's third short story collection. These thirteen twisted tales cross the genres of science fiction and horror with a dash of spirituality, and explore strange happenings with homeless people, science and technology gone awry, and some dark supernatural tales with gothic underpinnings.

Matt's work has appeared in Oui, New Dimensions, The Iconoclast, Starbright, Infinity, Passport, The Short Story Digest, Redcat, The San Diego Writer's Monthly, Connotations, Phantasm, Essentially You, The Haven Journal, The Hurricanes & Swan Songs Anthology, The Santa Barbara Literary Journal, The Closed Eye Open, The Montecito Journal, and many others. His fiction has been featured in The San Diego Union Tribune which he has also reviewed books for, and his work has been heard on KPBS-FM in San Diego, KUCI FM in Irvine, television Channel Three in Santa Barbara, and The Susan Cameron Block Show in Vancouver. He has been a guest on the following nationally syndicated talk shows; Coast to Coast with George Noory, Paul Rodriguez, In The Light with Michelle Whitedove, Susun Weed,

Medicine Woman, Inner Journey with Greg Friedman, Night Dreams, and Environmental Directions Radio series. Matt has appeared on the following television shows; Bridging Heaven and Earth, Elyssa's Raw and Wild Food Show, Things That Matter, Literary Gumbo, Indie Authors TV, Spiritually Raw, and ECONEWS. He has also been a frequent guest on numerous podcasts, among them, The Psychedelic Salon, Black Light in the Attic, Third Eye Drops, C-Realm, Psychedelics Today, Voices in the Dark, Adventures Through the Mind, Beyond the Veil, Mind Escape, and many others.

Matt received the Man of the Year Award from San Diego Writer's Monthly Magazine and has taught a fiction workshop at the **Southern California Writers' Conference** in San Diego, Palm Springs, and Los Angeles, and at the **Santa Barbara Writers' Conference** for over thirty years. He has lectured at the Greater Los Angeles Writer's Conference, the Getting It Write conference in Oregon, the Saddleback Writers' Conference, the Rio Grande Writers' Seminar, the National Council of Teachers of English, The San Diego Writer's and Editor's Guild, The San Diego Book Publicists, The Pacific Institute for Professional Writing, The 805 Writers Conference, The College of Central Florida, Yakima Valley College in Washington, The Yakima Public School System, and he has been a panelist at the World Fantasy Convention, Con-Dor, and Coppercon. He is presently Editor in Chief of Mystic Ink Publishing.

Matt was a featured lecturer and performer at the **Mysteries of the Amazon** exhibit at the Appleton Museum in Ocala Florida and The Larson Gallery in Yakima Washington. He frequently visits the mountains, deserts, and jungles of North, Central, and South America pursuing his studies of shamanism.

MATTPALLAMARY.COM

BOOKS BY MATTHEW J. PALLAMARY

THE SMALL DARK ROOM OF THE SOUL

LAND WITHOUT EVIL

SPIRIT MATTERS

DREAMLAND (WITH KEN REETH)

THE INFINITY ZONE (WITH PAUL MAYBERRY)

A SHORT WALK TO THE OTHER SIDE

CYBERCHRIST

EYE OF THE PREDATOR

PHANTASTIC FICTION

NIGHT WHISPERS

THE SANTA BARABARA WRITERS CONFERENCE SCRAPBOOK
(WITH MARY CONRAD & Y. ARMANDO NIETO)

n0THING

AFTERLIFE: THE ADVENTURES OF A LOST SOUL

THE CENTER OF THE UNIVERSE IS RIGHT BETWEEN
YOUR EYES BUT HOME IS WHERE THE HEART IS

DEATH: (A LOVE STORY)

PICAFLOR

PICAFLORES: THE NERVE ENDINGS OF GOD

HOLOGRAPHICOSMIC MAN

I AM CONSCIOUSNESS INCARNATE

THE THINNING VEIL

*9 7 8 0 6 9 2 5 1 8 1 7 5 *